# Aaron

*Amish and Gay*

A Novel
BY
**H. Milo Yoder**

# TABLE OF CONTENTS

# CHAPTER ONE

I was flat on my back, staring up at the blue sky above me. It's difficult to really be comfortable on meadow grass, no matter how bucolic it may sound, for grass is prickly and the ground is rough. Yet, I did not move. The sharp rock digging into my shoulder blade somehow made the memory of my dead horse more bearable.

"Prince was only an animal." Dad's voice still echoed down the corridors of my brain. "Only an animal."

I was born and raised on an Amish farm and I had seen animals die or be killed ever since my first childhood memories. Surely now at thirty-three, I should be used to the death of animals. And people.

But at least, when people died, there were funerals.

There was a closure for people. Of sorts.

"I can see what you are thinking" I used to tell my black horse, looking into his eyes, big and alive, and staring back at me. "You don't just think about oats and hay or galloping across the farm fields or dozing in the hot summer sun under a maple tree." I would lean closer and stare into one of his eyes, seeing my face reflected in his. I would feel my soul reach out and touch his wild equine spirit. And just as I would begin to feel that connection, Prince would jerk his head away and snort with flaring nostrils, as if he, too, felt the connection and it unsettled him.

Now, as I lay on the grass, I heard my dry sob come from deep inside of me. I opened my eyes and stared into the blue sky once more. A flock of starlings flew overhead, swooping and darting about in a tightly connected flock. Suddenly one bird banked and

1

flew off towards the east, leaving the safety of the rest. My eyes followed the lone bird until it disappeared into the distance, still flying steadily and all alone.

"We have to put him down." Dad's voice had not been unkind, just factual. "A gelding with a broken leg is useless. Good for nothing."

No one would ever know how it happened. What had caused Prince to break his leg? This morning, which already seemed another lifetime in the past, I had left my house in preparation for work when I had seen Prince standing in the corner of his pasture, favoring one of his hind legs, the hoof barely touching the grass. When I called him, he hobbled several steps towards me. That leg dangled and flopped about uselessly before Prince lowered his head and stood still, his flanks dark with sweat.

"Broken metatarsus," Doc Thornton said rather brusquely as his practiced vet fingers explored the bone between Prince's hock and the knee. "Clean break. Snapped in half." He had looked at the north end of the pasture where a low outcropping of a rocky ledge jutted upwards. "May have stepped into a hole. I know it hardly ever happens, but I guess your horse got unlucky."

Dad was in his 70's now, but he had always been a keen hunter and a good marksman. He handled his 22 rifle with confidence and I knew his aim would be on target. "You don't have to be here," Dad had told me. "If it's easier for you to leave, I understand."

"No," I had answered, "I want to be here."

When Dad had returned from my parents' house just down the road from my place, I had made sure I had already said goodbye to my horse. I wanted Prince to understand. But, how could he? Is it ever possible for an animal to understand why humans do what we do? I had looked deeply into Prince's eye once more and I saw the pain that clouded the usually clear gaze.

Then I had stepped away from Prince and turned my head so I wouldn't see Dad aiming the rifle at my horse's head. The sharp crack of the rifle and the whine of the bullet split through the quiet country morning and I turned quickly as I heard the impact of Prince's body hit the ground.

"Careful! His legs are still thrashing!" I dashed towards Prince and dropped to the ground to cradle my dying horse's head on my lap, ignoring all caution. When the thrashing legs stopped, the huge body finally heaved a long shuddering movement and then lay still. Tears blinded my eyes and I didn't move. I stayed there a long time and I heard Dad walk away. I must have been out there for more than an hour and only after I heard the too familiar chug of a truck and then I knew Dad had contacted Mr. Mac, the neighbor who hauled carcasses away to come and collect my dead horse did I go back to my house to shower and change out of my dirty clothes. I stayed inside until I heard the truck drive out my lane and turn onto the country road. It was then I had come up here to the top of Prince's pasture and flung myself on the grass. To think. Or try not to think.

Now I sat up and looked down the slope towards the only two buildings on my place. My eyes went immediately to the small shed built onto the side of my woodworking shop. Where Prince's stall was now empty. I had enclosed the stable to protect Prince from the winter snow and wind but under the shed part, my two buggies were parked side by side. The open buggy, light and easy to be pulled by a horse was by far my favorite of the two. "My convertible" I called my open buggy for it had a folding top I had made to provide shade from the hot summer sun or to protect me from light rains. I had made my closed buggy as well and used it in the winter or in heavy rains.

3

From my vantage point on top of the knoll, I could see how the sugar maple tree I had planted on the south side of my small house had spread several of its branches over the roof. The slate gray color had been a good choice for the tin roof. I was glad I had not chosen the darker gray, for the summer sun beat warmly on my house and the lighter color reflected more heat. Plus, ten years after I enclosed the house with board and batten siding, the hemlock wood had silvered to a hue I especially cherished. Dad had approved of my insistence on using nothing but hemlock wood for the siding of my house. "If hemlock is protected by eaves and rain gutters and downspouts, it is practically indestructible."

"Now Aaron, why would anyone want to make a house out of a granary?" Mom had asked me when she first found out what I was planning "Sisht yuscht episs!" ( It's just something! ) was her response as she had looked at me in surprise. But now I had to smile slightly as I remembered how often she would tell visitors about her son who had made a house "...out of what once was a granary and you could never tell."

My dad and my two married brothers, Jake and Levi, had helped me make skids out of timbers from the woods, jack up the granary and then hired an "English" ( as we called all non- Amish regardless of nationality or skin color ) neighbor to come with his huge tractor and drag the solidly built structure the short distance to my three acres. It had taken a lot of work, and even more time than I had thought it would, to turn the granary into my house. But I have never regretted it.

"Now you have your nest," Jake had teased me after I moved in. "It's time to find a birdie to keep you company!"

"Maybe you had to do it this way so you could get a bird," my younger brother Levi said quickly, staring at me. "Most birds do

4

want someone who can build a nest but looking at you, no one would ever know you had it in you."

"Nah, Levi!" Mom had come to my defense. "Aaron just needs to take his time. Like he does when he makes his furniture, still."

"Yah, when Aaron grew higher than Jake when he turned nineteen, I said it's a good thing for he needs height if he can't have weight."

"Boys, boys," Dad said in his calming way. "You know it matters not how we look on the outside, it's what's on the inside that counts."

"Well, I'm looking on the outside," Levi had laughed. "Susan's curls peeping out from under her cap makes her my birdie for sure." He had looked at his young bride with a possessive smile.

I knew I was often the object of chatter, or yes even gossip, in our Amish community in Pennsylvania. I wasn't the only bachelor among the Amish, but really there were very few of us unmarried men in our thirties. Then, I guess it was thought even more strange when I renovated the granary and moved in to live by myself.

As anyone who really knows about Amish culture and lifestyles, there is quite a bit of pressure to be conformed to the community. To keep the ways that have been handed down from generation to generation is highly prized and straying too far from the norm is often quickly frowned on with suspicion of restlessness and discontent with the confines of being Amish.

Most days, I walked the short distance to my parents' house and ate lunch, dinner we called the midday meal, with my mom and dad. Today I wasn't hungry after what had happened to my horse, but I knew Mom would want to know how I was doing. "Aaron, it is just too bad what happened with Prince," Mom shook her head slightly, her neat white cap framing her concerned face. "Can you imagine what happened? I know Dad said the vet thought he must have stepped in a hole up among the rocks. But that is hard to believe, because we had horses in there before we deeded the three acres to you. Now how could Prince have found a hole none of the other horses stepped into?"

Dad looked briefly at me and then took another bite of mashed potatoes. "Now, Emma," he said laying down his spoon and stroking his long white beard, " I don't think Aaron wants to think much about what happened. It is hard for him to lose his horse."

"Ach yes, "Mom said quickly. "Aaron always did feel things deeply. But he knows Prince was just an animal.

Animals don't have souls. Not like we humans do."

"Hey," I managed a grin, "I am here. You are talking as though I were somewhere else."

"We didn't mean to," Mom chortled. "Yes, I guess we did. So, what are you thinking? You will be looking for another horse, yes? Of course, you could use Nellie, I guess. At least for a while. If we don't need her. And," her voice lifted, "you can ride with us to church on Sunday. We can take the surrey. Plenty of room."

"Yes, I will be looking for a horse," I nodded, wondering why Mom's meatloaf, baked to perfection, tasted like sawdust. "Although no other horse will be able to take Prince's place. He was my favorite horse by far. In spite of his stubbornness when I trained him as a colt, he turned out very reliable. Spirited for sure, but true to his training."

"Aaron," Mom said with a quick nod of her head, "with all the things you are so good at, horse training, furniture making and look what you did with the old granary! Why, you shouldn't waste that

6

all on yourself! And on us! You could easily get a good girl for a wife. You know, Corner Jake's Mary is such a sweet girl. Always smiling and such a good worker, too. Not so young anymore, either."

I sighed and kept on eating. Dad said nothing but folded his arms across his chest, his plate cleaned of all food.

"Just last week, Aunt Edna's sister-in-law mentioned how she hadn't heard anything about you taking a girl to the singings, yet." Mom continued. "But I told Edna just because no one knows if you are taking a girl to the singings or home afterwards doesn't mean you aren't. Why, since you live by yourself you could be doing all kinds of things nobody knows about."

Dad ended the monologue by letting out a sigh, bowing his head and closing his eyes in silent prayer. Mom and I followed his example and relief flooded my weary brain. After the time of stillness, I would feel free to leave.

"Denge fah da mittag," I told Mom using our unique German dialect.

"You are welcome," Mom replied in Amish. "You are always so polite, thanking me and all. Of all three of the boys, you notice the little things. I wonder how it would have been if we would have had a girl? At least one? Would she be more like you, arranging flowers, making things look nice and, and interested in the feelings of others? Now Jake and Levi, they don't think of such things. Of course, they have their wives...." Mom's voice followed me out the door. I walked quickly, my hands balled into fists and my clenched teeth hidden behind my closed lips.

I walked down the quarter of a mile separating my place from where the family homestead was. My feet felt hot. I bent over and unlaced my shoes then pulled them off my feet. I took my socks off and stuffed them into my shoes. The grass along the roadside felt cool and refreshing to my feet. I walked on towards home, feeling slightly better. "There, I got rid of those 'prison walls of pride', as Whittier so poetically put it. Oh, and how about "with thy rolled-up pantaloons"? I might as well go all the way and once more be 'The Barefoot Boy' of my youth." I dropped my shoes and rolled up my pants' legs, each one exactly three times and as I straightened up I heard the clip clops of horse hooves coming up behind me.

I flinched and resisted the impulse to turn around to see who was coming. I would find out soon enough. I walked on, and when the trotting horse's nodding head came into my peripheral view, keeping time with the staccato steps of his shod hoofs, I turned my head and nodded in greeting.

It was "Essich Johnny" ( Vinegar John) who was given that nickname when he was young and had gulped down about a pint of homemade vinegar, assuming it was hard cider. It was as if the effects of vinegar never quite left him for Johnny was a sour faced man married to a barren woman, equally as unhappy with life as her husband.

The fast-trotting horse had taken his owner quickly past me but not quickly enough. John's piercing blue eyes had taken in my bare feet and legs and I was almost sure the corners of his mouth went into a deeper frown of disapproval than before. Then, I did something very uncharacteristic for me. Maybe it was the pain that had engulfed me when Prince had to be put down or perhaps it was Mom's wearisome and unrelenting topic about why I wasn't dating and her never-ending lists of girls she would recommend, but as I watched John's buggy draw away from me, I lifted my left hand and waved my shoes back and forth above my head. Back and forth, I waved my shoes and for some reason, I felt relieved. I'm quite sure John saw me in the small round mirrors fastened to the sides of the top buggy and so I waved my shoes some more. And just to celebrate the rush of freedom that flooded through me, I jumped up off the grass and tried to click my bare heels together. I didn't quite manage but landed rather ungracefully onto a sharp stone with my right foot. "Ouch," I yelled and then I as I heard my voice erupt into the quiet air I yelled even louder, "OOOOUUUCCCCHHHH!"

# CHAPTER TWO

I studied the address on the paper in my hand. "354 Candlewood Township Road, Babville, PA." Only a block down the road from Ted's Corner Grocery. A store with a hitching rack for us Amish to tie up our horses while we shopped. Babville is a small hamlet rimmed by the Alleghaney Mountains of Central Pennsylvania.

I walked up to the front door and read the small plaque, "Brian Downton, M.S. Counselor/Therapist. Clients please use side entrance." The arrow pointed to my left. I stepped off the small front stoop and followed the brick path. Orange and yellow nasturtiums spilled out onto the walk, bordering the foundation plantings. The side door was a full paned French door. I could see a light filled room furnished comfortably. I took a deep breath, pushed the doorbell button and I heard the chimes inside announce my arrival.

A man appeared and smiled at me through the glass and opened the door. "Hi, I'm Brian. Come inside." He had a shock of bedhead gray hair but I realized he was not much older than myself.

"I'm Aaron," I answered, and we shook hands. I took my straw hat off my head and Brian waved to a hall tree. "Hang your hat on the hook and come sit down."

"Aaron, what brings you here?"

I'm not sure how I thought our session would begin but I was not prepared for the direct question. I studied the pattern on the rug and cleared my throat. "I'm… uh… I guess I came because I have some questions that I wanted to be able to talk to someone about. Some things, yes, some questions."

We sat opposite each other on a pair of wing chairs right in front of a set of French doors opening up onto a patio. Tall trees cast dappled shade onto the well-trimmed lawn.

Brian didn't reply. He crossed his one leg over the other and his leather sandal dangled from the lifted foot. "Okay," I said. "I've been having a lot of depression recently. My horse broke his leg and had to be put down." I heard a small hiccup in my voice, and I wet my lips and tried again. "I can't sleep. I feel so tired, go to bed, fall asleep almost immediately but then about an hour later, I wake up. I have that wide-awake feeling and I know I will not be able to sleep for a long time. Then I get up and try to do something to occupy my mind or to make myself tired, and yet I stay up until about 3 or 4 in the morning."

"How long has this been going on? Since your horse died?"

I shook my head, "No, but it got worse. It's been over a month ago now that Prince died. At first, I thought I would eventually get over it, but I haven't. I feel tired all the time."

Brian nodded his head in understanding, "You haven't consulted a medical doctor?"

I shook my head. "I've tried a lot of natural teas and herb capsules and nothing seems to work. I went to a chiropractor and after he adjusted my spine, I did have one night of more sleep."

"Tell me about your horse. How that happened."

I told him about the incident. Brian paid keen attention to my story.

"That was tough for you. However, you seem to realize your sleeplessness worsened after that and did not begin there."

I nodded in agreement. "That's true."

11

"Then there is something else that causes your sleeplessness. Brian thought a moment. "What do you do at night when you can't sleep?"

"Sometimes I read. Or draw in my sketch book. And if I feel really stressed, I go out to my woodshed and work on whatever furniture I'm making." My mind went back to endless black nights I endured.

"That sounds amazing," Brian said. "I'm impressed! Drawing and making furniture! Do you make your own designs?"

"Mostly," I told him. "Sometimes I get an order for a specific design."

"Show…" Brian interrupted himself and chuckled. "I was going to say show me some pictures. But I'm assuming you don't have a phone. Or camera."

I smiled at him. "I don't. But I do have pictures at my house. I hire a photographer to take studio shots of what I make."

"Forgive me," Brian said apologetically. "I was born and raised here among the Amish and Mennonites and I could have known." Then he added, "I'm assuming you are not from the strictest sect?"

"We are considered more progressive. Instead of being Old Order, we are New Order."

For the rest of my hour session, Brian asked me a lot of questions. He wanted to know about my life. He asked about my childhood and my years in school. But not once did I detect any condescension or even a hint of disrespect for our people. "Relax your jaw," he told me when I was talking about my childhood experiences. "Are you aware you do that?"

I nodded and looked down on my knees as unbidden tears stung my eyelids.

"I'll remind you," Brain said kindly. "And hey, if you feel emotional in any of these moments, know it's okay. I'm a therapist and I encourage you to be able to stay in touch with your feelings"

I think after that I was able to talk more freely.

"Keep a daily diary. Not about what you do, but what you are thinking. Mostly what you are feeling. Paper holds still and doesn't talk back at you if you write things you wouldn't want to tell anyone. I've a suspicion you also write. You are quite articulate."

"I do write," I acknowledged, "and I also read, a lot."

"Is a check okay?" I asked before I left. "I could bring you cash. Or use my bank debit card."

"Check is fine," Brian said with a smile. He looked up at me,

"How tall are you?"

"I'm six, two," I told him.

"All that good Amish food must have helped to make you grow tall and strong," he laughed. "I rarely but sometimes go to that Amish restaurant over in Allentown. I try not to, but my wife Tansy especially loves the chicken potpie they serve."

"Ummm," I hesitated. "I'd like to come back again, Mr. Downton. I like the direction our conversation went today."

"Call me Brian," he said warmly. "Same time, same day next week?" He picked up the envelope I had mailed him and looked at the return address. "You don't live very far from here, do you?"

I liked how the light-colored maple wood created a contrast with the dark walnut. I gently tapped the mortise and tenons together for the counter height side table I was building. The north light coming in the big windows was perfect for my workspace. I felt the rough wood, but didn't stop to sand it. I could do that at night when the light wasn't as good. Most woodworkers go more by how the surface of wood feels even more than how it looks.

Our fingertips are one of the most sensitive parts of our body and I learned to put that to good use when the light was dim.

I stepped back to view the assembled table. It was counter height, the top a solid two-inch walnut plank with light colored maple legs. The lighter wood used for the sides also gave an illusion the dark walnut slab top was floating. However, on the edges where the finger joints intersected, the dark walnut grabbed the lighter wood sides firmly. I had gotten the idea to plane the sides to a narrow width from my admiration of Shaker furniture pictured in a much thumbed and paged book I had bought at a used book sale.

I realized my spirit felt lighter. I was enjoying working on my project. This table was only the second piece I was able to finish since Prince had died.

Now I had another horse. It had not taken long for me to take a shine to Lady, a rangy chestnut Standardbred mare an elderly Amish man in another church district was selling. "Since my Mattie died, I haven't the need for two buggy horses. She used to love to go visit the children and not want me to be missing a horse if I needed to go somewhere. And you are Monie Ben's son? Yes, I was in the same youth group with him. Of course, that was years ago. And who is your wife?" I was as polite as possible. Yet all I wanted to do was to buy this beautiful horse with white stockings and with a lightning bolt blaze extending down to her nose, and not once again be asked by someone about my wife.

14

"I'm not married." I reached out and combed Lady's mane with my fingers.

"Ach, yah, so is life. There will be a good wife waiting for you someday and I hope it is soon. Don't give up looking." I shrugged away the memory and turned my attention to my task. I still needed to create two narrow side pieces of maple, called the aprons, to support the walnut top so I went to my rack where I stored my lumber pieces and sorted through the maple wood.

"Relax your jaw." I knew Brian was not in my shop but the words he had said this morning reminded me again just how quickly I tensed up. I inhaled deeply and stretched my arms towards the ceiling. I felt my body respond to the exercise and reminded myself to replace the stretch band I had snapped the week before during my regular morning workout. I ran my hands down over the sides of my ribs and felt my stomach. I shouldn't procrastinate getting back into a workout routine for even though I wasn't sure if I actually had abs, I had worked too hard to get rid of the belly fat that had plagued me all during my 20's to have it come back! I had gotten into better shape after I had moved into my own place and away from my mom's heavy carb diet and now quite frequently, I skipped dinner in the evening, and replaced a cooked meal with fresh carrots, tomatoes and other garden vegetables. I dropped my arms and resumed my work.

That evening, as I climbed up the flight of wooden steps to my loft, I still felt the lightness of the afternoon.

Perhaps tonight I could sleep without waking up! I had my favorite gardening book by Ruth Stout, "How To Have A Green Thumb Without An Aching Back", hopefully to lull me into sleep. Although written and published in 1956, her words leaped off the pages as I read about her foray into gardening.

15

"Keep a diary,"

I undressed down to my briefs and climbed into bed. The all cotton sheets felt good on my bare skin. I ran my hand over the empty space beside me. "But do you think when you get married your wife will like so simple bedding? I mean, get some of the new sheets, easy to wash and never wrinkly!" Mom had clucked her tongue at my choice. I refrained from telling her I liked natural fibers, not only how they appealed to my eyes but also how they felt. Plus, the sheets went perfectly well with the jute rug beside my bed on the wood floor.

I lay on my back in bed, watching how the last light of the day created shadows on the wooden ceiling. Although I had painted the post and beam frame white and the planed boards were the exact same shade of white, it never ceased to amaze me at all the different variations the same color created by all the different angles and corners. I visually checked to make sure my octagon windows at the top of the end walls were open to ensure a heat escape and cross ventilation to keep the house cool even on the warmest nights and the windows beside my bed were all open. Then I reached for a notebook. "Dear Diary". I wrote. "It was good to talk with Brian. I wonder if he ever had an Amish client before? Although I have had quite a lot of interaction with English people, I don't think I ever talked about my feelings as I did today. Guess that's what makes him a good therapist. I'm going back next week."

I continued writing. *"I've been thinking about how he asked if I had childhood trauma. I really think I had a good childhood. Even in spite of Levi able to outdo and outperform me in almost every way when we were young. Run faster, lift more weight, and make friends a lot easier than I was able to. Maybe it was trauma to have to be on the lookout for his temper. Like the time he chased me with the hayfork when he got mad at me for something. I can still feel the fear of feeling the sharp tines in my backend at any moment as I ran*

16

*screaming at the top of my voice and I still don't know what would have happened if Dad hadn't come around the corner of the milk house just then. Of course, Dad had heard my screams of panic, for that was one thing I could do. Scream. 'Screams louder than a girl' my siblings used to tell me.*

*"Is it considered childhood trauma if you constantly feel you are different from the other boys in your family? Or even any other boys? Is it trauma to wonder why I don't like hunting and seeing animals bleed and then be told I'm a sissy? Is it trauma to want to feel safe even though the memories of our neighbor's house burning down in the early morning hours one winter seems branded on my brain and the nightmares about our house being next to burn is haunting me for years? Do I feel such incidents more keenly than others? Is it wrong to crave beauty and love the way words convey feelings and make pictures for our minds and to wonder if a person can ever actually experience what the mind can create? Is it trauma to feel that I have to change myself somehow or I will feel the fires of eternal hell in the next life? Why do I wrestle with the feelings of being flawed and in need of healing? Diary, I'm going to stop now for I think I'm actually getting in a worse state of mind than when I started writing. Good night."*

I blew out the kerosene lamp, then lay back on my bed. I cradled my head on my hands behind my neck and stared up into the dark. I felt my body sink into the memory foam and released my thoughts into sleep.

That night, sitting downstairs right beside the screen door leading out to the deck, I watched the moon light up my world as it rose above the tree line. I felt the cool night air caress my bare legs and blow gently over my chest and arms. It felt good to be undressed in the dark. Tonight, I didn't want to work in the workshop, or sketch or read. I wanted to think. To exist. To be me. Aaron Peachy. And just perhaps explore more who I was rather than who I should be. I

17

longed to talk with Brian again. Someone I could be totally honest with and not have to worry if they would think I'm weird. Someone I would not have to pretend to be a man I wasn't. A feeling of loneliness wrapped stifling tentacles around me in spite of the cooling breezes. I jumped up and ran outside. Dressed only in my briefs, I ran all the way up to the top of the knoll. I heard Lady snort in the darkness and I realized I must have startled her for she lifted her tail and trotted stiffly away from my running figure and then stopped, snorting again. "Lady!" I called her softly and as soon as she heard my voice, she dropped her tail and came towards me. Even though I knew we had bonded earlier, I felt a surge of companionship flood through me, not like the connection I had with Prince, but still good. I chuckled slightly. Equine companionship. That was probably the closest connection I could ever expect with another living creature. I pressed her head against my chest feeling her warm breath on my bare skin.

# CHAPTER THREE

"**I** don't know how you do it, but your furniture designs keep improving, getting more sophisticated." Jamil aimed his zoom lens in to detail the mortise and tenon work on my table and clicked his shutter. "Let's move the table closer to the window and I'll take a shot of it from outside the open door. The maple wood is so light and if I take the shot with the right light, it is as though the walnut top is floating in place. This is probably my favorite piece you have made."

We moved the heavy workbench to one side and then placed the table in front of the windows. Jamil knelt on one knee just outside the door, the sunlight streaming in behind him and I thought what a nice picture he made, dark curly hair and brown skin he got from his Persian heritage, framed by the door frame. Sunlight gave him a halo and turned the curls on his head to gold where the light shone through.

Then I turned to look at my table, and I was quite pleased to see how well the table looked as Jamil had posed it. "I really, really like it," the young man said. Then he straightened his back and glanced around the shop. "Just a few props," and he selected a wooden mallet, two wooden clamps and placed them on the table. He picked up some wooden shavings from the corner where I worked on sizing wooden pieces and placed them on the table.

"Then you will need to include this," I suggested and put a hand plane beside the shavings. Jamil nodded and began focusing his lens.

Giving legs to my impulse, I went outside with a pair of scissors and clipped a medley of wildflowers, including Queen Anne's lace, the bluest chicory blossoms I could find and added early black-eyed

Susans and then I clipped grass stems with silvery seed heads and took them back inside the shop. I knew just where a glass vase I had admired and purchased at a yard sale was, and I arranged the wildflowers by staggering the stems into different lengths. I put the bouquet on the table.

Jamil saw what I was doing and began clicking away. "I am early in my career as a photographer, but I really don't think I have ever met anyone as multi-gifted as you are." he told me as his brown eyes looked directly into mine. "You have a special quality I haven't met before. You make such beautiful furniture, you have an eye for design, and what you do, you do so well."

I felt an embarrassed flush sweep over me. Amish people seldom praise each other as it is thought to generate pride. And to be proud is one of the deadly sins the preachers talk about at length on the hour-long Sunday sermons.

"Plus, you are very handsome. Tall and slender with an approachable face," Jamil said. Then a little hesitantly, "Maybe I shouldn't have said that. I'm sorry."

I shook my head. "No, it's okay. I'm actually quite flattered, really. Thank you."

"I sense our lives are quite different from each other, but I also see many practices among the Amish that echo a lot of my upbringing and traditions. Strong family ties. Rigid rules to keep us in control. Fear of eternal fires if we aren't good people. No?" his young face, surely he couldn't be more than about 23, registered his hesitancy to talk about this.

I didn't reply immediately. I knew how my community would feel about any Muslim, or Middle Eastern people, comparing their lives to our own. "I see what you mean," I began. "You are very polite and careful not to cause offense. You, like you said, have customs and traditions you follow closely. Yes, we are probably more alike than we want to admit. I'm wondering if that applies to most strict religions."

Jamil nodded and then came over beside me to show his camera shots. I felt his shoulder brush against mine as we put our heads close together in order to see. The digital screen was small but even though it was difficult to really see well, I realized that Jamil had done a great job. We decided on four of the pictures we felt showed the table to the best effect and then I paid him. "I'll mail the printouts to you as usual.

"You need to enter your pieces in handcrafted furniture shows. Do you mind if I Google and see if there are shows we could submit photographs for consideration?" Jamil put his camera in the leather case and buckled the strap.

"Hmm... I guess that's okay. If you really think the pieces are good enough." I didn't think anyone in my church would disapprove. I wasn't the only furniture maker among the Amish by a long shot. Hundreds of men and boys worked in furniture factories, churning out "Amish" furniture.

"The furniture is good enough, I know. But the most important part is that you are good enough," Jamil's eyes twinkled at his comment.

"Well, denke", I said with a smile. "Do you know what "denke" means? It means 'thank you'.

"Denkkee," Jamil tried out my word. "I'll have to remember that. Dennkee for the good time and for letting me photograph your craft."

"Jamil" I called out after he had left the shop. When he turned and came back inside, I thought I would lose courage to speak to him. But I managed to say, "You are quite handsome yourself."

I didn't know dark complexioned people could blush but I know he turned at least a shade darker as his white teeth flashed against his swarthy skin. "Thank you. I mean dennkee" He reached out and we shook hands and then he left. I heard his car tires crunch over the gravel of my driveway and I stood still for a moment. Then I shook my head slightly, jiggling my straw hat and bringing me back to reality. Or had that moment been reality? "Stop it," I scolded myself mentally. I was Amish. Born and raised Amish, living in an Amish community and adhering to the Amish way of life as much as I could.

Most of the time, I felt I was doing a good job being Amish. I didn't know any other way. I wasn't really wanting another way. I didn't feel hemmed in or restricted. At least not most of the time. There were a lot of traditions and customs we Amish had that I greatly appreciated and was glad to have been born into. Most of the time I felt satisfied. To be honest, I hated the depression that wanted to come in like a heavy fog and color my world gray. But I also knew life was to be endured, to be lived soberly and simply, in hopes for a better life after death. I knew other Amish who battled with mental disorders. Why were my people becoming so depressed? More and more were seeking counsel and asking other Amish and even Mennonites to help them work through troubling issues and trauma. Our community was much more open to getting help rather than just boxing it up inside than it used to be. That's why I had decided to meet with my therapist. We were not frozen in the past century like so many people think we are, I told myself. We New Order Amish were actually quite open and willing to learn about life and wanted to deal with the everyday problems all people face.

"I am okay," I told myself out loud. "Plus, I'm going t Brian next week and I have my Diary I 'talk' to." For some reason this made me smile as I began putting my workshop back into order.

I looked at the blank page of my diary. I wanted to write the flood of words that were building up inside of my brain, yet it was as though my left hand couldn't lift the pen and begin to write. I had lit the kerosene lamp and sat at my desk beside the loft window. The dim flame illuminated my face enough to see my reflection in the glass. I stared at my image. Medium brown hair with a slight wave, parted in the middle like the men were required to do in our church district for years, and I tilted my face slightly to one side to see my profile more clearly. My short beard showed in the window and I rubbed my hands over the brown facial hair. I sighed and looked back down at my diary. I reached for the pen and placed the tip on the blank page. *"Dear Diary. I have a beard. Not a long one but short, much like the other younger men in my church have. I've had a beard for a little over a year now. I thought long about it before I decided to grow the beard and also tried to prepare myself for the reaction from the church community. You see, Diary, we Amish men usually don't grow beards until we marry. I mean until they marry. So, since I'm not married, it is not expected for me to grow a beard just yet. As if I am telling the church community I'm planning to stay single for the rest of my life. Oh, by the time an unmarried man reaches the age of 50 or so, it's no big deal if he lets the beard grow. So, when I grew my beard out, I did get reactions but not as much as I thought. 'How will the visiting girls from other communities know you are single?' Mom asked. 'At first I thought you forgot to shave, but then I told myself Aaron doesn't forget such things and then I decided you must want to feel how it would be like to be married.' Diary, I like my mom, but really, I believe she begins talking most of the time without ever knowing where her sentences will end. Oh, and I need to tell you I don't have a mustache. Pretty much throughout all the church districts, the mustache is forbidden.*

*No need to ask why, it's just that way. So, Diary, that's why I have a beard and no mustache. Oh, when Levi asked why I have a beard now and questioned me whether I had convictions for a beard I told him, 'I have a beard because I like it and because it grows there. I'd think I'd need a conviction to shave rather than a conviction to grow one. Beards grow without convictions. Kind of like fingernails. They grow without conviction as well.' He had looked at me and shook his head and said my thoughts were strange.*

*"Strange. Different. I have heard…"* My eyes caught a burst of red and orange in the darkness of the night outside. Fire! The night sky was being lit by a building on fire! I stood up quickly and focused as much as I could in the night. It looked like Car Johnny's place up against the foot of Jack's Mountain!

I ran downstairs and went outside. Now the glow of the fire had grown and flames leaped upwards into the night, sending fiery sparks out in flashes of orange. I heard the wail of fire trucks start up from the volunteer fire department in Babville, staffed by English and Amish men and boys who all lived close by to the all essential fire station in our rural community. The flames leaped higher and higher! I was quite sure it must be the huge barn on the farm. I hoped all the animals were out of the barn. But it could also be they were not. The dairy bull in his sturdy pen or several newborn calves perhaps. Although barn fires are not frequent, I had been still in school when one winter one of my relative's barns had caught fire and more than twenty animals had perished and several more were scorched so badly they had been put down.

I thought briefly about hitching up Lady and going to the fire. Joining the community spectators as they showed up by horse and buggy if Amish, by car and truck if English plus black cars and trucks if from the Mennonite/Amish community which Car Johnny and his wife had joined when they left the New Order Amish. Much like the Amish, except they allow more modern conveniences like electricity, telephones and cars and trucks, the Car Amish still try to maintain a strict control over their members including requiring them to paint all their vehicles black in an attempt to curtail pride and vanity.

Yes, many in the immediate community would be there, assisting in any way possible. It was the way of rural folks, including the Amish communities. But the flashback I had to another fire kept me at home. It had been a terrible night, waking up to hear my mom scream "Fire at Gleener's!" when I was ten years old. Why had my mom taken us to see the fire? I don't know if the memory of that night will ever leave me.

The burning timbers of the two story farmhouse walls and rafters, the twisted metal of the tin roof, the scorched and burned skeletons of the shade trees next to the house, the firemen training their hoses on the periphery of the fire and spraying the several outbuildings close by, the noise of men shouting and the crackle of the fire all flooded my memory. Then, there had been the black tarp. Covering the bodies of Mrs. Gleener and her sister Sadie. They had perished in the fire. Mr. Gleener, an elderly man in his 70's was walking around in a daze, staring at the fire one minute and then going back to the black tarp to stand there with tears streaming down his face. "I tried to keep them from going back in, but I heard a scream from Elma, and she ran back inside, and Sadie ran in after her! What was she trying to save from the fire? Oh, Elma, nothing was that important."

Only after I became a teen-ager did I become aware of rumors suggesting Elma may have started the fire and ran back inside after she discovered Mr. Gleener and Sadie in bed together.

So no, I didn't go to the scene of the fire. I would go when the barn raising was scheduled. I would join the Amish, the Car Amish and the Mennonites and any other people who would volunteer from

25

two to three days to do what the Amish did so well, volunteering their labor and to help rebuild after disasters. This is what being Amish meant and I was a part of that. Helping people, especially of our own communities and also in English communities where fires, tornados, hurricanes and floods devastated communities. But tonight, I didn't go to the site of the fire, I stayed home, by myself, walking around inside my house, sleepless and trying to erase the haunting memories. Then I went outside and climbed the knoll of Lady's pasture. I could see the fire still blazing and hear the far-off roar of the fire engines and see the flashing emergency lights in a rotation of red, blue and white. I sat on a rock and hugged my knees to my chest. I wasn't cold and yet I found myself shivering and I realized I was clenching my jaw until the muscles in my neck began to hurt.

# CHAPTER FOUR

"**U**ncle Aaron, draw a horse," my five-year-old niece Bertha begged, thrusting a pencil into my hand and giving me a piece of paper.

"Yes, Uncle Aaron, draw animals," her seven-year-old brother Benjamin echoed. "We like when you draw pictures." "You do?" I smiled and took the paper from Bertha.

"What would you like the horse to be doing?"

It was Sunday, and my brother Jake and his wife Mary had invited my parents and I, and my brother Levi and his family to their house for supper. My oldest brother and his family lived in the original farmhouse and my dad and mom lived in a small house on the opposite side of the barn. Levi had bought a rundown farm two miles down the road and worked hard long days salvaging what he could and with help from the family was getting on his feet financially. Quite frequently our family, hosted by my parents or by my married brothers, gathered together for supper Sunday evenings. Not only with my immediate family but also with the aunts and uncles, cousins and other relatives living in the area. It was not uncommon for any family to arrive unannounced in the evening and to spend time together, eating and visiting, swapping events of the week or discussing community news. This connection among the Amish continues to be as strong as it has been for generations. I think the community connection springs from our traditions of helping each other, joining together to accomplish laborious tasks and make the barn raisings, the quiltings, and other work-related work parties really be "frolics" as we called them. We had already had the frolic to clean up after Car Johnny's devastating fire and

27

there would be another one when the lumber was cut for the new barn to be raised.

"Running," Bertha had decided, so I took the pencil and began sketching. I drew several outline marks on the paper and Bertha and Benjamin crowded closer. Levi and Susan's three-year-old daughter, Miriam came over to watch. I heard Mom and Mary in the kitchen making popcorn. Dad was on his rocker and my brothers were relaxing on the couch.

"There's the horse's ears," Bertha chattered.

"One ear is going like this", Benjamin held up his hand, palm facing away from him. "And the other ear is facing back."

"Why do you think the horse is doing that?" I asked with a smile.

"I don't know," Bertha said. "Why?"

"So he can pay attention both to what is happening behind him and what is going on in front of him," I said. "When I trained horses, I learned to closely watch their ears. Do you know how a horse feels if both ears are turned backwards and lowered towards his neck?"

The three children continued to watch as I sketched the horse's legs, the opposite legs lifted and going at a trot, his tail flowing out behind him.

"When horses lay their ears backwards, they are mad," Levi told the children. "Like this," and he grabbed both of Benjamin's ears and pulled them backwards.

"Ouch!" Benjamin whimpered. Levi released his nephew's ears and laughed. "Last night Susan's ears were facing backwards," he chuckled. "She was outside hanging up the wash on the clothesline and had her back turned to me as I came around the side of the house.

So, I sneaked up behind her and grabbed her around the waist. You should have heard her scream and seen her jump." Levi turned to look for his wife. Susan was in the kitchen nursing their four-month-old newborn, Eli. "Susan, didn't your ears lay backwards last night when you got mad at me for scaring you?"

"Ach, Levi!" Susan's voice was dismissive. "You are always scaring me. But not as much as you did when we were first married."

Levi and Susan's relationship was always lively and yes, sometimes strained. Levi's somewhat heartless manners and crude behavior clearly rankled Susan and there were times I was aware she resented his treatment of her but for the most part she managed to keep things from getting out of hand.

"All done," I said and gave the sketch to Bertha. "What will you name your horse?"

"Nellie," she decided, choosing the name of their family buggy mare. "Look Dad," she showed the drawing to Jake, "see Nellie?"

Jake took the drawing and lifted it up for a better view, "Well, it doesn't look much like Nellie, since she is quite a bit heavier so she can haul our big buggy, but she does look really good. Aaron, I never stop marveling at how well you can draw. A few strokes of your pencil on a piece of paper and you come up with this."

"Takes after my Pap," my dad said reaching for the paper. "He could draw horses and animals and one summer he took a job with a sign maker and went around the eastern states painting signs on roofs and on sides of buildings. A good drawer he was."

"Draw me," Benjamin had found another piece of paper.

"Now Benjamin, Aaron doesn't draw people. You know it's not the Amish way," my dad said seriously. Benjamin stood silently for a while. "Why not?"

"God told us in the Ten Commandments not to make graven images." Dad had his answer ready.

"What's 'graven image?'" Benjamin's voice stumbled over the unfamiliar term.

"Likeness," Levi said quickly. "Like drawing. Or pictures." Then he got up abruptly. "Funny thing is, the Bible says not to make ANY graven image of anything. Not of anything on earth or in heaven. The horse Aaron drew is also a graven image." He walked to the window and looked out into the gathering dusk of the evening.

"Well, Levi," Dad said slowly. "We Amish have decided a long time ago it is best not to have pictures or drawings of people, for that can promote pride. I remember when I was young, we were not to have big mirrors. lest we become too concerned with our own looks. So, you know, even though we do allow pictures of animals and other natural things, we don't have cameras and frown on our people having pictures of ourselves and so that includes drawings." Dad's voice was not unkind, but it was strict. Even in his old age, he had not lost his authority when it came to such matters.

"Here, I'll draw you stick figures," I told Benjamin. "See, this is you…. and here is Bertha… and here is Miriam." I sketched three stick figures and drew little caps on the heads for the girls.

"We look funny!" Bertha giggled. "My legs aren't that skinny!"

"Popcorn time," Mom bustled in from the kitchen with a huge stainless-steel bowl of popcorn. "Bertha, go get the small bowls and pass them out." Mary followed behind my mom with a tray of glasses and a pitcher of homemade grape juice.

Perhaps drawing for my nephew and nieces sparked a renewed interest in me to sketch, for later, after I walked the short distance home in the dark from my brother's place, I opened the bottom drawer of the chest in the loft and removed my sketch pad out from under my winter underwear I stored there.

I flipped open the cover and looked at several sketches I had done. I had another sketchbook out in the workshop where I sketched my ideas for furniture, but this one was the one I had been using for random artwork the last five years. There had been, and still were, certain scenes that I've seen I wanted to draw, like a red-tailed hawk, talons outstretched, plummeting to earth after prey. Or a sketch of the cornice of an historic building in town. Yes, of horses as well, but mostly just the head, or a detail of a hoof, working to get the right amount of shading to show the strain of the tendons as a horse galloped across the field.

Then I flipped to the last page I had made a sketch on. I had seen an English neighbor's teen-aged son come riding down the road on his horse one evening while I was weeding my vegetable patch and when the setting sun had shone on the horse and rider, turning them into not two, but one living creature, I had tried to capture the feeling I felt.

Instead of using detail, I made lots of quick strokes of my pencil for I wanted to keep the movement active and at the same time release a sense of carefulness to the sketch. Now, studying it, I felt frustrated by not knowing how to draw the horse and rider to match just what I saw in my head. So, I flipped to a new page and began again. I sketched the galloping horse and then I sketched the rider, using the same kind of broad, bold strokes to draw the man as I did to draw the horse. Almost without realizing it, I was drawing a mature man instead of a teen-aged boy. When I drew the rider's legs and then his feet, I erased the boot I had sketched and made the man barefooted. Then I began working upwards from the foot, drawing his leg, then his butt sitting easily on the horse. Swiftly I drew the torso of the man, then I placed his arms, one grabbing onto the wild

31

flowing mane and one arm reaching down and his hand grabbing his own naked thigh and finally I drew the man's head, thrown back and with a wildness matching the horse's mad gallop. I drew the horse without a saddle or bridle or halter of any kind. I was swept up into a different world, one of excitement and a readiness to explore an artistic outlet I had never experienced before. I felt exhilarated as I drew, pausing to hold up my sketch and then allowing myself to be drawn back into creating my vision.

At one point, I lit my pressurized gas lantern so I could see better with the much brighter light than the dim kerosene lamp I had been using, and continued sketching. I drew small details on the man's foot and then let the outline of the leg carry the image upwards. I carefully drew his fingernails, the knuckles and the veins on the back of his hand. More than once, I used my own right hand for a model, gripping my own thigh. The artistic high kept me up for hours as I moved from one point of my sketch to the next, at times drawing with only several strokes to depict movement or strength and other times I got so detailed it took me long minutes to draw what I was seeing in my mind. My thoughts flew back to what my dad had said just that evening about small mirrors as I brought out the behind-door-mirror I stored in the back of my closet. "Why do you have such a mirror, Aaron?" my mother had asked once when she had brought my clothes to my place.

"I have no one to tell me if my hair is a mess or if my shirttail is hanging out in the back," I had smiled.

But now I propped the mirror against the wall close to my desk and I studied my face in the mirror. I decided to draw his jawline in great detail. That and his eyes and use just enough shading to show his lips and nose. I drew the hair on his head short with a slight curl. I selected a wide tipped pencil and paused a moment and breathed slowly in and out. Then, I made several quick broad strokes of a rough image of his scrotal hair and penis. I used the same pencil to go over a number of the other places I wanted to have blackened. There was a point where I thought maybe I should erase the marks I had made for the genitals but then I dismissed the thought for I was drawing it for myself. I couldn't imagine letting anyone else see it. It would be scandalous, not only because I had drawn a person but also a naked person.

The ring of black dogs facing me were barely distinguishable, for it was nighttime. Their eyes glowed green, their white teeth shone in mocking, leering and vicious grins and I could hear them growl. It sounded like what I would imagine the cackle of witches and they moved in restless motions as they whined and growled. I couldn't move. I wanted to raise my arms and shout at them, to dash towards them and make them run away, but I couldn't. It was as though I was bound by ropes, held immobile and helpless. Then, one of the dogs jumped towards me and with a mighty effort, I flung my arms upwards.

I felt my body jerk on my bed and I woke up, sitting bolt upright, my breath coming in gasps. The morning sun shone into my windows and outside, the freshness of the day was in stark contrast to the nightmare I had woken up from. I looked at my drawing on the desktop and then I looked away again. It had been after two o'clock when I had finally stopped drawing and gone to bed to fall asleep almost immediately.

Not once had I awoken all night and actually slept in, for when I looked at my alarm clock, it was already 7:30, an hour later than my usual wake up time.

My nightmare stayed with me all day on Monday. I had gotten an order to make an extension dining room table for a cousin whose large family had kept on growing, so I used the pattern I had and began cutting out the pieces. My gasoline generator hummed noisy outside and air-powered tools made all the sounds of air expulsion I was used to. I know among the English, it's always fascinating for them to see how we Amish power our tools without electricity, but for us, we are so used to it we hardly think otherwise. But today, the growl of the dogs was echoed somehow by the noises in my shop.

I was so thankful I could work by myself. Ever since I was seventeen, I had worked in furniture shops, making chairs and tables and dressers. Yes, it had gotten monotonous and boring, doing the same thing day after day but it had finally paid off when I had asked if I could use the shop equipment to make some pieces I wanted to construct. "Hardly enough work for specialty pieces. You have to charge much more and it's the price that is the final decision for many people," my boss had told me as he ran his hand over the top of the Shaker nightstand I had made. "It's much more fragile looking than the rest of the furniture. Those legs don't look like they could withstand a lot of roughhousing. I'm thinking people like more sturdy looking furniture. Let's put it in the show room and see what happens."

The nightstand had stood there for two months and Shorty Jake, the salesman said a number of people admired it and then shook their heads slightly as they read the price. Then one day, Shorty Jake opened the door to where we workers were busily making furniture and beckoned me to come. I left the noise behind me and brushed the sawdust off my shirt sleeves. "There is a lady here and she wonders if you could make a matching table. I told her I'm sure you could but wanted to ask. She wants to meet you."

"Hi, I'm Annabelle Romana," the woman introduced herself. Dark hair framed her brown skin, her lipstick framing perfect white teeth. Her white blouse had a lay down collar and was buttoned with pearl buttons, draped over the waist of her black skirt. "You are younger than I expected. You designed this or copied it? It looks Shaker, a line of furniture I admire and actually have the privilege

34

of owning a bench. It is extremely rare and highly sought after, you know."

"I did design it myself," I told her "although I copied a lot of the design from a book about Shaker furniture I have. I raised the height to accommodate our higher beds and here," I showed her the drawer, "I used several pieces of narrow wood for the bottom to minimize the possibility of warping for I don't know how long the lumber was cured."

Annabelle nodded, "Small but interesting changes." She ran her hand over the square top. "I like the proportions."

I waited as she had examined it. "So, you can make a matching piece?" Her dark eyes looked up at me.

I had nodded. "Okay," she had said. "I'll pay for this one and leave it here so you can copy it and then you will let me know when the next one is completed. I'll leave my telephone number. Can you have the piece completed in a month?"

I nodded my head, "Probably earlier. I'll do my best."

"You are Amish, aren't you?" she had asked, looking at my suspenders and handmade shirt and pants. "I am," I replied.

"Well you have talent," she said. "That is some fine design and workmanship."

That had been the springboard for my business and five years ago, I had created a niche with my originally designed pieces and was able to work on my own. I had two studios in Philadelphia that assured me they would sell my furniture on consignment and then eventually began buying my furniture to resell.

But today, I was glad for the easy piece I was making as the nightmare continued to plague me. "You won't charge them the expensive prices you charge the English for the other pieces, will you?" Mom had said somewhat admonishingly when she heard I was making the table. "You know with all those children to feed and clothe."

"I'll charge them the going rate," I told Mom and refrained from reminding her how Cousin Andy had inherited the farm from his parents and as the only child, was probably wealthier than even a lot of the other wealthy Amish farmers and businessmen.

That evening, I took out my sketch pad and looked at the drawing from the night before. I studied the man, and then I studied the horse. I examined the crosshatching on the man's hand on his thigh. My technique was definitely different from my other sketches. I liked the feeling of wildness, of unrestrained freedom that came to me from the horse and rider, unencumbered and without a bridle or a saddle, and the man without clothes.

Then doubts began creeping into my thoughts. Was this departure from my normal way of sketching or drawing responsible for the nightmare? Was this a punishment from God for drawing a naked man? I looked at the sketch again. It was as if the contrast between the detailed areas and the rather abstract lines delineating the outline of the horse and rider gave it motion. Fluidity.

I wished I could talk to the rider. He looked strong and full of life, sitting confidently astride his mount and I wanted to know who he was. I felt as though he had always been there, and my pencil had merely been the tool by which he was revealed to me. I felt slightly uncomfortable, as though my thoughts were taking me places I shouldn't go. What had I created?

I'm hardly ever impulsive, but suddenly I reached out, lifted the sketch pad, ripped the drawing out of the book and then tore the picture into small pieces, hot tears streaking down my face as I destroyed my creation, and feeling as though I was killing a part of myself. I went to bed and lay on my back, staring straight up into the darkness. My bedside clock ticked steadily, and I felt my heart beat rapidly under my crossed arms. I heard my teeth grind together and I sighed and tried to relax my jaw. I remembered I hadn't written in my diary for two days, but I didn't want to move. Or to think.

# CHAPTER FIVE

"**H**ow was your week?" Mr. Downton asked. "Have you been writing in your diary?"

"I have. But not every day. I skipped the last two days." I adjusted myself on the chair and looked at the therapist.

"I see," Mr. Downton replied. "Was there something that happened that made you quit? You got involved with something or what?"

"Mr. Downton," I began, and he interrupted quickly. "Call me Brian."

"Brian, something did happen," I said simply. "I drew a picture." Then, I chuckled a little bit at how silly it sounded.

But Brian didn't laugh. "You drew a picture? Of what?"

"A man riding a horse."

"Did you bring it along? I'd love to see it." Brian said with interest.

"No," I shook my head, "I didn't bring it along. You see, I tore it up. To shreds." I'm not exactly sure why I trusted Mr. Downton, err, Brian, so easily, however I think I may just have been so relieved to finally find someone to talk with. So, before he could even begin asking questions, I told him. About my bold departure from not drawing people to drawing the man riding the horse without clothes on. Yes, I told him about the dark dogs in my nightmare and I told him about the depression that had sat on me for the next two days

38

and then how last night, I had tore my picture to shreds. Then my spate of words ended.

"You didn't write about this in your diary," Brian said. "Was it too emotional for you?"

I blinked my eyes and looked away. I nodded my head.

"Like I said before," Brian encouraged me, "it's okay for you be emotional with me. I'm thinking you may not be used to speaking into words your feelings. That's why I encourage you to keep a diary as a way of learning to release your emotions. Trying to clamp the lid too tightly on a teapot on the stove results in the pot blowing its lid. Much better to let the excess water escape as steam."

"Or remove the teapot from the heat?" I smiled.

Brain shook his head. "The heat is life. We have very little means of controlling how much heat life gives us. But God has given us mechanisms on how to release the steam."

I nodded. "I like that. Did I let the lid blow off when I drew my picture? Then I got a nightmare? And sleepless nights? You know what? Like I told you, I stayed up late to draw and went to bed around 2:00 a.m. I never woke up once until the next morning and I even slept in." I shrugged my shoulders.

This was not making sense.

"Aaron," Brian said kindly. "Don't overthink. You recognize God gave you these talents and you enjoy using them. For sure, you can abuse talents but do you really think God would punish you with nightmares because you drew what was in your imagination? Maybe your sketch was a release for something he wants to show you about yourself. Something you may have been trying to clamp the lid on. I don't know if that's the case, but I do know God is not punishing you. He's not that kind of God."

When I had searched in the local phone book for therapists, I had zeroed in one Brain Downton's ad because his ad had included the words "Christian Counseling". So, I was not surprised to hear Brian speak easily about God and I'm sure it gave me a lot of confidence to talk easily with him about my depression.

"You don't think God punishes people in this life because of what they do?" I now asked.

Brain shook his head, "If he did, we all would be suffering. Not one of us are that good. I know, I know! So many people go back to the Old Testament and bring up verses about God punishing the wicked. King David actually asks God to do some terrible things to his enemies. But you must put that all aside! You know why?"

"It's confusing," I confessed. "God seems to be... to be complex," I said feeling like maybe one shouldn't talk about God this way.

"I'm going to suggest something to you," Brain said with warmth. "I want you to put aside all you know about God except what is revealed in the four Gospels. I want you to not think of God the way Moses and Abraham and King David and King Solomon or any of the prophets thought about God. I don't want you to think about God the way the Apostle Paul, or Apostle Peter or the believers in Acts thought about God. I want you to think of God only the way Jesus reveals his thoughts about God. Either Jesus is true about who God is and no one else did or really can understand who God really is, or Jesus is a liar. We cannot have both. The God who was seen in part by the early Fathers nor the God that was by early leaders of the church outside of how Jesus shows us who God is, is not accurate." Brain stopped himself and bit his lip. His eyes filled with tears as he struggled to contain his own emotions.

"I'm not being very professional," Brian said wryly "but this is such an elemental truth for Christianity. If we can't embrace this, we confuse and muddy all of humanity's way of looking at God. So," he said with a smile. "I would like you to try this. Write your thoughts in your diary. Speak your words to whoever you speak with. Live your life fully and openly but in all things, put everything to the test you hear about God and what is right and what is wrong by asking yourself, *What does Jesus say?* and *'Did Jesus leave an example for this?'* Then and only then can we get a picture of who God is and life makes so much more sense."

"So, it wasn't wrong for me to draw the naked man?" I said rather slowly.

"That's not for me to say," Brian said simply. "Too often we want to know what is right and what is wrong. Not necessarily a bad thing but I feel strongly God guides us more than what we give him credit for. Should you have torn up the picture? As much as I hate to say it because I would have loved to see it, it's okay for you to have destroyed it if it bothered you. Do I believe God punished you with a nightmare? No."

That evening, I drew another sketch. Much the same as the first, but I drew the man, fully clothed. And the horse had a bridle. I tried to make my sketch come alive, evoke the same feeling of movement and light and fluid motions but even as I was sketching, I knew I was failing. When I finally lay my pencil down in frustration, I felt empty. I put the sketch pad away. I toyed with the idea of tearing this one up, too, but I didn't.

*"Dear Diary. I'm not supposed to tell you what I did today but what I felt today. Hmmm, let me see where to begin. This morning, I felt good because I knew I was going to see Mr. Downton, cross that out, Brian today. Then after I was there and he told me to put aside what I had thought God is like to only what Jesus taught us*

41

*who God is, both by his example and his teachings, I felt bewildered. Yes, because I had never separated the two. All my life I thought about God as the Creator who made the heaven and earth, gave lots of rules to the people in the Old Testament, destroyed people because of the bad things they did, favored his people, the Israelites over any other race and then added the teachings of Jesus to those ideas about who God is, plus attached the teachings of Paul and the Apostles as rules to follow and tried to make sense of it all. Now I'm supposed to try to see God only through the eyes and life of Jesus. I did feel bewildered, as though I was questioning the very existence of my faith.*

*"So, back to my feelings. Yes, strange. Even revolutionary. When I stopped in at my parents' house to pick up my laundry, I saw my mom in the kitchen sitting at the table writing a letter. She had washed her hair and was letting it hang to dry it. I've seen her without her cap before, although not frequently, but this time I thought of what a nice sketch that would make but of course, I rejected the idea right away, both because we are not to draw people and because she would not like to be drawn without her cap. In fact, so strong is our teaching about the women wearing caps, when she saw me come in, she jumped up and got her cap off the shelf beside the door and put it on her head, her gray hair hanging around her shoulders but her cap securely on her scalp.*

*"Normally, I wouldn't have felt anything about it, but on the rest of the way home I examined what I knew about the caps the Amish and Mennonite women wear. The shapes and sizes, the different styles, the disputes of how big they should be or how much hair could be shown in front of the cap. The many times sermons are preached about it and how history supports how women for centuries wore caps and how the idea of women not wearing caps nor cutting their hair was only recent, like in the last hundred years or so. In my mind I saw a sea of caps, stretching from the present*

42

*where only the Amish and Car Amish wore caps, back to the years where all women wore caps. Or a veiling or shawl. Like the Muslims. I have heard Amish men comment on how they appreciate seeing Muslim women heavily veiled. Yet I knew the Amish would never accept Muslims as Christians for the Muslims had Mohammad as their prophet instead of Jesus. All because the Apostle Paul wrote a letter to the Corinthians telling them their women should cover their heads and the men shouldn't. Then why were we men expected to wear hats when we went away? Wasn't that covering our heads? Oh, Diary, I forgot. I'm supposed to write about my feelings. Well to be frank, I'm feeling confused. So, I will do what Brian said. I will take the teaching of Jesus about the caps and hats and because he didn't say anything at all about who should and who shouldn't cover their heads, I will not bother myself about it. I feel good. There, those are my feelings. Oh, and I feel good that I tried to sketch the horse and rider again but I don't feel good that I wasn't able to make it alive like the other one. I feel like I should maybe try again. Now, I feel sleepy."*

The very next day, Aunt Katie walked over to see me. My mom's unmarried sister, Katie, lived about 5 miles away in an Old Order church district in a small one-bedroom apartment annex built onto a farmhouse where my grandparents used to live. While my grandparents were still alive, Katie had her room in the upstairs of the big farmhouse where my Uncle Ammon and his family now lived but after the death of Dawddy and then of Mahmmy, as we called our grandfather and grandmother respectively, Katie had moved into the annex where she now lived. About once a month except in the winter, Katie, now in her upper 70's came to visit my mom and spend the day. After i moved into my own home, she began coming over to spend time with me. "I get lonely because I live by myself. You live by yourself and you get lonely so it is good for lonely people to meet other lonely people so we can be lonely together. Except then we are no longer lonely." Katie enjoyed distilling ideas into cryptic anomalies and they were usually followed by her infectious laughs.

"Aaron, now you yust keep on working still," Katie was a little out of breath as came into my woodworking shop. "If I could have some water yet, it would be good" and thankfully accepted the water I offered from the thermos I kept in the shop. "So now, what are you making now?" She peered over her rimless eyeglasses. Her white cap matched her straight white hair tucked back severely underneath the covering. "Didn't wear my bonnet to come see you, even though I am supposed to. Too hot and the walk here too short. There you have it. Too hot and too short," she chortled.

I laughed with her. "I just started making a coffee table," I told her. "It's going to have three legs, each one supported in part by the others. Then I'll make a wooden top on it but I will cut the wood apart, making mortises and tenons as I go, and then I will cut out spaces between the joins and put it back together again."

"Ach Aaron! It makes no sense. Your words and why would you cut something apart just to put it back together?"

I laughed. "Look Aunt Katie, like this," and I showed her the sketch.

Katie peered through her glasses at the paper. "Ah yes, I see. You are such a good drawer I can now understand your words. But still, taking the time to cut wood apart just to put it back together. Such waste of time."

"Ummm, isn't that the same principle about jigsaw puzzles? You and Mom spend a lot of time putting a picture back together that at one time was already in one piece. Then, when you start another puzzle and there are several pieces in the box still together you take even those apart, mix them up and then spend time trying to fit the right pieces together into a picture that was already together!" My woodshed filled with our laughter and Katie shook her finger at me. "You are just the limit. I guess we do the same when we make quilts. Cut apart material into pieces only to move the colors into the right places and then sew them back together."

"Katie, when you think of God, do you think of him as angry or do you think of him as loving?"

My question made my aunt look sharply at me. "Now Aaron, why do you ask that? I can read in the Bible who God is. Sometimes he is angry and sometimes not. The God of the Bible is the God of Katie." She shook her head slightly. "That's the Amish way."

I hand sanded the wooden piece I was working on. A faint dust filled the air around us. "I've just been thinking," I told her. "Jesus hardly ever appears to be angry. And He said if we want to know God, we can know him through Jesus."

"Jesus was angry," Katie said emphatically. "He was angry at the Jews for selling stuff in the temple and he called King Herod a fox. That was anger."

"Whoah," I laughed raising my eyebrows, "you know the Bible well. And have thought about whether God is angry or not."

"Yes, when Mahmmy was sick in bed, I read the Bible to her for hours. The Gospel of John was her favorite. Of course, I used our German Bible to read but sometimes later I would look it up in the English Bible to see how they explained it. But such stuff is better left to the ministers, anyway. That's why they are made ministers. To help us understand the Bible and tell us how to live."

I thought about Katie's church. Old Order ministers spend a lot of time preaching from the Old Testament, using the examples from the history of the Israelites and teaching how God was angry with the heathen and with those who disobeyed Him. When the New

Order congregations split off the Old Order groups, our preachers, as we call them, used more examples from the life of Jesus and taught more from the New Testament.

"When English women who believe in God, die, do they go to hell because they don't wear caps?" I gave voice to some of my recent thoughts.

"If they don't know better, then we leave that up to God. But if Amish women leave the church and stop wearing the caps, it is sin! The Bible teaches us what to do!" Katie's voice rose. "Now Aaron, what is wrong with you? Such questions you are asking. Come, Mom said you lost your driver and got another horse. Let's go see this new one. I've always been one for horses" and Katie rose up with determination and went for the door. "Time to speak of normal stuff."

We went outside and I whistled for Lady. I got her grain bucket and when she heard my whistle, Lady lifted her head and looked towards us. I rattled the oats against the tin side of the bucket and Lady came up to the fence at a trot, her white stocking legs a dance of elegance and beauty, her ears pricked forward in anticipation of the grain and her flowing brown mane and tail undulating, my horse trotted towards us.

"Oh, ho," Katie laughed, "quite a looker! Now Aaron, if you can find a sweet girl as easily as you pick good horses, you will get a good one." Then Aunt Katie laughed at her own quip.

"Yeah, that's the normal stuff it's alright to talk about," I mumbled under my breath as we turned to go to my house. If Katie heard me, she didn't reply.

"This is just the best way to have a house, although I wouldn't have to wash all those windows," Katie said looking at my bank of windows looking out in all directions of the main floor. Only the corner where I had put the bathroom had no windows. I had used the original granary tongue and groove boards to build the walls for the bathroom, leaving their natural patina untouched. "But the way you have your bedroom up there, all open and everything, gives you no privacy."

This wasn't the first time Katie or other relatives and friends had chided me for making the choices that I have made in building my house. I had learned to mostly listen to their comments and let it slide but now I said, "Privacy from whom? I live by myself, just as you do. Do you worry about privacy?"

"I pull the shades every evening on all the windows. I wish sometimes my windows were bigger for I don't have good daylight but at night, the shades must come down. I don't want people spying in on me. It isn't seemly!" Katie shook her head in a decided manner.

"Dear Diary, I feel more quiet in my spirit since I stopped trying to live my life in fear of the wrath of God. Yes, I still think about hell and how I must live in order not to go there, but I also can think more about life without thinking always I must not do certain things because it would make God angry.

I feel more at peace."

# CHAPTER SIX

T he late summer morning was already warm enough to make Lady's flanks dark with sweat, and the harness she wore was outlined in damp lines. I, too, was warm and glad for the shade of my straw hat to keep the sun from shining directly on my face. I was headed to the sawmill in my dad's spring wagon. That is what we called the elongated buggy without a top and with only one double seat up front and the cargo space in back big enough to transport half a dozen bags of animal feed, a newborn calf, or as was in my case, lumber I would take back to air dry on my rack. Even with sunglasses the light was bright and warm, and the brisk trot of my horse was almost the only sound on the deserted country road. A male red-winged blackbird sat on top of a weathered wooden fence post and slightly lifted his black wings, emblazoned with the yellow edged bright red epaulets and sang his cheery "Okaa-ka-leeeee" into the lazy morning. To my right, the fields of wheat had already turned into a sea of golden stalks, the seed heads full and heavy although standing up straight on the sturdy stalks.

"Oh, Aaron," I heard a woman's voice call to me when I neared a typical white farmhouse built close to the road. Hannah and Homer Stoltzfus are the Amish woman and man who have lived here all of their sixty plus years. They inherited the farm from their parents, of whom I only had faint memories, before they passed on when I was but a young boy. Neither Hannah nor Homer had ever married and anyone who didn't know them would have taken them for a childless Amish couple. As twins, they must have gotten along quite well and they ran the farm as efficiently as any married couple, Hannah baking bread, cleaning house and making both their clothes, and entertaining friends and relatives. Homer took care of their herd of beautiful doe-eyed Jersey cows, around 30 in number and seemed quite content to follow in the wake of his chatter-box sister, who made the business of everyone else her business as well.

"Whoah, Lady," I said and pulled on the reins to stop my sweating horse. "Good morning, Hannah."

"Aaron, when I heard hoofbeats on the road, I said to myself, 'Now who could be coming this way in the morning? Farmers are busy in the fields and us womenfolk are busy in the house, getting the breakfast dishes away and the house all read up. So, when I looked out the sink window, I saw a new horse and so I thought, who could that be?" She laughed and smoothed her work worn hands down over her half apron, pinned together in the back with the obligatory straight pins all Amish women use to fasten their clothes.

"It's me," I smiled. "I got Lady about a month ago so I guess that's why you didn't recognize Dad's rig."

"Ah yes," she chortled, "that's why. I did hear about your other horse, what was his name? that broke his leg. So shaauttt." She looked at Lady, who was making her bridle jingle as she tossed her head to get rid of the annoying flies. "And still no blinders," Hannah said, referring to the black leather squares usually fastened to the sides of the bridle flanking the horse's eyes. They were originally used to keep horses from shying from unexpected objects coming up beside them and spooking them and eventually they became fashionable way back before the automobiles were invented. As is the way among us Amish, it was considered best not to mess with traditions, so this practice of having blinders for horses was not mandated but considered to be a sign of conformity.

"Well Hannah, as you obviously remember, I didn't use blinders on Prince either. I think it prevents most horses from being able to see on the sides as they have always done. I know there are

49

some exceptions where a horse actually feels safer by not being able to see out the side and only have tunnel vision, but they are in the great minority. So, that's why I don't use blinders."

Hannah's laugh rang out, "Aaron you have always been different. Your explanation makes so much sense, but you know we Amish don't always make sense, we just do as we are told. Works the best, you know, keeps us in the way of the fathers before us."

"You have always lived here, haven't you Hannah?"

"Yes," Hannah nodded and I thought I may have seen a slight cloud cover her usually cheerful countenance. "Born here and will die here. It is my lot. The furtherest distance I traveled was to Ohio for a funeral of a cousin who used to live here. When I came back, I told Homer 'If the world is as big the other way around I don't want to go again' and he said well, he's never been to Ohio." Then all signs of wistfulness left her face as she laughed again.

"Oh Aaron, I wanted to tell you please ask your mom I need another quart of her elderberry syrup. Homer and I used the last of it in the spring when we got that nasty flu that was going around and now, with summer ending soon and colder weather coming, we want to be prepared for the crud when it shows up again. That elderberry medicine sure does the trick. Does she make you use it, still?"

"Oh yes, I do. Great and powerful stuff. " I smiled. "I will tell her you asked for some."

"Well, I should go on," I told Hannah.

"Are you maybe going to your brother Levi's?" Hannah curiously questioned me.

"No, not today."

"Well, maybe to get horse feed for your driver, here?"

"I get my horse feed from Dad since I only have one horse."

"Ah yes, I should have known that. No sense getting your own. Good parents you have."

"I do. Well I should be going."

"Then I'm thinking maybe you decided to get some more wood working equipment for your shop. Since you have your dad's spring wagon."

"Not today, Hannah."

"I don't see any tools on the back and I didn't hear of any frolics today or work bees. But maybe you have been asked to help somewhere?"

I gave in to her questioning and told the inquisitive woman, "No Hannah, I'm on my way to Lapp's Sawmill to get some more maple lumber, and while I'm there I might get some walnut or other kind of hardwood lumber so I can air dry it and then when I am ready for another project, I will have the lumber I need."

A pleased smile spread her mouth into a triumphant grin. "Well Aaron, that is wonderful! So thinking ahead you are! Well, you have a good day. Wait! I just finished a batch of oatmeal raisin cookies and it will only take a minute to get you half a dozen. Living by yourself as you do and without a wife yet, you could use some cookies, now couldn't you?"

Someday I will sketch this Amish woman, probably as I saw her just now, bustling her portly self through the front gate of the white painted wooden fence and up the straight concrete walk to her front door to fetch me some of her cookies. Never have I sensed any regrets for having lived her entire life on the farm, never married, no children, caring for her twin brother as well as any sister could and happy at having bested "that different young man up the street who lives by himself and hardly works" in wearing me down by her indirect questioning to find out where I was going.

"Happy enough," I told myself between bites of the still oven-warm cookie. "Maybe by the time I'm that age, I will have learned to be the same. I wonder if she ever battled depression."

"We are not put on earth to try to figure out how to make ourselves happy and fulfilled. We are put on earth to serve, to work hard, to honor God and to make the world a better place by our lives, the way we treat our neighbors and to provide a good home for our offspring. It is the way of the world to seek happiness to sacrifice the ways of holiness for the ways of the appetite." Preacher Dan stood upright in the archway between the large living room of the farmhouse.

Preacher Dan was in his seventies, a kind and round faced, pink cheeked, long white bearded man with past ears-hair whose ends curled up at the ends, probably the result of years of wearing a hat day after day, season after season. I sat in the middle of the room on a wooden backless bench, leaning slightly forward to change my position and ease my back where I had been for over the last hour. I was surrounded quite tightly by the other males of the congregation and because I was an older single man, now with a beard, I had adapted my seating position at church in a seat usually somewhat between the young unmarried boys and older married men. For anyone not familiar with the seating arrangement of Amish services, held in turn by the families of that district, the men and boys usually were congregated in the living room and the women and girls in the spacious kitchen/ dining room and if the house was unusually small, there were extra backless benches placed in the halls and even occasionally the downstairs bedrooms had the beds pushed against the wall and the overflow crowd was seated in all available spaces. It was not uncommon for summer services to be held in a large outdoor shop, even in buggy sheds, for when it was warm and humid, it was way more pleasant and less easy to get away from the sweaty smell, both in the women's area and of course in the men's section, that was sure to make houses stuffy, and to be honest, at times just gross.

"We must live our lives in the constant knowledge of the end days," Preacher Dan continued shaking his hoary head slightly. "So many people die with such great regrets. I have stood beside the death beds of men who have moaned almost with their last breath, 'I wish I had done more. More for others and for God and less for myself.' It is one of the saddest things I have ever heard. So now is the time, my dear people, now is the time to live like you should. None of us have the guarantee on one more day, or even of one more hour. How clearly I remember, and I know I have told you before, when I was only a twenty year old boy, not even married yet and all at once, there was this noise and old Roy, true he was already more than 80, fell off his seat and died of a heart attack." As he continued telling the now very familiar story of how imminent death can be, I studied his facial expressions as he talked about the finality of death and how it hovered about all living people. What made this man, usually so friendly and happy, seem so obsessed with dying?

"If a bird would once every hundred, no, make that every thousand, years fly to Jack's Mountain and take a beak full of dirt, then fly to the Atlantic Ocean and drop the dirt, when the mountain would be totally removed, eternity would have just begun. And if we miss heaven, and are cast into the lake of fire, that is hell for eternity it will be without time. That is how serious it is to be prepared the best we can to be ready to die. Even then, the best we be or do is not enough. We have to believe God in his mercy will allow us to live in heaven with him."

Preacher Dan's analogy of eternity will probably be emblazoned forever in my memory, for as a young boy my vivid imagination tried over and over to imagine just how horrible hell would be. I would try over and over to comfort myself that, well, at least, sometime, hell would have to be over. Nothing could last forever! Plus, when I helped my dad clean up dead branches and burn treetops after having made firewood and the flames would shoot upwards, usually after a rain to keep wildfires from spreading, I would look intently into the flames, and try to imagine being in there. Even as I backed away from the intense heat, there was a morbid fascination to try to get used to the heat, hoping somehow to make the expected agony more bearable.

I exhaled slowly and sat up straight, slightly arching my back. Thankfully, I was wearing my white shirt Mom had just finished that summer. I had selected the fabric and even though I really wanted to choose the fabric that was loosely woven and more breathable, I instead chose the cotton that was heavier and opaque. Now, there was a word we Amish learned early. Opaque. All clothes had to be opaque. No transparent stockings for the women and girls. No see-through fabric for the dresses. Caps were to be opaque. The capes and aprons the females wore over their dresses could be transparent but that was about the extent transparent fabric could be used for any clothing. And men never wore transparent clothing. Well, except for well-worn everyday shirts at times were worn and washed so often you could see through the worn areas.

"We must say 'No' to the devil and his whispers tempting us to follow the lusts of the flesh. You young men," he turned his attention fully to our room, "have to be so careful in the summertime. You must be willing to do everything you can to stay away from the nakedness of the worldly. I told one young man, who came to me for advice on how to avoid temptation; to avoid going to town in the summertime. When he said he went past a neighbor's house where the teenaged girls were outside sunning themselves with such skimpy bikinis it left nothing to the imagination, I told him he should go the other direction to get to his work. Better to go the long way to and from work rather than to be in torture forever in hell."

My mind wandered, back to a childhood memory. I was about fifteen years old. I had just finished the obligatory eighth grade education the Amish school provided, and which was required by the laws of Pennsylvania. I was not yet sixteen, when the Amish youth are permitted to join the rumspringa years of attending the Sunday evening singings, holiday outings and other youth activities. I had been sent to our nearby neighbor to return a cow halter we had borrowed to tie up a recuperating sick cow outside. Uriah was a newly married young man with a sweet-faced wife, and, I think, an infant daughter. When I rounded the side of his barn, Uriah was forking loose straw onto a farm wagon. His strong muscled arms bulged and flexed as he effortlessly tossed huge mounds of straw onto the wagon. His shirt, perhaps at one time a blue chambray, had worn to its current threadbare state and when he saw me, he stopped work. "Hi Aaron," he said with his friendly smile and his white teeth flashed above his short Amish beard.

"I, I brought the cow halter back," I heard my voice stammer. "Dad told me to say 'Denke " and just as I ended my sentence, my voice changed pitch, for I was going through the awkward stage of dealing with my voice changing.

"Tell him he is welcome," Uriah laughed with a twinkle. "I remember when my voice did that. Made me realize I was growing up." He poked the pitchfork into the ground and put one foot on the side. "Sometimes I think it was one of the best times of my life. Waking up to the changes going on inside of me. Watching my muscles grow and me getting taller." Uriah flexed his right arm and I could see the muscles on his chest push against the thin fabric.

I wanted to say something in reply, but I could only swallow deeply and nod. I smiled at him.

"How old are you?" he asked.

"I'm, I'm fifteen," this time my voice didn't embarrass me.

"Fifteen and I think you are already almost as tall as I am. Come here."

"Let's take our hats off and see."

We stood back to back. "Yep," I could feel his hand on top of our heads. "Feel up here."

I lifted my left hand and he took it and put it on our heads. His hand felt strong and warm, pulsing with energy. I was very aware of his body pressed against mine. I felt my body respond to the pressure of his buttocks against mine.

"Bout same, actually," he said and stepped away and put his hat on again.

I placed my summer straw hat on my head and turned to leave. I took a quick look into Uriah's face and was warmed by his friendly smile. Then he put his hat back on and thrust his fork into another bunch of straw. "Bye, Aaron," Uriah called and turned back to his work.

"Bye" I called out and made sure he could hear my departing word. But I didn't turn my head. In fact, I didn't want to do anything that might make the feeling I had go away. Or disappear. For I could still feel his hand on the top of my head, now covered by my hat. I could still feel the touch of his strong hand on the top of my hand, helping me feel how close to the same height we were. I could also feel where his back end had fit against me, just below mine for most of my height is in my legs. His strong back had pressed against mine and every move of his body had filled me with something I had never experienced before. I was aware of my body responding in ways I had never, ever known were possible.

Preacher Dan continued on with his warnings. I tried to jerk my thoughts from my past and into today. "It is so serious Jesus even said it is better for a man to cut off his hand rather than go through life using his hand to cause offense. Same with the eye! Can you imagine cutting out your own eye because you looked at a woman to lust after her? Jesus wanted us to see how serious life was. And still is."

I remember how embarrassed all of us young boys in our youth group were and I can't imagine what the girls thought. My mind darted back to a story my dad told us boys once when were all still at home. "Jacob had to stay at the hospital overnight and of course someone found out he had been pleasuring himself so often he finally decided to take literally the teaching of Jesus and having helped his dad to castrate the newly born bull calves, he took matters into his own hands, literally, and castrated one of his testicles. He began bleeding so much he panicked and screamed for help from the bathroom and his parents got a neighbor to take him to the emergency room. After he recovered, he moved to another state to an Amish community where he wasn't known, married and has a family, it is told." Dad's voice had been grave and somber and I know it was his way of telling us about the birds and bees and making sure none of us boys would spill our honey by ourselves.

Preacher Dan's voice droned on and on. In front of me, three of the young men bent forward, resting their beardless chins on their knees, the back of their suspenders flat against the tightly stretched white shirts. Lean and strong, I could see the outline of their spines pushing against the restraining opaque fabric.

"In closing, I want to go over several things yet," Preacher Dan said and there was a perceptible movement among the listeners.

Several of the men pulled their watches from their pockets and then put them back again. The boys in front of me sat back up and one of them reached back and scratched his back. His hand was short and his fingers stubby and as he leisurely scratched his back, the dirt under his fingernails showed evidence of the morning chores he had probably done. That was not uncommon, for work came before hygiene among the Amish many times. I checked my own nails and picked at some dirt lodged in my thumbnail.

But no, I knew the "in closing" did not necessarily mean our two-hour plus Sunday morning services were really ending. It just meant it was more a sign that the services COULD be winding down soon. For even after Preacher Dan ended his sermon and we all knelt backwards facing the rear ends of all the others behind us as Preacher Dan read an obligatory prayer from the small Black Prayer book the preachers all carried, it would be time for the other preachers, and perhaps two or so elderly men from the congregation to bear "witness" to the sermon. This witnessing could become quite lengthy sometimes and only when the final song, lasting as long as ten minutes or more, was sung would the youth boys rise and leave the house, and from the women's area, the young girls following their lead and leave the room.

This is all so familiar to me I hardly ever really think of how all this ever came into being in the first place. Oh, and the entire services are held in German. Not in Amish German, although the preachers are beginning to use more and more our common vernacular to deliver their sermons. It is still considered more holy to use as much High German as possible. Plus, all the prayers and songs are in German and were written during the Reformation Era in mid 1500's a time of much persecution and executions of the Anabaptists, from where we Amish originated.

"Aaron," Uncle Ammon extended his right hand towards me and we shook hands. "Vee gehts?"

"Vee gehts?" I echoed our customary greeting which literally translated is, "How's it going?" and really doesn't require an answer at all.

"Aaron, I remember you told me there was a man down the valley who sharpens planer blades for large machinery. I couldn't remember his name and where he lives. Do you remember?" Uncle Ammon owned a large wooden chair factory and employed over 50 people.

"Yes, it was...."

Uncle Ammon lifted his hand stopped me with a laugh. "I won't remember. I have so much information on my mind all the time. Here," he fished around in his capacious Sunday pants pocket and drew out a small spiral bound tablet. "Write it in here," he said giving me a stubby pencil. He offered the pencil towards my right hand and I used my left hand to take it and began to write.

"Left-handed. And a wood worker. How does that work out for you?"

A wood worker himself, Uncle Ammon knew many of the early woodworking tools designed and crafted were made to be used by the right hand.

"Ambidextrous," I said with a smile and to show him, switched the pencil to my right hand and wrote the name of the man and then switched to my left hand and added the address. "I don't remember his telephone number."

"Was that hard to do? To use both hands to write and to work with?" I could see he was intrigued, glancing first at my right hand and then at my left.

"Yes," I told him. "Very."

"Hmm, interesting. But I'm sure you are glad you learned to use both hands."

This time I corrected him. "Either. I use either right or left and only both like anyone else."

"Whatever," Uncle Ammon shrugged, and I knew the point was lost.

Then we joined the rest of the men as we filed outside, some to help the boys set up the tables beneath the maple shade trees in preparation for the Sunday meal of sliced homemade bread, peanut butter and marshmallow spread, pickles, pickled red beets an during the wintertime, huge pots of bean soup followed by an assortment of pies. Other men would "go visit the barn" and everyone was ready by the time the women and girls would have swiftly set out the food and then the men and boys ate first, followed by the women, girls and children.

That evening, I had a lot to tell my Diary. Plus, there was an idea I wanted to sketch.

# CHAPTER SEVEN

I stood frozen to the floor of my house. The evening light outside had the fascinating yellow-gold light happening only when the clouds gathered in the west and soaked up and then reflected the sun in order to give off their own golden glow. Even though I was aware of the luminescent sheen outside and spilling in through the windows, it was as though I were not even present in my own body. I was sure I felt small atoms dislodge themselves from the top of my being and slowly yielding to gravity, flow down my body and gathering up more of who I was, melting everything except my center core, then to puddle onto the floor about me. In my consciousness, I could see my melted cells begin to spread out around my feet, as though my entire facade had completely melted away. I read the note on the ripped envelope again.

"What in tarnation is this? Are you gay?"

The note was placed on my open sketch book, flipped to the page I had been working on last evening. I pushed the paper slowly off my sketch and looked at what I had created.

Like I said before, Amish frown on having pictures and I knew Dad especially didn't approve of me drawing people. I realized the sketch I had made of the two men lying in the shade of a sugar maple, the younger one resting his head on the chest of the older man was still mostly unfinished but I had drawn the faces, both with contented half-smiles and closed eyes reflecting the perfection of the moment. No, the sketch was far from complete, but the faces reflected how they both felt.

The note was written by my brother Levi. I knew his handwriting, bold and messy. Why he had been at my place or why he had come into my house and why he had flipped through my sketch book had hardly any bearing on what I was feeling. No, it was the word "gay".

Everyone's universe has a center. Around that center are people, usually family, relatives, friends and community. For us Amish, the furthest out from our universe is usually the English. That was where the word "gay" belonged. To the English. The Amish don't do gay. Don't acknowledge it except as a deviation, an unnatural feeling and an abomination against God and all people.

So, now as I stood there looking at the note, I felt that was where Levi had put me in his mind. Cast me into a world away from the Amish, away from my family and away from my community.

I began experiencing an unusual phenomenon I had felt several times before. It was a supernatural experience of being very present in myself, but also detached and aloof from reality. As though my spirit was floating above my body about ten feet and was looking down at myself standing in front of the sketch.

I imagined Levi, coming into my house, maybe for a drink of water or something for an empty glass was on the table next to my sketchbook and the note. I could see him idly flipping through my sketches and then coming to this one. The one of two men showing affection, both very happy with what they were experiencing.

When life changing moments occur, the mind can do some strange twists and turns, trying to take in the enormous changes. Did Levi see this as something I had been wanting all my adult life? Did his mind race back into our mutual past and was he seeing the signs or evidences he could have picked up?

I shook my head slightly to bring me out of the floating space and I heard a soft moan escape from somewhere deep inside of me.

Gay.

Only yesterday after work had I ever even first written the word "gay" and how I felt affected by it. In my diary.

Funny how small details work themselves into the bigger picture only later. Like now.

My sketchbook, the drawing, the note Levi had written, the empty glass of water had told me enough of the story to freeze my feet to the floor. I had overlooked the small blue covered spiral bound notebook I used for my diary lying on the tabletop next to the sketchbook. Usually in the morning after I heated the water for my coffee and ate my slice of homemade bread with apple butter, I cleaned up the kitchen before I left, but that morning I had been in a hurry for I had promised one of my cousins I would come and help him frame the addition of another bedroom onto his house. So, I had left my house in a rush and left. Left my sketch book and diary lying on the table. Now, prickles of apprehension gave me goosebumps. Had Levi read my diary! Is that why he asked if I was gay? Was the drawing enough to make him use the word gay, or had he read my diary?

"Read your entry again," the voice inside of my head demanded. "Read what you wrote!" I heard the voice scorning and accusing me, the echo growing louder and louder.

I reached for my diary. I flipped to the last entry. *"Diary, Brian told me to write about my feelings. So, I'm going to write how I feel. I feel attracted to men. I like the way they look, the way they talk, and the way they feel. These are my feelings. I've known ever since I was young that I had these feelings. I remember when I realized these were not feelings other boys shared. That I was different. At first, it had only been a feeling of excitement, like as when we boys wrestled and then lay laughing, the one pinned down underneath the other, waiting for the word, "Give". The feeling of another boy's body against mine. Sometimes it was like what I had felt when I took the borrowed cow halter back to Uriah and we had stood back to back to compare our heights. Nothing out of the ordinary for any of the Amish boys and men to do, and yet I realized my body responded differently to those incidents than theirs did. I was responding to males just as they would towards females.*

*"Am I gay?"*

That is what I had written. I had wanted to write more, but I had felt as though I had opened the door into the forbidden room of thinking. For some reason, I was not ready to walk into that room. Not even with my pencil.

Prickles of fear made me first hot and then cold and I felt the strength leave my legs and so I pulled out a chair and sat down. Why had I written that? Why had I let my sketch book out and my diary exposed? Why had I finally after all these years, had to sketch, to write and to try to answer questions that I had felt had no answers?

I heard my alarm clock ticking up in the loft beside my bed. I heard the "blip" as the pilot of my propane powered refrigerator lit the burner and the noise of the refrigerant liquid expanding through the lines to cool the interior. However, the house seemed very quiet. As though even my environment was waiting for something to happen. Even though none of the foundation blocks that given me my life and existence had been removed, I knew one of those foundation blocks had now been exposed. Both by me to myself and now to my brother Levi.

"Hardly any sleep," I told Brian, "for the last two nights." I forced my voice to speak calmly. "During the days, I avoided as much contact with any people as much as I could. Didn't even go to my parent's house for supper."

Brian smiled at me and then surprised me by saying, "Aaron, you are stronger than this! I look at you and I see someone drowned in pity." My face must have registered my shock for he said, "Don't look so shocked. Even though this is only our third session, I see you as you need to see yourself. A self-made man. Strong enough to navigate as a gay man through a strict and controlled environment, knowing who you are and yet moving on, willing to live your dream of making a house out of a granary, designing and making furniture and becoming quite successful and only in your thirties. You have succeeded in achieving your goals at an early age. I'm sure you had to overcome a lot of obstacles to come to the place where you are and in spite of the setbacks, you kept on building and making and creating.

"You are not a different man now that Levi knows you are gay. You don't know exactly what this disclosure will mean to you, but the same man that sits in my study with me is the same man that will be able to know what to do when the need arises. I'm not being unsympathetic. I'm telling you what you need to know. You are not all at once a different man than you were before! You are still Aaron, still a talented craftsman, still a man who thinks deeply about life," he paused, "and knows how to express some of his feelings in written words." Brian waved his hand towards my diary.

I wasn't even sure why I had brought my sketch book and my diary when I came for my therapy session. Perhaps as props so if words failed to express my feelings, I could show Brian what I was going through. Yes, I had cried as I told Brian about finding the note. And about wondering if Levi had read the diary.

"Crybaby" had been thrown at me often when I was younger. Then, as I entered my teens, I had learned how to control my emotions and not cry in front of people. I had learned how to blink away tears when I became emotional reading books, or even at times when I came across unexpected kindnesses.

65

"I imagine you write poetry as well," Brian added. "If you haven't, you should."

"Let me change the subject," my therapist said quietly. "Aaron, you have to know this one thing in order for you to cope with what you now acknowledge. You are gay."

"I have a question," I interrupted. "Am I gay if I've never... ah never DID anything with another guy?"

"You mean, if you never had sex with another man?" Brian asked. "You can say it, you know."

I nodded.

"Yes. You are gay whether you have had sex with a man or not. Because gay does not, contrary to many people's definition, mean having sex with men. Or lesbians having sex with each other." Brian smiled. "It's so interesting that sometimes people, straight as well as gay, religious as well as non-religious, get so obsessed about sex, that they immediately think about people having sex when they hear the words "gay" and "lesbian" and "straight." As though our natural attractions mean ultimately culminating in sex. True, it often does. However, there are straight people, attracted to the opposite sex, who never have sex. Do you know of such people?"

"Aunt Katie has never been married. And our neighbors, Hannah and Homer, are twins and single, in their 70's. I am quite certain none of them ever had sex." Then I added, "And me. I've never had sex," I smiled at him. It felt good to be able to talk freely about sex with my therapist.

Brain tossed his head back and laughed loudly. "Being gay has nothing to do with what you do. It is all about who you are."

I know he continued talking, but my weary brain closed in on his last statement with the tenacity of a drowning man. "Being gay

66

has nothing to do with what you do. It is all about who you are." That meant I had nothing to do with being gay! If it wasn't my fault, whose fault  was it?

"Then God made me gay?" I couldn't help myself.

Brian stopped what he was saying. "What?" he asked.

"If what you said is true, about me having nothing to do with being gay, but being gay is who I am, then God must have made me gay?"

Brian smiled and waited. "Not any more than you can help you were born left-handed. You didn't choose that. You were born that way."

"But I learned to use my right hand as well. One of my earliest memories is my dad gently taking my spoon out of my left hand and putting it in my right hand. I remember crying and wondering why he wouldn't let me eat. 'Ach, leave him alone,' Mom would say. 'There are a lot of left-handed people who make out all right' but dad never stopped. By the time I was seven and started school, I had learned to eat with my right hand, but when I was tired or cranky, I would use my left hand. I know my dad had a talk with my teacher, and she was just a young Amish girl in her first year of teaching, but she insisted I learn how to write with my right hand."

"Interesting," Brian commented. "Did you know at one time left-handed people were not allowed to be members of some church congregations for it was considered unnatural? But back to you, what do you think? Are you glad your dad insisted you learn how to use your right hand?"

"Yes, I am," I admitted. "I'm glad I am ambidextrous. Glad

I don't always have to search for woodworking tools made for left-handed craftsmen and actually, it comes in handy when I carpenter, for when my left hand gets tired of swinging the hammer, I can use my right hand." I had to laugh along with him and felt myself relaxing.

"What would you do if you had a child and it was lefthanded?"

"I'm not sure," I said slowly, then added, "probably let him be left-handed. It's different but eventually hardly anyone even knows." Brain looked at me keenly, then asked, "What?"

"I didn't say anything," I chuckled.

"You did with your eyebrow. Your left eyebrow goes up if you are quizzical," my therapist smiled.

"You know how to read people."

"Yes, it comes with the vocation. Now what was your question?"

"I think I would at an early age talk with my child and explain that there is nothing wrong with the way God created him, or her, but it may mean there are some difficulties that come along with being left-handed and if they would want to learn to use their right hands as well, I would be glad to support them and help them as much as I could." I heard my own words and realized the words I was saying directly reflected my own feelings of being gay. My eyes filled with tears and they streaked down my cheeks and ran into my beard, almost scalding my skin. This time, I didn't lift my hands to wipe them away, I let them fall.

"Very good," I heard the catch in Brian's voice, and another volley of salty rain fell from my storm-weather eyes.

"Okay," Brian said, "I'm going to put into words how I understand you. You can tell me if I'm correct." I nodded.

"If you had a child and you would find out that child had same sex attraction, you would first tell your child he is created perfectly the way God planned, however if they wanted to learn to like opposite genders you would support them and help them in any way?" Brian summarized his understanding of what I was saying.

I thought about that statement a long time, then I finally said, "But I don't know if they could. Do you know of any gay people actually changing? I have read much on the subject from books I checked out or read in the local library and you don't know how many times when I read about people who wrote they have changed to now liking the opposite sex, I still wonder if they really have. I'm not sure why, but I have not read a convincing story yet."

"That's because you have such a strong attraction to men," Brian said bluntly. "But back to my question, would you tell them you will support them if they DID want to?"

I shrugged and felt uncomfortable. "I don't know. It seems like a lot to tell a child."

"It is," Brian said, "but it happened to me. My oldest son is seventeen now and both my wife and I thought he might be gay even when he was as young as five. We talked about it together and agreed to not stress about it. We often prayed and by the time he began asking questions which we felt indicated he was questioning his feelings we actually steered the conversation into an area where he felt comfortable in telling us."

"But you guys are Christians!" I was amazed at my outburst.

My statement must have hit Brian hard. I saw him clench his fists and his smile was a straight line in his face. "Yes," he said softly. "We are, and my son is also. Being gay doesn't mean you can't be a Christian."

That very same evening, when I went over to my parents' house to get my weekly milk and eggs, before I went into the house, I heard Dad calling, "Aaron! Can you come over here?" and saw my dad standing in the doorway of the shop, where he often tinkered making repairs and building projects of his own, like marble rollers for the grandchildren and at times dollhouse furniture.

I entered the familiar shop, dim now for the sun had already set, but I could see he was not alone. Levi was there with him.

Dad nodded and sat in his wooden swivel chair beside the wood stove he used to heat the shop in the winter. Now the summer night air came in easily through the open door and exited out the windows. I leaned against the workbench. Levi was balanced on a three legged stool Dad had made years before.

"It has come to my attention you have unnatural feelings for men," Dad's normal Amish was substituted for a more High German, like the preachers used on Sundays. He had always done this when he spoke to any of his children about Bible subjects or about God. "Levi told me what he found."

I looked at Levi. His face framed with his straw hat on his head, his Amish beard growing chin-style as is often done by the younger married men. His blue eyes looked straight into mine and I felt I saw more than the usual condescension I often felt from him. "I do… I do have feelings for men," I said as calmly as I could.

Dad didn't reply immediately.

"That's sin!" Levi almost hissed. "The Bible is very clear about that. God clearly forbade it in the Bible. Not just in the Old Testament but also in the New! Aaron, you know better than this! That picture you drew is terrible! Have you been having sex with animals as well? Is that why you wanted a mare? This is so disgusting!"

"Levi!" Dad's voice was firm. "That's enough! Listen, both of you. Levi, if you can't control yourself, you must leave now. You are suggesting Aaron having sex with animals is indecent. Aaron is your brother. If you don't apologize for that question, I want you to leave right now." Then turning to me he said just as sternly, "Aaron, I expect you to answer some questions and to tell us the truth. This is a serious matter and as your father, I demand you respect that."

"Sorry," Levi said in a softer tone, "I shouldn't have said that."

I nodded my forgiveness but didn't trust myself to talk.

No one said anything for several minutes, and we three sat in silence as the night folded in around us. We heard footsteps approaching on the cement walk and we all knew immediately it was Mom. "Ben?" her voice came into the door before she switched on her flashlight in on her husband and two sons sitting inside in the dark. "Vas gebbt?" ( What gives?) I blinked against the bright light as she identified each one of us.

"Vernie," Dad said calmly, "we are talking about things that pertain to men." His words fell without emotion and I thought I could almost hear them hit the rough wooden floor beneath our feet.

"Monsleit, Monsliet", ( Menfolks, menfolks.) My mom clucked her tongue. "Sometimes I think the only reason women exist is to make sure there will be another generation of men to make decisions and keep us women out of their business." She sniffed indignantly and snapped off her flashlight, then turned and we heard her walk towards the house.

"How long has this been going on?" The question from dad didn't have to be addressed to me.

"I've always known, "I said. "Even as a young boy, I knew I was attracted deeply to certain boys. When I got older, my

71

attractions were toward other men, usually around my age."  I couldn't believe how easy it was for me, not only to answer Dad's questions, but add my own information.  I didn't want this to be an inquisition, but a discussion.  I didn't really feel as though I should be on trial.

I heard Levi snort softly in the dark but at least he didn't say anything.

"Levi, go ask Jake if he could come out."

Levi left and the skies outside became dark.  I heard a cow mooing from the pasture and the sound carried easily through the quietness. There was enough breeze to turn the tall windmill and the familiar clanking sound of the long metal shaft pumping water up into the storage tank from the well was a constant backdrop sound of the farm. I benefitted from the water pressure as well as we had dug trenches and laid a supply line to my house. Water was plentiful in the valley and the farms close to the mountain ranges were fortunate to have artesian wells supplying the enormous water needs of the dairy farms in the area. But our family depended on the windmill for our water.

Dad said nothing and I wondered what he was thinking.  We heard a double set of footsteps and Jake followed Levi into the shop. Jake is the shortest of us three boys.

"Did Levi tell you?"

"Yes."

"Aaron, what do you want to do? How are you planning on dealing with this?"  Dad's question caught me off guard. I was expecting him to say what he was thinking.

"I want to live my life like I always have," I answered. "I'm not a different man than I've ever been. I'm still the same Aaron."

"But you have to agree what you feel is wrong," Levi retorted, and I could hear his voice reflecting his conviction.

"No," I answered. "I did not choose to like men, so I don't feel it is up to me to say I'm doing something wrong in order to deal with my feelings." I know I wasn't very clear telling them how I felt but I was trying.

"Do you agree the Bible says it is wrong?" Jake asked, not unkindly.

I've always admired and respected my older brother. Like Dad, he was not outgoing and verbal like Levi and I knew he had a gentle and caring spirit. So, when he spoke in a normal tone, it moved me deeply and I fought back my tears. I was glad it was dark, and I answered, "Yes, I know the Bible has clear teachings about men having promiscuous sex with men. But I'm not having sex with men. I never have. I am gay because I have attractions for some men and yes, I am sexually attracted to men and not to women."

"Well, I guess that is obvious because you never had a girlfriend," Levi's voice was more like normal now.

"So. you never fooled around with boys or men? Ever?" Dad asked.

I shook my head and said, "No."

"But you want to," Levi said, not asked and I could hear disgust creeping into his voice. "You want to put it up into a man's behind!"

"Levi!" Dad's voice came out strong again.

"It's okay Dad. Let me answer." I turned towards my brother. "You know the feelings you have for your wife? Of being with someone who loves you and someone who enjoys being with you and you want to show affection and how special she is to you? How when you are away from home and want to see her and if she is gone you miss her? You know that feeling when you are at church and maybe during church there is a time when you see your wife and she looks at you and a happy smile flits across her face because she sees you? You know that feeling? That feeling of putting your arms around her and holding her tightly against you? How you feel when there is something upsetting going on and how other people sometimes don't understand and accept who and what you are, and then you come home and there she is, waiting to listen to you and welcome you home? Those are the feelings every human has, and they are not wrong. Maybe what they do sometimes with those feelings are wrong but not to have those feelings. Those are the feelings I have as well. But my feelings like that are not for a woman. And I didn't choose my feelings for men, I was born with them, so if it is wrong to have those feelings, then God made a mistake when he made me and thousands of other men like me or there is something that is so flawed inside of me that I can't fix it.

"Do you think one evening when I was a teen-ager I decided, 'I want to have feelings for men! I want to be different from most of the Amish men and boys I know, and I want to make life difficult for myself and for my family! I want to choose a path so painful I can't talk with anyone about it and try to hide my emotions and feelings inside of me and be lonely and face life without the possibility of ever having a companion that is natural for me?' Levi, do you think this is what I chose for myself? How ridiculous would that be?" Tears were streaming down my face, but my words spilled out into the farm shop, splashing against the ears of my brothers and my dad, carrying through the open window and into the night air.

I wasn't finished. "You said, Levi, about me wanting to put my penis up another man's bottom. You are wrong. I don't want to. And if I never am able to find someone to share my life with, to be a companion to, it will not be easy, but I'm not the only one. Do you

74

think Homer never wanted to get married and have a companion? What about Aunt Katie? We know of other people in the Amish church who never find a companion. If they can do it, I can do it as well."

"Well said," Jake said simply. "I was just thinking the same thing."

"Don't blame God for making you this way, Aaron," Dad said sternly. "That is not right. We are all born into sin and our sins will keep us out of heaven. God doesn't want men to be with men and women to be with women as a man and a woman are created to be. We have the clear word written and obeyed by his people for thousands of years and God does not change."

"Do you still believe in God?" Levi asked. "And that the

Bible is the Word of God?"

"I believe in God," I answered wearily. I was getting extremely tired and exhausted from my sleepless nights. "I believe God's Word is in the Bible." And then I added, "I believe in God as Jesus has revealed him to us. Jesus didn't give any teaching on same sex attraction. Surely there were people with same sex attraction among the people he met. It was all around him as history has proven."

"By the heathen," Levi said with a laugh. "You want to justify what the heathen did and still do?"

"I also have a lot of questions. Earlier I thought I wanted to ask you why went through my sketchbook and whether you also read my diary, but now I don't care anymore. This may sound strange to all of you but I'm glad you did, Levi. I am exactly the same person, the same son to you Dad, and the same brother to you Levi and Jake, the same uncle to your children, the same cousin to the cousins and the same man to the community I always have been, but now you know something I have always known and didn't share with anyone. Except Brian," I remembered. "I told Brian just today." I was barely aware of what I was saying.

"Who is Brian?" Dad and Levi asked as one voice.

"My therapist. I go to see Brian Downton, a Christian counselor in Babville." I might as well tell them everything. "I have nothing to hide anymore. I'm sure it's not easy for you to hear me say these things and if you want to try to help me, I'm not going to turn you away. Like I said, I too, have lots of questions. But one thing I am sure of, I never chose to be gay. I was born this way. I can wish God wouldn't have made me gay and pray to him to make me straight, but at least I know it's not on me for I didn't choose it."

I walked home in the moonlight, my legs wanting to crumple in weariness. But as I climbed the steps to my loft, feeling lightheaded with sleeplessness, it felt as though I had lost something. In my sleep-muddled brain, I wondered what I had lost. I undressed completely for I didn't feel awake enough to take a shower, nor did I want to sleep in my sweat dried underwear and fell asleep almost instantly. That night I never once woke up.

# CHAPTER EIGHT

"Good morning," Jamil's friendly smile greeted me as he came into my woodworking shop the next day. "You may wonder why I came without an appointment. I could have written a letter, but I was too excited about the invitation and wanted to be able to tell you."

"Well this sounds interesting. What invitation?"

"I submitted the photos of the table you made," he looked around trying to spot it, "as a potential entry for the Pennsylvania Original Design Studio competition. Here, look at their brochure and I have more information on my laptop. Do you want to see?" His dark eyes were bright as he gave me his exciting news.

"I would like that," I said.

"Okay," Jamil replied. "Let me go get the laptop." He turned to go back out to his car. I followed him to the door.

It had rained overnight, and this morning, the world was as bright and fresh as a late summer morning could possibly be. Birds had already begun to do their preliminary practice migratory flight patterns and I watched a small flock of about a dozen red-winged blackbirds dart overhead. "Jamil!" I called. "Bring it, your computer to the house and we can look at the information there. Okay?"

"Sure," he replied.

I led the way up the pebble walk I had made by placing a border of four by fours along the sides and then putting a layer of medium sized river pebbles in between to create what I called a "chatter pebble" walk for footsteps created a conversational tone as people walked over them. "Great front door. I suppose you made it, " Jamil said when I opened the pine door I had made with tongue and groove two by eights.

"Thank you, I did. At first, I thought I would put a window in it but since I have a window on this side of my house facing the drive, I decided to make it a solid door."

We entered my house and I pulled a chair away from the table for Jamil and then I sat down as well. Jamil opened up his laptop and waited for the screen to light up. "Great space," he said looking around the loft. Then his computer came on and he opened up a page and there was the table I had made!

Jamil turned to me with a smile and pushed the laptop towards me. "See here is the homepage for the design studio. They accept entries only from crafts people who have never entered competitions before. That would be you, right?"

"I've never entered any competitions. I may have to check with the studios in Philadelphia, however I think they would have contacted me if they ever entered any. Should I contact them and ask?" I leaned forward to read some more.

Jamil moved his chair closer to mine. "Well, I already entered your table but yes, if you would feel better to make sure, I think it is a good idea." He gave me time to read the information. I could feel his warm breath on my ear as we both read from the small screen.

"Look, right…"

"Is that…"

My left hand and his right hand collided as we both began pointing to the screen. We looked at each other and laughed and I dropped my hand to the table. "What were you going to ask?" he asked, his hand poised in mid-air.

"See here?" I asked pointing to the small words "Winning

Entries from Previous Contests". "Have you looked at them?"

"Yes," Jamil replied, and he clicked on the tab. "They have the winning entries from the last 10 years. I don't think any of them are as good as yours." He clicked on the photos one by one and showed them to me. Tables, desks and chairs were the most common, but a tea cart really caught my attention.

"Interesting to me how some really contemporary pieces won, and other years traditional styles were chosen. Really good designs. I'm impressed." I knew the hours and hours of design and thought and work it had taken to make each piece of functional art. We continued discussing the winning entries and our dialogue was easy and relaxed.

"Let me show you how to see what you would like to see," Jamil said. "Take your finger and place it here. Now click downwards." I pressed but nothing happened. "No, like this," he smiled, and he took his hand and showed me how to click towards the bottom of the entry board. "Then if you want to make it larger, take your thumb and finger, or two fingers, and do like this." He moved my hand onto the sensor and then spread my fingers apart. "Yes," he said as I navigated around on the screen.

"With a lot of jerks on my part and a lot of patience on yours, I can do this!" I laughed.

"These are excellent," I reiterated as I studied the winning entries again and again. "Really, really good!"

"But none as good as yours," Jamil said, his face only inches from mine. He smiled as his gaze met mine. I saw his Adam's apple ripple as he swallowed, still looking directly at me. I gave him a quick smile and then I exhaled slowly and said, "Maybe you are biased. Plus, remember who took these excellent photos. Hey, would you like some coffee? Or something cool to drink?"

"A glass of water is fine," Jamel replied. He looked down at the computer.

I brought two glasses of water to the table. Jamil took a drink and then set his glass down. "I have been too forward," he said in a subdued manner. "Please forgive me."

"Jamil, no. You have not been too forward," I reached out and lay my hand on his. "It's fine. I understand."

"Sometimes I get so lonely," he confided. "I am different from the rest of my extended family here in America. They all want to keep the old ways from Iran, and everyone is trying to make sure no strange influences come into our lives. But we all are learning it is not so easy to come to America and pretend we still live in Iran. For me, coming to the States has been the best thing that ever happened. I am finding there are others who I can connect with. People outside of my family and my faith. I meet many nice people in photographic appointments."

"Then you know how life is among the Amish. With even more restrictions. No electricity, no computers, no cars and it is even more difficult to be "different" as you say." I said with a little laugh.

"You are gay?" Jamil asked.

"Yes," I replied, "I am gay."

"Me, too," Jamil smiled. "I thought maybe you are gay the first time I came to photograph your furniture pieces. But I didn't know if Amish are gay or not."

I didn't say anything as I thought how to say what I wanted to. "Amish don't do gay, but some Amish are gay. Not openly, for even though I think I may have met other Amish gay men I don't know for sure."

"You are like they say here, 'In the closet'? Jamil asked.

"I was," I admitted, "until yesterday."

"Was it hard coming out?"

"Here, let me show you what my brother found." I opened the drawer under the table and pulled out my sketch book. As I showed him the drawing, I heard Jamil take a quick breath in and hold it. "Then here read this," and I showed him my diary entry. Afterwards, I told him about my meeting with Dad and my brothers.

"Wow," Jamil kept saying over and over again. He studied my sketch and held it up to the light. "I'm not out," he said softly. "To no one."

"And I wasn't sure about you," I chuckled. "I guess I haven't been around gay people enough to know how to tell."

"That's the good thing," Jamil said quickly. "It is much better if being gay or straight is not what connects or separates us. We are all people and that is what connects us."

"We are all people, and that is what should connect us," I repeated. "That is a profound statement. I will remember that. Thank you, Jamil."

"So it's okay for your table to be entered in the competition?" Jamil asked getting up from the table.

I nodded, "I think so. Sometimes it is frowned on among us Amish about entering competitions, but I know there are times when other people, English as we call non-Amish, have entered Amish crafts in fairs and competitions instead of us, so I think this is all right. I will also check with the studios."

"But I am not English," Jamil said a small crease furrowing his forehead.

"I realize it's a strange term to use for non-Amish, but you may understand why when your realize we Amish have for hundreds of years used a German dialect among ourselves and when the first Amish settled in America before the Revolutionary War with England, they lived right among many English speaking people. So the Amish simply began calling all non-Amish English since the majority of the people at that time in America were from Great Britain. Gradually the term 'English' meant exactly the same as 'Non Amish' no matter what race or nationality. Does that make sense?"

Jamil laughed, "You are a good teacher but yes, it does. We, too, have a term for all non-Muslims. "          ">

"Aaron!" I heard my mom's voice calling my name and then the gravel began the conversation as she walked towards the front door.

"Yes, Mom in here," I went towards the door.

"Aaron, I saw a car here all morning and I thought oh well, maybe you aren't feeling well so I came over," Mom began speaking in Amish German of course and then she came inside and saw Jamil. She shot a quick glance at him and then looked at me and cocked her head slightly to one side. "He's here on business?"

"Mom," I said in English, "this is Jamil. He's the man who comes to take pictures of my furniture and he was showing me a furniture competition he entered a table of mine in. Jamil, this is my mom."

"Nice to meet you, ma'am," Jamil was the perfect gentleman. He reached out to shake her hand. Mom responded, and they shook hands, but Mom made sure the handshake did not last longer than it had to.

"Your son is a fine man," Jamil said warmly and looked around my house. "He has made a wonderful home for himself."

"Well yes," Mom tried hard to look friendly, "but now he needs a wife to keep it in order. I won't interfere with what you were doing." Her glance towards the open computer on the table seemed to cause her concern, "but I will just check to make sure my son is doing his housework well." She started for the loft. "You know men. They sometimes forget to look under the bed for dust and things can just pile up something awful."

I was ready to protest but all at once I understood so I closed my mouth and said nothing as Mom slowly climbed the stairs.

"I should be going," Jamil said. "Thank you for the water and as soon as I hear from the selecting committee, I will let you know."

"If you hear," I corrected him and as we laughed together Jamil said, "I don't have any fears about that. This is just the entry level and your table will be accepted." When I turned to face him, I saw my mom up in my loft bedroom, standing back in the shadows, looking down at us. The corners of her mouth turned down and her eyebrows bunched together in the middle.

I accompanied Jamil to his car and as we shook hands in parting, I held his hand tightly in mine. "Until next time," I told him.

"Yes," he smiled and then drove off.

"Now Aaron, how could you waste a whole morning looking at the computer with that young man?" Mom's voice was indignant and I turned from watching Jamil drive off to face my Mom in the doorway of my house. She came down the two front steps and looked at me.

"Mom," I went towards her. "I wasn't wasting my time with Jamil. We were talking about my furniture and then we began talking about our lives. You know, I'm learning Muslims aren't so much different from us Amish as I used to think they were."

My mom is not often at a loss for words, but her expression was quite interesting to see as she opened and closed her mouth more than once. "Well, I declare! I never thought I would hear a son of mine say such a thing."

"He's really nice, Mom and I think you'd enjoy getting to know him." Then I grinned at her, "Did you find any dust bunnies under my bed? Am I keeping my house clean enough for your standards?"

Mom bunched her hands under her half apron like she does when she is uncomfortable, "Ach Aaron, I didn't come for that. I, I heard what you told Dad and the boys last night. I was outside listening through the window."

"I know, Mom," I told her. "It's okay. I don't mind."

"Oh, Aaron," she said, and I heard the hurt in her voice, "I am so disturbed! I don't know what to say. How can you say these things? Oh, Aaron, are you gay? Say it isn't so!" I heard a sob in her voice.

I hardly ever remember hearing my mother cry and to hear her now made me turn my head away sharply to hide my tears.

"I used to wonder about you sometimes, and thought about it, but I kept saying surely not. That's why I kept talking about you

84

getting a girlfriend and getting married. I probably shouldn't have," I heard my mother sniffle. "I know I meddle into things I shouldn't."

I turned and walked towards my mom. She was twisting her apron into a tight knot and looking down at the front steps. "Oh, Mom!" I wrapped her in my arms and hugged her tightly. I put my head on top of hers and huge tears rolled down my cheeks. I felt her body quiver as she tried to stop crying. "I love you, Mom, " I kept whispering as I hugged her.

In that hug I thought of the years and years my mother had worked hard to make a home for her husband and us boys. Not only had she worked at home, there was a period after we boys were all teenagers she had baked for the Amish market and her delicious homemade bread and cinnamon buns sold out quickly. Yes, baked, cleaned, sewed dresses and shirts and pants and washed windows and painted walls and in her own way showed us how much her family meant to her. She had beamed happily when my brothers got married, loved her grandchildren and was often the life at get togethers as her ready laugh and easy talk kept conversations flowing. But now I felt her as a person. Not just a wife and a mother, but as Vernie, a woman. Did she have dreams beyond the farm, beyond this community sometime when she was young? But I never sensed any dissatisfaction and I felt now she would never have traded her life for any other. Except now she had a gay son. And her pain was not only for herself, but for what she feared would be mine.

Finally, our storm of weeping subsided. She pulled away and using her apron she dried her eyes and then she lifted her arm towards my face, the hem of her apron still in her hand. "Use the other corner," I managed to say, then laughed through my tears, "The one that isn't already wet with your tears."

Mom's sobbing turned into giggles and she complied.

"Okay, Aaron, " she cleared her throat and then said quickly, "Now that's enough of that. I'm not going to get my housework done standing down here with you." She turned and walked towards her home.

I stood still and watched my mom's retreating back, feeling extremely sad and strangely relieved at the same time. No, not only relieved, but also happy. And light. As I watched my mom's steady gait take her further and further away from me, her familiar form becoming smaller and smaller, I remembered last night when I had been walking home in the moonlight and how I had the sensation of having lost something. Now I realized what I had lost. My secret was no longer a secret. I no longer carried the secret of being gay. I had no idea how much this would change my life in my Amish community, but at the moment just being out from under the dread of being "found out" was enough. I lifted both arms above my head and tilted my head towards the sky and I breathed a deep sigh and felt the tension of the years melt away. I looked to see if I could still see my mother, but she was gone, following the road around the barn and out of my vision. I found myself whistling that afternoon as I worked in the wood shop.

"Hey Aaron, how's the new horse doing for ya?"

I tied Lady up at the hitching rack and then said, "I like her. She's not as fast as Prince but she is long winded and easy to manage." I smiled at Yonni's Johnny who was tying up his horse next to mine.

"Oh, that Prince! I remember how he was very unpredictable when you first drove him. Big and strong, I knew he could do some damage if not trained right. But you did a good job with him." Johnny's voice was friendly. "Well, let's get to work. Looks like the bean field already grew a lot of workers," and then he laughed easily in his friendly way.

"Just take these baskets along with you," a Mennonite woman waved towards stacks of bushel baskets. "Then drop them off at the ends of the rows so the pickers don't have to come back here when they fill theirs. You can pick any row that's not started," she added. This was "Efficiency 101."

"Then stay on the row until it is finished. We don't want rows begun and then not finished for that would mean we don't get all the beans. They are for canning for relief, you know. And thanks for coming. There is a water table down there and there will be snacks afterwards. The Lord bless you," and she smiled at us. Then, she looked closely at me and said, "Are you Ben and Vernie's Aaron? Why I thought you might be. You probably don't know me but I know your mom real well. I used to haul her to the market when she still went and as we would go past your place she would say, 'There's Aaron. She how he made the granary into a house?' You tell her Frieda asked about her. She'll know who I am." With a laugh, she waved us on.

"Has your brother Jake started cutting his oats yet?" Johnny asked. "We started our first field today and so I dread tomorrow. Shocking oats is not my favorite farming. Sometimes I wonder if I should do something else. Worked on the farm all my short life."

"How old are you?" I asked, "About 23?"

"I'm 24," Johnny replied. "I'm going after church baptism and probably get married this fall, but sometimes I think I want to do more than farm. I know Dad will build me a small house to start off, but I'm just not sure. Did you ever want to do more than make furniture?"

"Yes, I have," I told him. "I enjoy my work and like where I live but I have thought it would be interesting to travel. Not just here in the United States but also other countries. I'd like to visit Germany. And Italy sounds nice from what I've read."

Every year, several farmers would donate the use of one of their fields to raise crops and then donate the food to charities where the crops were processed and then shipped to third world countries where the Mennonites often had small mission outposts. When the crops were ready for harvest, there would be announcements sent out for volunteer pickers for the beans, or perhaps tomatoes, or cucumbers or whatever the farmer had grown and then there was a community effort, many Amish and Mennonite districts gladly helping, to get the food prepared. That's the Amish and Mennonite way. "Many hands make light work" is an old saying, not only handed down verbally but in practice as well.

Picking beans is hard work, I decided about an hour later and I stood up to ease my back. All over the field, girls and boys, men and women, but mostly young people labored to help get the beans picked before dark. The scene before me was timeless for I remembered oil paintings I had seen in art books at the library painted by the masters of peasants working in the fields, bending over their tasks, harvesting crops from the earth. This was my life, my people, my heritage and I felt I belonged. Always have. Even though I went through the years of hiding my secret of being gay, that really didn't matter in the bigger scheme of things. I was but one man in a community of thousands. It felt good to belong. To be Amish.

"The shadows are getting long. That sun is setting fast," I heard Yonni's Johnny say as a gentle reminder. "Ach yah," I laughed and bent over and began picking beans again.

# CHAPTER NINE

"It has been brought to our attention you have erred and fallen into a trap of deception." The Amish bishop spoke gravely and firmly. "Men lying with men and women lying with women is an abomination to God and to his people!" Bishop Henry's eyes bored into mine. He threw his words out into my parents' living room with measured tones.

Preacher Dan was there, older than Bishop Henry by almost twenty years, and Preacher Monie (about the same age as the Bishop) from our district, and the deacon for our church, Lewis who was called Louie. As is common among the Amish, the Bishop may have several churches under his rule, and I think Henry had three churches he was responsible for. He officiated in weddings, funerals, and in baptisms, but most notably in presiding over church matters such as excommunication and shunning.

I waited. Dad had asked me to come to the house this evening and told me the preachers wanted to talk to me. So, here I was and Henry, ( Amish hardly ever give titles to each other ) had opened the meeting. The schoolhouse clock on the wall kept on ticking, measuring the silence into small bites and then moving on to the next moment. I wondered if Mom actually had left the house as is often requested by the preachers for women, or if she had sequestered herself in my parents' bedroom.

"Aaron," Preacher Dan said matter of factly, "maybe you can tell us how this came about."

I wonder if I was the first gay man they had ever had to "deal" with or if some other Amish man had ever been in my situation. I'm thinking any Amish boy or man would have probably left the Amish and gone "out into the world" before they came out.

"I hardly know what to say for your question makes it sound as though my attraction for the companionship of men hasn't always been with me. Ever since I was quite young, I realized I was attracted to boys. That interest and attraction , like straight men and boys have for women, is inside of me. I didn't choose it, nor did I want to be this way and so I hid it from everyone as much as I could." I tried to state the truth without being flippant in any way. I respected and yes, even admired the preachers in my church and although I didn't know Henry that well, I did feel he was a nice man and I never felt him to be overbearing or harsh.

Henry shook his head slightly and closed his eyes for a moment, then he looked at my dad. "Ben, did you know how Aaron was when he was young?"

My dad took his time to answer. "No. His mother and I knew Aaron was different than Jake and Levi. More like a girl, I guess. Very sensitive and always mild mannered and particular. But I did not know about this." I could hear the pain in his voice, and I went into "you cannot shed tears" mode. Then my dad added, and his voice was in the serious tone he used when we had done something wrong as boys, "It is a sin and must be dealt with."

Human feelings and emotions always had to be brushed aside when it came to religious matters and I knew that. It is a part of being Amish.

"Do you acknowledge that, for men, being intimate with men is a sin?" Monie asked me, his words sharp and to the point. His red beard, streaked with gray, was sparse and many times when he preached, I had to think of a bantam rooster we had on the farm when I was young. Like the rooster, Monie seemed to dart around, intent on finding information and being quite willing to impart such "news" quite readily even as the cock was eager to breed any willing hen.

"I am attracted to men for companionship and I think I always will be," I hedged. "I have never been "intimate" with men." Maybe this would suffice.

Monie gave a little chuckle, "That is not answering the question. We already know what the Bible teaches. Do you know in the old times you could have been stoned to death if you would have been brought before the elders? It is that serious."

I heard Louie clear his throat, "It is our intent, Aaron to help you. You say you have always felt this way. You are now how old, in your thirties?"

"I'm thirty-three," I nodded.

"So young yet," Monie said quickly.

Louie continued, "Since you have for years felt this way it may not be easy for you to suddenly change your mind, but we are here to help you see the error of your ways. We are not here to make life harder for you but to make it easier. I have heard of places where such boys and men as you, can get help. Now, our people do not quickly send patients there, but I am wondering, what would be your reaction about maybe seeking help?"

Louie began to speak but Henry with quiet authority shook his head, "Let Aaron speak."

My thoughts went to the sessions I had with Brian. Why had my therapist not suggested this? "I would consider that," I said.

"You have been going to a counselor," Dad said. "Did he suggest getting help?"

"Was it a Christian counselor?" Monie asked. "You know, those secular counselors tell their patients it's okay to be gay. Look what we have now in this country. Gay marriages!" His rather high-pitched voice ended in a squeak. I wished I could say, "Cock-a-doodle-do!" but of course I couldn't show such disrespect.

"No, Brian didn't recommend a counselor." I took a deep breath, "He told me his seventeen-year-old son is gay and they have known about it ever since he was young, and Brian and his wife are supporting him."

The look the preachers exchanged at my reply was not sympathetic.

Henry began talking about how the Bible is the Word of God and how throughout the years, the Amish have not changed any of their views on the holiness of God. He talked about how God hates sin and how unrepentant sinners are cast into hell. He also talked about the gravity of hardening our hearts and not wanting to be open to the Bible. I heard the mini-sermon with my ears but my mind traveled in its own direction.

I wondered how religious people can get to pick and choose what they want from the Bible. We Amish know there many verses in the Bible on how to live, what to wear, what not to do and what we must do. In the old times, children could also be stoned for not obeying their parents. There were so many rules, no one could keep them all and some rules were insisted on and others were ignored. I heard Brian's words echo in my memory. "Concentrate on the life of Jesus and only on that".

So, I had been doing that. The stories of people interacting with Jesus as though he were an ordinary man. Ordinary but extremely kind. Loving and forgiving, nonjudgement and not threatening to anyone. Not once did he turn anyone away or turn away from anyone who needed help. Kind. Like Jamil.

In spite of the drone of Henry's voice about the righteousness of God and how we must daily try to live up to his rules the best we could and still recognize we can never do enough, or be enough to be as holy as God is, I thought of my young friend. Never had I heard or seen anything unkind from him. He was not a milk-toast sort of guy, he knew his profession and carried himself with authority but not in an intimidating way. But I knew he was kind. Loving. And I was sure he could be very affectionate. I remembered the good feeling when our hands touched at my house. When we shook hands to say goodbye. Yes, more people needed to be like Jamil.

Would Jamil go to heaven if he died? Was it possible for him to be serving God and be in a "false" religion?

I had a mental image of Jamil and I meeting Jesus, maybe at a grocery store. Would Jamil like Jesus? Would Jesus like me? Would Jesus like Jamil and I together? "I'd ask him," I decided and almost smiled at my vivid imagination.

"Aaron, can you give us privacy for a bit?" Henry had finally stopped his diatribe. "We will reach a decision and let you know what we think is best."

"Okay," I answered and got up from my chair. "Do you want me to wait here tonight or will you let me know later?"

"Tonight," Henry said. "We hope you won't have to wait long."

I went outside and closed the door behind me. I walked around the side of the house and as I passed my parents' bedroom window, I saw Mom's shadow move across the drawn roller shade and knew she must have been listening.

I wished I had someone I could talk with. I thought of how easy it is for the English to be able to use their cell phones and talk with each other. If I had a cell phone, I could call Jamil. Or maybe Brian. Someone who would at least try to understand. I already felt pushed outside the safe circle of the Amish. I would now be considered different. And I knew as long as I was different, I would always be looked at with suspicion. Anyone who fell into grievous "sins" was marked for years, even if they didn't do anything else that was outside the rules of the church.

I thought of other Amish people who didn't fit in. Some were too bold in their speech and dared criticize the preachers and their decisions. Some went against the rules of the church and when confronted left the Amish church for other more liberal churches, like the black car Amish or even more liberal churches like the Mennonites.

I knew there were people in my church who had cell phones on the sly. Used them surreptitiously so no one would know they had them. For it was okay to "borrow" cell phones from the liberal car-Amish or English people but not to own the phones. But I have never felt comfortable to do so. Now, I wished I had a cell phone. To talk with Jamil.

"Aaron," my dad's voice came from the doorway.

The four ministers were all seated in chairs, in a row. My dad sat at the end, across from my empty chair, waiting for me, facing them.

Henry waited until I was settled in my chair. "Aaron, after much consideration and we feel under the direction of God, we have agreed on the following.

"You must stop going to the counselor, Brian."

"You must destroy the drawing of the two men." Henry paused and looked at Dad. "Have you seen the drawing?"

Dad shook his head and Henry looked back at me, "I want you to give the drawing to your father. He can get rid of it.

"You must not be alone with any English man. You must not talk about your poisonous position with any of our young people.

"You must be willing to go for help to an approved facility. We will be in touch with you once arrangements are made.

"You will be placed on proving with the church and you will not be allowed to vote on church matters or to take communion."

As my "Sentence" was given to me, I listened intently, trying to remember word for word what Henry, the Bishop of our churches, was saying. I tried not to think of how my life would be impacted, nor of the changes I would need to make, but I concentrated on how I could live my life in order for these requirements to be met.

As is common among the Amish and the Car Amish, once a baptized member is put on proving, it is a time of walking on thin ice. In a sense, this is a time when the entire congregation, who would be notified at our next Sunday service, would be asked to watch carefully how well I complied with the restrictions placed on me. So, my mind was now occupied how I could live, probably for the next six months, in a way that would "prove" that I was not headstrong and disobedient.

I had been a part of this procedure of agreeing to put members on proving and I had been a part of restoring the repentant and also a part of the group agreeing to shun the unrepentant.

Those in error were given at most, a year and a half to

"shape up" and if they didn't during that time, they would be excommunicated and shunned.

"Dear Brian,

My brother Levi found a sketch I drew of two men, the one resting his head on the chest of the other, both of whom are fully clothed. I think he also read the last entry in my diary and I had for the first time written about my attraction for men. He told Dad and tonight, the preachers made some decisions for me. They put me on proving and one of the stipulations they made for me was I would no longer come to see you as my therapist.

This is very hard for me, for I felt you were helping me with some deep questions I have about why I am gay and about how God looks at gay people.

I will not be coming to see you for I do not want to be shunned from the Amish people. I don't know if this makes sense to you but I hope you can understand the bind I am in.

Thank you so much, Mr. Downton, for the help you gave me.

I continue to benefit from your wise words and will always be grateful for your wisdom.

Sincerely, Aaron Peachy

My kerosene lamp was enough light for me to write my letter. My sketch of the two men lay face down on my desk, ripped out of the sketch book. I hadn't looked at it again, just ripped it out and lay it down. I felt drained and empty and any earlier feeling of lightness I had for no longer carrying my secret was gone and instead I felt heavy and dull. I wanted to rip up the sketch. Why did Henry want my dad to see it? Were the preachers afraid I would keep it and not tear it up? I wanted to rip it into shreds right now and not let my dad see it at all. Did they want to shame me by having me give the sketch to my dad? I grabbed the paper and turned it, face up.

I hadn't even thought of anyone in particular when I drew the picture. The older of the two lying on the grass was maybe in his late 40's, perhaps even in his 50's. The younger one I drew as someone in the age bracket when it is difficult to tell how hold they are. I studied the face I had drawn. He could have been in his 20's, or 30's or even 40's. Maybe they were almost the same age? What did it matter? They were just lying there, enjoying being together. Touching. Being affectionate. Was that so wrong?

"Like David and Jonathan in the Old Testament." My mind went to the story of the two young men who foraged such a strong friendship, a closeness that was recorded as "one surpassing the love of men for women"! Had David and Jonathon lay out on the hills and had they dared show affection like this? There is no recorded history of anyone scolding or reprimanding them.

I had begun to sketch their hands, one using his right hand and the other one using his left hand, with fingers entwined, but I hadn't completed that. I wanted to see them that way. I wanted them to be able to feel the other one's hand. Skin to skin, hand in hand, feeling the intimacy of the moment. I looked at my pencil.

It takes a while for me to sketch. For at first, I draw the outline and that must satisfy me, and then only can I fill in the details. i sketched the fingernails. I looked at my right hand and bent it at an angle so I could get a better feeling for my sketch. So many fingers, the thumbs touching, each finger echoed by another finger, the pointer finger, strong yet supple, the middle finger longer than the rest, the ring finger, bare and naked and of course if either of these men were Amish, they would not wear rings anyway, married or not for rings are considered jewelry and Amish don't do jewelry.

Suddenly I pushed my sketch away from me as a rush of emotions surged through my mind and through my body. Amish don't do this and Amish don't do that! I knew it, have always known it but right now in my loneliness and with all I had gone through in the last several days, I was sick of it! "I can't even think my own thoughts!" I said out loud. "I have to think Amish!"

I broke my pencil in frustration and was getting ready to rip my sketch in half when I remembered again the words from the bishop. "I want you to give the drawing to your father. He can get rid of it."

I got up from my chair and undressed then flung myself into bed. I was also going to write to Jamil and tell him I couldn't see him again unless I made sure we were not alone together. I rebelled at the thought of writing something like that to the young man I was learning to like very much. I knew he also came from a very religious family but I wasn't sure if he would understand. I didn't want to write to him. I wanted to tell him but I didn't want anyone else there to hear me tell him how much his friendship meant to me and how we had to break it off.

I did not cry. But I froze into a still form of a human. One I did not like, and I had no idea how to change that. I tossed and turned all night.

# CHAPTER TEN

When you live by yourself, you become very aware of sounds. Just like now, I heard the car approaching my place and instead of going on past, I heard the sound of the moving vehicle slow down and then the crunch of automobile tires on the gravel. I was in the middle of marking a piece of walnut with a pattern I had made and so I kept on tracing around the template on the dark wood. I heard the slam of the car door and by the time I could leave my work to see who was coming, I heard a young man's voice, "Hello! Anyone home?"

The door to my shop was open and I expected perhaps to see someone I knew, but the twenty-some young man was someone I had never seen before. "You must be Aaron," and the young man dressed in tight jeans and a tank top stuck out his hand. "I'm Trevor. Well, not really but that's the name I go by. Here in the valley I'm known as Sam's Sam's Sam, but really," and Trevor waved his right hand dramatically, "can you imagine introducing yourself as 'Sam's Sam's Sam' anywhere in the city? Everyone would think it's a name I gave myself," Trevor chortled.

"Well, Trevor, come in," I invited. "I'm all dusty with sawdust as you can see, but welcome."

"This is really a swell place," Trevor walked over to my workbench. "Such cool furniture. And…" he looked me straight in the face and then I felt as if he was mentally undressing me, "such a good-looking man you are." He winked and laughed.

My head was spinning. Everything about Trevor was moving rapidly into a really new space I was not used to.

"Do you live here by yourself? I really like the house I saw when I came in. You are still Amish I take it?"

"Yes to both questions and thank you for the compliment," I smiled. "Obviously you know me but I don't think I've ever heard of you."

"Oh, some old biddy told my mom you are in trouble with the preachers because someone found out you were drawing men being 'intimate' ," he winked and made quotation marks with his fingers. Several braided leather bracelets laced with blue turquoise beads flashed in the sunlight.

"Oh?" was all I managed to say.

"Yeah, as you well know, it doesn't take long for such scandalous news to spread among the Amish. The Amish pretend to be so holy and righteous, but you know they all love to spread any rumors they can. "Please pray for Aaron, he has fallen into the sin of liking men', " Trevor sounded for all the world just like an Amish woman.

"How long ago did you leave the Amish?"

"More than five years ago. I was nineteen and I got too fond of a young man two houses down from our farmhouse. At first, I tried to keep it a secret but I guess the parents found out and thought I was maybe sneaking out to see a girl but then, one evening Eric insisted I go with him to a bar in the next town, and someone must have seen us kissing for just like that, my dad was all down my throat about it and told me I was grounded. Couldn't leave the farm for anything. Well, I grounded him. Packed up a few of my things and that night I left home and stayed with Eric for awhile. No more Amish Sam's Sam's Sam for me." Trevor hoisted himself up on my workbench and swung his legs back and forth. His tight jeans left very little to the imagination and I tried to focus on his face.

100

"It's okay to look," Trevor laughed. "That's how we know who's gay and who isn't. It helps our 'gaydar' work properly," Trevor laughed. "Now your Amish pants, they are maybe just a little tight to be considered modest. Maybe you make them yourself? You look like you are quite 'handy' in more ways than one," then he laughed suggestively.

I was mesmerized. Never before had I met someone quite as brazen as Trevor. There was something that repulsed me about him, but he also intrigued me. Not only by his name but also by some of his mannerisms it had quickly become apparent Trevor indeed had at one time been Amish. None of the swagger with which he talked and moved around quite covered all his Amish roots.

"So, tell me, Aaron, what about you? Surely you must have experimented with guys. Have you ever dated girls? I know Amish supposedly don't have sex before marriage but in Hayfork Andy's church district where I grew up there was a lot of hanky-panky going on. Everyone involved just tried to make sure no one got pregnant, but sex is sex and it happened every once in a while. Then it was hurry up and get married before the baby bump shows or if they waited too long, it was the 'get married right after church' without a wedding. Tell me about yourself," Trevor jumped off the workbench and walked back and forth.

"Umm," I replied, "there really isn't much to tell. I've never been with a guy. Or a girl," I added.

"So, you got put on proving because you drew two men together? Did you draw them naked? Did you draw them having sex?" Trevor stared at me and laughed.

"No, they had their clothes on. The one had his head resting on the other onc's chest. They were lying under a tree."

"Let me see it," Trevor demanded. "Did you draw them with erections?"

"I don't have it," I told him. "I gave it to my dad."

"Whaaattttt??" Trevor asked his voice rising into an incredulous note. "You gave it to your dad? How old are you? You are not a little boy anymore. Man, I almost forgot how controlling the Amish are. But what made you give it to your dad?"

"The preachers told me to," and I told him the story.

"Well, you sound like a really tame guy," Trevor said shaking his head, "and you got a bum rap for only having drawn a sketch of two men cuddling. Damn!"

Trevor paused, as if to collect his thoughts. Then, the questions continued flowing.

"So, what are you going to do? Leave the Amish church? You might as well. You can't be gay and stay Amish. They would never leave you alone. After I left the Amish, I thought I could hang with Eric, but he soon got tired of me. I was still too Amish, didn't know the current songs, the gay culture and I didn't have a job. That's when I moved to Altoona and I tell you, it was rough. At first, it was really fun going to the gay bars, and I have to tell you, I was pursued a lot by some really hot guys. I was having sex with guys almost every night, thought I fell in love with one guy, but he was like, 'whoah, I'm not looking for a husband!' I learned pretty fast. Now I'm pretty much like all the rest. I have a boyfriend, sort of, but we still see other guys. I probably shouldn't tell you too much, you look pretty stunned at the little I am telling you." Trevor rattled on.

"Yes," I said rather slowly, "this is a lot of information. You asked if I was going to leave the Amish. I'm not planning to. I have a lot of questions and I'm trying to sort things out in my mind, but leaving the Amish is not what I want to do. I like my family and I can't imagine living in the ban and being shunned."

"Yeah, well I at least escaped that," Trevor laughed. "I never joined the church nor was baptized so now they can't shun me. Although I feel shunned. Dad hardly talks to me when I come home and I'm not invited to any family get togethers. I might as well be shunned."

"Uh, you know I am not supposed to be alone with any English man," I suddenly remembered. "I know you used to be Amish but I'm thinking I probably shouldn't be here by myself with you. I hate to ask you to leave but if I'm questioned it probably wouldn't help even if I said you are Amish or used to be."

"Oh my gosh!" Trevor said and walked towards the door. "That is just too rich." He held up his hand and said, "No, not against you and yes, because I was Amish I understand, but really, Aaron do you think you have a chance to get back in good graces with the Amish? You are gay and Amish don't do gay. Surely you know that."

"But," I protested, "I'm not intimate with guys. That's not what I want. I just want to be honest about my feelings. I'm sure there are other Amish who have the same feelings. Maybe the Amish will learn to accept it's the way we are born and not our choice to be gay."

"Much luck with that," Trevor snorted and said, "Okay, I'll leave. I don't want to make more trouble for you. Yeah, they might think we are making out or something if I'm here too long. But I tell you, it doesn't take long to have sex. We could have already had sex in the short time I was here. You are hot enough!"

Then Trevor left. I stood in the doorway watching his car recede in the distance. I looked towards my parents' farm. Had anyone seen

Trevor's car in my driveway? Would they think I had invited some guy to come over? I made a quick decision, pulled my shop door closed and walked towards the farm. Even though I forced my feet to go fast, my heart felt heavy. Had I already violated my proving period?

I found my dad in the shop. "Hello," I greeted him as I stepped inside.

"Well, Aaron," Dad replied, "how is your day going?" I heard the strain in his voice, but I was pleased he was making an effort to be friendly.

"It was going well," I told him. "Then I had a visitor, Sam's Sam's Sam, who used to be Amish and he wanted to talk so he was in the shop for a while. I remembered, then, I was not to be alone with any English boys or men, so I told him, and he left."

"Had you met him before?" Dad asked, his face becoming lined as his eyebrows furrowed.

"No," I told him. "At first, I didn't think about it and then I wasn't sure if he would be considered English, because he used to be Amish, but then I decided to come and tell you. He wasn't there more than maybe 15 minutes, if that long." According to Trevor that would have been long enough to have had sex!

"Well, I didn't see his car there. You know, since you are on the other side of the big barn, we often don't see if you have company." Dad said slowly. "Was he from Hayfork Andy's district? I mean, his parents? I know of Sam's Sam, but I didn't know he had a son Sam."

"Yes," I told him, " he was from that district."

"And he was driving a car? 'Gone off' Amish?"

"Yes, he ran away when he was nineteen."

Dad cleared his throat, "Why did he come to see you? Was he queer like you say you are?"

"He is gay," I replied, "Like I am."

"You did the honorable thing to tell your dad about that young man coming to see you," Preacher Dan said from his buggy seat. His driving horse stood patiently in my graveled driveway, ignoring Lady who had cantered to the fence when she saw the preacher's rig come into my drive the next evening.

I had gone out to see what he wanted, and Dan had seemed relieved he didn't have to get off the buggy. I knew he was suffering from arthritis and it must have been an effort for him to come pay me a visit. "Yes, honorable, " he repeated. "And he must have heard about your problem and wanted to come talk to you. I hope you didn't listen to any of his false ideas about the problem." Dan looked at me keenly from beneath his bushy gray eyebrows.

"I don't think I changed any of my ways of thinking because of his visit," I told him. I didn't tell him actually I was repulsed by much of Trevor's actions and words. I had not been impressed by that young man. Really, I had been shocked by his flippant speech and bold actions. I knew if that was the "gay lifestyle", I didn't want it. Also, I didn't like being told I had a problem.

"Well, I did talk with Henry and he and I decided it would be best for you to move back home to be with your parents. We want you to know we do appreciate how you went and told your dad about your visitor, but we also know how easy it could be to yield to temptations and think it would be safer for you to live at home. Your mom and dad have agreed." Preacher Dan said some more words, but they didn't really register.

Before he left, Dan said in a kind voice, "Aaron, this may not be easy for you and I do want you to know it is not with hard feelings we ask you to do these things but for the good of your soul. Please look at it as a way to change your ways and to be content with how God ordained men to be. You are meant to be married to a woman. 'It is not good for man to be alone' is the Word of the Lord and we must abide by that."

For the rest of the evening, I walked around in a daze. I fed Lady her evening oats and stroked her muzzle as she munched. Would I be allowed to keep my horse over here? What about my work in the shop? I knew I could sleep in the one extra bedroom my parents' house. They still enjoyed Amish guests or relatives who wanted to stay overnight but of course I would be expected to eat my meals with my parents. For living with them meant living with them. Before I went to bed, I walked around in the main room of my house. I liked having my own place. I enjoyed making the food I wanted to eat and not the usual diet heavy with carbohydrates. Sure, fried potatoes and fried chicken and cooked vegetables were tasty, but I preferred roasting or broiling most of my potatoes and meat and eating my vegetables raw. How could I leave my home, the house I had designed and enjoyed for the past five years? Who would live in here if I moved out? I didn't want to rent out my house to someone else.

I tried to be submissive, to give in to the orders from the preachers. I shouldn't have told my dad about Trevor! Why had that young man even showed up? Just because we were both gay? I didn't feel any more connection with him than I did with any other English man. Not even as much as I had with my male Amish friends. Trevor seemed to have lost something and I didn't think he was really happy. Oh, I was sure he thought he was having fun, but it also sounded like he had gotten his heart broken more than once.

I felt a shudder go through me as my vivid imagination gave me mental pictures of Trevor out carousing with his "friends". That was not what I wanted. I wanted a meaningful friendship. Like I had with Jamil. Caring. Respectful. Oh, and I hadn't written to Jamil. I had decided I wasn't asked to, and I would just tell him the next time I needed him to take pictures. That was not soon for I had been having a difficult time coming up with any new designs for furniture. My creativity seemed stifled since all this mess had started.

Brian. I wanted to talk with Brian. But I had been forbidden to see him. Maybe I could walk over after dark, anyway. I needed to talk and confide in someone. The days were getting shorter as late summer faded into fall and I could walk the two miles to the therapist's place without anyone knowing. I didn't have an appointment but maybe he would have some time for me. I could see myself in that pleasant room looking out into the back yard, talking with a man I respected. But that would be direct disobedience. Which might mean being shunned.

"I won't go. I won't move." I am not sure where the strength came from to say that to myself. "I am not a small child. I am a grown man. I have made a home for myself and built my shop and I need to know I will not have to move back home to my parents' house like a disobedient son. I have not gone against the rules of the church. I have agreed to the preachers' stipulations and I have voluntarily told my dad about Trevor's visit. I will not give in to more restrictions." My words filled the main floor of my small house and I tilted my head towards the sleeping loft. "I have given my sketch to my dad and he didn't rip it up but looked at it briefly and put it back in the envelope. If I don't stand up to be the man I am I will lose even that. I will not stifle the man I am, the man I am becoming."

I looked around for my work shoes and without bothering to put socks on, I tied my shoes and walked out the door. I would tell my parents I would not move in and then wait. I had no idea how I could evade the shunning but one thing I did know, I had to live with myself and who I was before God. Before Jesus.

"Uncle Aaron!" I heard my nephew Benjamin's voice calling me before I had reached the farm. He had a flashlight and was running towards me. "It's Dawhddy! O come, quick! Something's wrong with Dawhddy!"

I ran the short distance to my nephew. "He fell down and Mahhmy ran over to get help. Mom told me to come get you because my dad is not at home this evening."

We ran to my parents' house. My sister in law was kneeling on the floor beside my dad's prone figure and my mom was wiping the white spittle oozing from the side of my dad's mouth. "Aaron, go call the ambulance! Or maybe we should just get Randy to drive him to the hospital, do you think?"

Then she said, "Ben, can you hear me? Say something." My dad moved his lips and the garble of sounds coming from his mouth made no sense. The right side of his face was drawn and he was curled up on the floor on his right side.

Stroke. My dad had suffered a stroke, the doctor told us. Severe enough to partially paralyze his right side and his face. Just like that my dad's life changed. And mine. For I moved home to help mom take care of Dad's physical needs. He was a big man and Mom would never be strong enough to care for him.

# CHAPTER ELEVEN

"**M**om, I don't want to leave you alone!" I faced my aged mother and tried to get her to understand.

"Aaron, I'm not alone," my mom said and I heard the quiver in her voice and knew she was bracing herself up. "Levi and Mary and the children live right across the yard." Mom's voice sounded tired and she looked all the world like the painting a famous artist, Whistler, I think his name was, had done of his mother.

My mom was dressed in black, as were all the women in the family for when there is a funeral in the Amish family, the women all wear black. We men, of course mostly wear black pants and suit coats all the time. I knew Mom would probably wear black for the rest of her life, as many older Amish widows do.

After the stroke Dad had not improved and about three weeks later, he died in his sleep one night. I don't do well with funerals, and the following days after Dad passed, I basically functioned out of habit. The streams of relatives and neighbors coming to the viewing the night before the funeral, that night knowing Dad's body was lying in a black homemade coffin of pine, trying to take care of mom and all the moments of having taken care of my dad's physical needs had pretty well already drained me of all my emotions, but now I was facing one more.

"Aaron, Dad would want you to go," Mom said. "You need help with your problem and there is no better time than now. I'll need something to do and I can go look after your place and feed Lady. You will only be gone three weeks, maybe not even that long if you get healed."

I looked down at my mother, standing in front of me. Mom was having one of her moments.

We all knew my mother as a woman who talked a lot, bustled around and tried to make sure everyone else was comfortable but occasionally she would get that look and then everyone knew unless we listened to her, and yes, obeyed her, Mom would not be happy and we all hated when that happened. I used to wonder if she ever gave Dad that look, but never mind now, I was getting the look.

So, I went to Healing Meadows.

"Welcome," Freeman Miller came towards me as, suitcase in hand, I stood outside the building that had one time been a farmhouse but now the building had so many additions added to it the original structure had become overwhelmed by annexes and shotgun rooms. Maybe it was meant to be healing but whoever had designed or added to the building had managed to make it look anything but peaceful.

"I'm Aaron," I said. "Aaron Peachy." We shook hands and I was surprised at how genuine and pleasant Freeman was.

"Oh yes, Aaron!" He looked me over and smiled. "I'm not sure why, but I thought you would be younger. And here you are, a man! I mean a mature man, of probably about thirty?" his laugh was easy and not forced. "Isn't it interesting how we mentally picture someone in our brain. Anyway, when your bishop came to talk with me, I guess I never thought to ask how old you are."

"I will show you your room and you can get settled then come to the office," and he waved to one of the additions, neatly labeled "Office" "and then we can get you enrolled in the program."

The two-story addition to the right of the main house had a staircase leading upstairs and a central hall. "Bathrooms on each end of the hall, shared with the other residents, and downstairs is the kitchen, the dining room and a living room, plus several offices."

I saw an Amish man come out of one of the bedrooms and when he saw us, he melted back into his room and closed the door. "It's okay, Jonas," Freeman said cheerily and added in a loud tone, "You are safe," then he turned and smiled at me but offered no explanation. "At present we have two couples here, three men and I think about twelve women. We have been here for over ten years now and we are devoted to walk with anyone who comes here on the journey of life, learning together how to handle problems and overcome obstacles Satan wants to trip us with. God is bigger than any problems any of us have, we just sometimes need to learn what tools to use to get into our stride."

My room had two single beds in it, a closet, two wooden dining room chairs and a small table between the beds. It looked like a typical Amish bedroom, except the two windows had white curtains that could be closed at night. A kerosene lamp was on the table, but Freeman flipped a switch and a bare lightbulb lit up in the center of the ceiling. "We do have electricity but also provide for those who feel uncomfortable living with it. Our guests come from a broad spectrum of churches, so we do want everyone to feel at home as much as they can."

"Thank you, Freeman. I appreciate this." I suddenly realized I had not said much to this man and I wanted him to know I felt a respect for him. I liked how he was at ease and did not come across to me as pompous or know-it-all.

"Okay, see you soon in the office," Freeman said and smiled a cheery smile and went down the stairs.

I sat on my bed, and I'm not sure why, but I felt eager for this season. "Healing" and "help" and "journey" were all positive words.

I opened my suitcase and took out my clothes, then hung my shirts on hangers and put my underwear and pants on one of the shelves, and then I saw the envelope I had gotten in the mail the day before I had left. From Bruce.

"You are a good man, Aaron. I'm glad to have met you and I will always be interested in how life is treating you. I'm sorry we couldn't continue with our sessions but I totally support your position of discontinuing at the request of your ministers. I honor that. Thank you for letting me know. I'm proud of you to have the grace to write and let me know about this."

This was the part I read over and over again. I don't think anyone had ever told me they were proud of me. We Amish avoid using the word "proud" in a good way. For pride is considered sin. Now I began to understand it in a different manner. Encouragement.

"Dear Diary," I wrote after being there for two weeks. "I long to be back home, building furniture, taking Lady out for a drive to see the beautiful fall colors, going on a walk up the hill behind my house and I wonder how Mom is doing and how my brothers and their families are. I'm tired of reading. I'm weary of yet another book. I find inspiration and strength from some of the words I read but many of the authors are saying the same thing in a different way. Where are the people who used to be gay and now aren't? Outside of Freeman, no one has even talked to be about my desire for companionship from a man. Even though Freeman tried to help me during a talk session, I could tell he doesn't understand. And, how could he? I'm "different" and "have a problem". I'm not blaming him for I think he definitely cares but he, too is caught up with trying to please the Amish and be liberal enough for the Car Amish and the Mennonites. Sometimes I think he thinks he's Amish and other times I think he thinks of himself as a liberated or free Amish.

*"Diary, the first week I was here, I thought maybe I was "healed". I went through so much inner cleansing and rejecting thoughts and questions and felt so traumatized by Dad's sickness and dying and the funeral, I felt as though I was not even attracted to men. I had reached a place where I was almost devoid of feeling and I'm like, 'Okay, I'm not attracted to men, it was just a phase' for I didn't want to talk with anyone. The dogs in the night turned into snakes. The demons became monsters. I felt like running away from this place and the darkness wanted to swallow me up."*

Maybe it was strange that I still wrote in my Diary but there are times I think my little book is the only place I can totally be myself. I won't make the mistake to let it lay about for someone to be able to pick it up and read my thoughts.

I wrote this poem in my diary.

*"The snakes came out again last night*

*With gaping jaws and slitted eyes*

*They hissed and sprang with oily coils*

*The dark night listened to my cries.*

*A vicious vice held me in iron grips I could not move or flee away*

*The black night sat upon my chest I groped in vain for the day.*

*Then this morning when light shone in*

*I lay exhausted on my bed*

*The struggle began to subside The dark ink went from my head.*

*What are these snakes tormenting me Why do they come in the night? Why would they come with hissing breath What do they get from my fright?*

*So I took my own mind in my hand*

*And walked back into the den*

*I no longer saw them as a crowd I looked at them again and again. I began to give them names*

*Shame and Fear and Rot and Pain I reduced each one to his proper size I unlocked each heavy chain.*

*The sun shone on the den of snakes*

*They basked in the warmth of the heat Never once did they strike at me But lay placid by my feet.*

*I will remember the change that came*

*As light reveals their true size*

*I will not fear the snakes at night I will not startle in surprise.*

*It is the light, the light, the Light,*

*Drives all my puny fears to flight*

*And I stand tall and tall and tall*

*I'm not afraid at all, at all."*

Afterwards, I felt ten feel tall. I did not feel as though I had a problem. How that was possible I don't know, but that's what made me able to get through the darkness.

"This is Andrew Waldorp," the moderator introduced the speaker, an elderly portly man with a gray beard. "The author of "One Man, One Woman" which some of you may have read." Then the moderator talked about Mr. Waldorp's education, his experience as a speaker and a lecturer and when he finally ended, Mr Waldorp got up and said, "Now that you know all that about me, let's get right on with the subject."

I looked around at the audience of perhaps twenty-five or so, all men. I was the only Amish. Was everyone here gay, I wondered. Freeman had clearly told me, "Aaron, after counseling with some of the people on the board at Healing Meadows, we felt it would be good for you to go and listen to Mr. Waldorp. He has been successful in helping some with your problem get healing. If you are interested, I will arrange for you to go."

"The lack of affection in your young years comes out in your adult years and it can manifest itself in lots of different ways. For some, it is to be attracted to their own sex." Mr. Waldorp smiled at us. "For many people, including the families of those affected, that can be frightening. And what do frightened people do? They either push away those they are frightened by or they ignore them, hoping this will go away. I'm assuming many of you in here have frightened someone by telling them you are gay.

"To be gay is to be attracted to someone of your own sex. That is the definition the world gives you and we know there are many that now say you are born gay, or you might be gay because you are the oldest, or the youngest and if you are the only one would you be doubly gay because you would be both?" He laughed at his own joke and a ripple of laughter swept through the listeners.

"But God calls it abomination. Man calls it gay. That's it. So, we as Christians, want to examine this from the Biblical viewpoint. As I speak, any questions you may have, you should write them down and then as time permits, we can address them at the end of my presentation.

"So what's the first letter in 'Gay?" He lifted his hands, palms upwards and waited.

"G" came from somewhere in the audience and Mr. Waldorp beamed and nodded. "I came up with an acrostic to help us renounce the idea that gay is acceptable." He flipped on a laptop computer on the podium and punched a few keys.

The cartoon figure of a man in bold checked pants, a ruffled shirt and high heeled boots was on the side of the slide and the words

G = Gag

A = Awful

Y = Yuck finished off the design.

I wonder if it ever occurred to Mr. Waldorp that he may he have lost the respect of over half of the audience by the time he had been speaking for the first ten minutes. He tried, I must give him that. I'm not used to sitting in classes taught by the English, but this man's crass manners and choice of words to describe what he thought of gay people did not build a rapport with the audience. His sole purpose was to make us feel how disgusting and unnatural and deviant it was to have any kind of sexual feelings for men to have for men.

He was quite lurid and vivid with his descriptions and talked about how impossible it was for some sex acts to be done man to man until I wanted to cover my ears.

"Now after our break, I'm going to give you the real goods. How to overcome your problems and be healed! Hallelujah! Once and for all! Yes, you go for a ten-minute break and come back for the real goods."

When I got to the hall, I went to the water fountain to get a drink. "Sorry, the water fountain doesn't work. There's a Seven Eleven next door and they sell bottled water," the receptionist told me. I went out into the sunshine and took a deep breath. I headed to the convenience store.

I paid for a bottle of water and went back outside. I felt the need to take a brisk walk and instead of going back to the building where Mr. Waldorp was conducting his meeting, I went the other way. A small pocket park with a few benches and a fountain that no longer founted looked sad, so I went on past it and then turned to go down an alley. It was the backside of the main street and I could hear the whine of air conditioners and I saw the tail end of a cat digging in a garbage container. When I got close to the next street, I saw a man sitting on the brick steps of a small stoop. I thought he looked somewhat familiar but walked on past.

"Hey, I saw you in Mr. Waldrop's class," his voice reached out and made me turn to face him.

"Yes," I replied. "You were there, too?"

"I'm Alex Tremont," he stood up and we shook hands.

"Aaron Peachy. I needed to stretch my legs and thought

I'll take a quick walk before heading back in."

Alex nodded. "I, too, needed some space. Are you headed back? Mind if I join you?"

I smiled my invitation and we fell into step. He was older than I am but still athletic and trim.

"So, what do you think?" Alex asked. "How are you liking the lecture?"

"Hmm," I hedged. "There is a lot of subject matter to think about. I guess maybe I was hoping for some answers to my questions, but so far I'm feeling Mr. Waldorp is basically spending his time wanting to convince everyone that to be gay is wrong and disgusting. I was looking more for something I could really understand about myself." I found it easy to talk with Alex.

"I'm wishing it was over," Alex said bluntly. "I, too, have questions but I'm not even sure I want to ask them. Such a bunch of nonsense! Sorry, I'm not usually this negative."

We matched steps as we walked back to the building. I took my water bottle with me into the auditorium.

"Welcome back," Mr. Waldorp beamed. "Oh, I must remind you it is not in the best interest for the health of this class to spend much time together out of class, so we have planned for a lunch break here in the classroom. I think Edna has a delicious lunch planned for us," and he nodded towards the closed glass door leading to the corridor. "Our receptionist has agreed to bring the lunch in here so we can eat together and get to know each other."

Why would I have thought the next part of the meeting might be different? Why did I have hopes to hear some original thoughts or perhaps a new perspective on my "problem"? Mr. Waldorp's "real goods" was hardly different from the morning's diatribe. Being gay was wrong, being gay was not natural, being gay made the world a darker place and being gay was not beneficial in any way to anyone on the planet.

Lunch was a dismal affair of white bread, slices of cheap bologna and cheese. Mayonnaise, iceberg lettuce, anemic tomatoes and condiments offered a make-your-own sandwiches opportunity.

118

Several boxes of glazed doughnuts accompanied by coffee ended the meal and I was thankful the coffee was piping hot so I could dunk my doughnut into it.

"You dunk, too?" Alex saw what I was doing and smiled. "I always liked to do so and when I was young, I had to do it when Mom wasn't watching for she thought it was not mannerly. Then, I married and my wife didn't like it either."

"Oh, I didn't know it wasn't considered mannerly," I said, wiping my fingers with my paper napkin. "I think it freshens up a doughnut that otherwise is a little sad."

"I like that," Alex laughed. "Some doughnuts ARE sad."

Then he pretended to be horrified and said, "I'm not saying THESE doughnuts are sad, just SOME!"

Perhaps it was because I was really getting frustrated by the way the lecture was not delivering for me or maybe I was tense from all the questions banging around inside my brain, but when Alex quipped about the doughnuts, I began to laugh. "Oh, you SAD poor doughnut," I said and dunked the last half into the coffee. "Now you are a GLAD doughnut!"

Alex let out a quick shout of laughter and we began to laugh together.

"What's so funny?" Mr. Waldorp asked. "Tell us the joke so we can all share it together."

"Oh, we were talking about dunking doughnuts," Alex managed to say with a snort.

This set us both off again and the rest of the men looked at us with uncertainty. "Well, it must be some kind of private joke but I don't get it," Mr. Waldorp decided and turned away.

During the afternoon lecture we were given sheets of paper and asked to fill out a questionnaire. I'm afraid I was not in a very receptive mood by this time, and when I was asked about my childhood, and whether I had been molested and if I fantasized about being held by my dad when I was young, I tried to answer truthfully, but I know I only gave curt and brief answers. When I was finished, I looked over at where Alex was sitting, penciling answers on his sheet. Was he still married? He had mentioned his wife. Did he have children? Did his pastor send him here to help him with his "problem"?

I guessed he might be almost 50. Short gray hair, strong jawline and his upper lip dipped into a vee right in the center which I found very attractive. Instinctively I wet my own lips. He had small wrinkles at the corners of his blue eyes and his face was tanned a warm brown. He wore his fitted white shirt with an open collar and a natural colored leather belt cinched his khaki jeans. Brown wing-tipped shoes finished his wardrobe. I saw him glance my way and when his eyes found mine, he smiled a little and then bent over his paper again, then once more took a quick look at me. I forced my gaze onto my own paper, but I wondered what he was writing.

"Now I see from some of your answers here on your sheets there really are a number of similarities. Edna did some tallying for me after I collected your papers and look, over half of you are the youngest in your family!" Mr. Waldorp beamed as though he had just discovered a new species of mammals. "Isn't that a telling bit of evidence?"

He droned on and on. About how he noticed "patterns" and "probably not everyone felt comfortable in writing about nasty childhood experiences" but statistics he had studied showed him most gay people were the victims of some kind of abuse. I could tell where he wanted all his evidence to point to. He wanted to find a culprit, a reason, something explainable to prove being gay was not

120

the way we were born but rather the result of some activity or trauma.

Then it was the last hour and I wondered when we would have time to ask questions. Well, it never happened. "Look, if you have questions, feel free to write me and I'll answer them. You have my email on your information sheets and also my home address. So sorry we couldn't have the Q and A time, but I felt it was more important to let you know about the new findings we found on the statistics about gays. Now, just remember as you go out now, equipped with this new information, anytime you get tempted, just do the GAG, AWFUL, YUCK and let God show you again how depraved it is." That was it.

I was so glad it was over, but also so disappointed to not have answers to my questions. I got up to leave. I saw Alex get up and make his way to the door and his face reflected the same frustration I was feeling. I slowed down and waited for him. "It was nice meeting you, Alex," I told him. "Same here," he said. "How did you come?" "I came by bus," I told him.

When he found out where I was staying, he said quietly,

"I'll take you back. It's right on my way."

"Oh," I protested weakly, my manners melting underneath his steady gaze, "you don't have to."

"But I want to," he smiled in a thin line. "I want to talk with you some more. I think we may have some things in common."

# Chapter Twelve

" I 'm sorry for your loss," Alex said holding the steering wheel with his right hand. "Death is so final, and I'm not sure anything can quite prepare us for when it happens. Were you close with your dad?" His left hand was on the console between us. Strong fingers, tapered at the end and close clipped nails, clean. On the back of his hands, I could see the network of blood veins and a scattering of brown hair with some silver hairs here and there. He had rolled up his sleeves elbow length and I could see his arms were not overly muscular but toned.

"Thank you," I said. Telling him about my dad's stroke and death had not been easy but Alex had drawn my story out with genuine interest in his eyes when he glanced at my face as he drove expertly on the highway while I told him my story.

"I think I've talked enough about me," I said. "What about you? Tell me about yourself."

"Fair enough," Alex said. "You told me your story and it's only fair you ask me about my life." But he didn't say more for a while and kept on driving. "I was a pastor," he said abruptly. "Not of a big church, but still of some size. Baptist."

"Are you married?" I asked, remembering his remark about his wife.

Alex shook his head, "No," he said quickly. "Not anymore."

I sensed his reluctance to talk about himself, so I didn't ask any more questions.

"Aaron, I'm not being fair to you," Alex said. "I really want to tell you all about my life but there are some things about me I cannot talk about yet. I too have always known I'm gay, even when I was a young lad. I think I might have been twelve when I had my first crush on a friend of my older brother. Nothing happened, nothing developed but I knew. Of course, as a pastor's kid, myself, I knew I had to hide my emotions so that's what I did. Hid it and did fairly well. Wanted a family so I married a girl I went to high school with. We have three children, first a son and then two daughters. I married when I was 21 and by the time my marriage ended, the oldest two were already on their own. My youngest daughter Alicia lives with her mom except weekends she often stays with me. She's enrolling in college this fall and will be moving to Michigan. "

Then he turned his head slightly and looked away from me. "You see, I too, came today to see if I could get some answers. I, too wish we could have gone somewhere to have listened to an informed person speak about what it is we are to do when we don't fit in and how to handle what life is shoving at us." He gripped the steering wheel with both of his palms but lifted his fingers. "See, no ring."

"That's right," I said, "I could have noticed but since we Amish don't wear jewelry, I'm not quick to check someone's married status."

"I don't really know any Amish," Alex said, "but for some reason I don't think you seem Amish. Not the Amish I had in my mind. You know how to express your feelings. You are in touch with who you are."

"I remember the first time I had the same feeling about you English. I think I was twelve and one day I saw a girl about my age running down the road past our farm and she was calling for her cat. I was out by the road, trimming the long grasses away from the fence

123

and she came up to me with tear-streaked eyes and asked, 'Have you seen a cat around here? A really big black cat?'

"I told her I hadn't. 'I brought him along with me when I came to stay with Aunt Katrina and last night he must have gotten out. I'm so afraid something happened to him' and she started crying. I didn't know what to do or say but as she ran on down the road calling out for her pet, I remember thinking, 'English people are just like us, but different.' If you know what I mean."

"I do know what you mean," Alex said and reached over and gripped my hand for only a moment and then pulled away. "I like that. English people are just like us, but different. That says volumes for it is true about people all over the world no matter what race or religion. Or lack of religion." I heard his voice quiver just a bit.

For the rest of the thirty minutes' drive to Healing Meadows, neither of us said much. Yet, I felt as though we communicated as well without words as we did with words. "Thank you so much, Alex." I opened the car door on my side to get out.

"Aaron," Alex said and I faced him. He turned in his seat and took his hands and gripped me on my shoulders and said, "You are a good man." He smiled at me and then he added, "You have a beautiful soul and I believe nothing will ever take that away from you."

I wasn't sure what he meant but I knew for him, the words meant something very deep. "Thank you."

"May I have… no, how about you give me your address? We can write. Or I'll give you my phone number. Maybe sometime you can find a phone and call me. I would like to stay in touch with you."

I must have hesitated for Alex said, "Maybe you are not comfortable doing that? It's okay, I may have spoken out of turn." He reached across my legs and opened the glove compartment. His arm rested on my knee as he opened the small door and then he found what he was looking for. "Here's my card. If you ever want to, or feel like it you can get in touch." He lay the card in my hand and I took it but he didn't move his arm.

"Not sure what I'm supposed to say," I said, "but I know I would enjoy seeing you again. Just not sure if I were going against the preachers…." my voice trailed off. I could feel the warmth of his arm on my leg. Not only then but even after his car had disappeared down the road and all that evening, it was as though I could still feel his touch on my leg.

That evening, I wrote to Jamil. I told him briefly about what had happened with my dad, and told him I had moved home with my parents to take care of him, and then after Dad passed away, I had come here to Healing Meadows. To learn how to deal with my problem.

"I have so many questions and no one seems to have answers for me. I am just told how wrong it is. How is it that our feelings are wrong, and we need to be fixed but we have to go through so much to find healing. We are told it is not natural but if something is not natural, then how do we go about fixing it? Jamil, I know you believe in God and you can understand the frustration I am facing. This is my last week here and I have learned a lot about humans and how we are to say no to the things that are sin, or bad, but I have not gotten any answers for my bigger questions.

"Jamil, I don't even know if I should be writing you, but I like you too much not to let you know what is happening in my life. I respect you too much to just leave you wondering what happened. I'm not supposed to be alone with you after this, but they didn't tell me I couldn't call you, so I'm going to try to find a phone soon and call you."

I poised my pen above the letter, then added, "Your friend, Aaron". I found a pencil and sketched the two of us, shaking hands. An Amish man and a Muslim, recognizing the bond of humanity that bound us together. That, and the common knowledge that we were both gay.

"It was good to get to know you, Aaron," Freeman told me before I left. "You are a strong man and I do believe as you trust in God to give you grace to overcome, you will walk in that knowledge. Try not to understand issues with your human heart but by faith believe the Word of God. You are earnest in your seeking and God rewards that."

"Thank you, Freeman," I replied. "I thank you for all you tried to do for me and for the many things I did learn. I see your work here is not easy and I appreciate your genuine desire to make a difference and offer healing for people's hearts. How do I pay for the time here?"

Freeman shook his head, "When Dan came to me, he handed me a donation and that was generous. Your church wants to see you healed and since we only take donations and do not charge, God has blessed us so richly."

On my way home on the bus, I thought about the people I had met there. Chupp Sam and his wife Miriam had come, sullen and silent and as the days went by I could see a softening in their manner towards each other. Then there was Jonas, who had seemed to be afraid of his own shadow and now could be seen evenings in the common areas, not conversing much to be sure, but feeling brave enough to venture out of the dark shell life seemed to have thrust him into. I had acquired a greater appreciation for the work at

Healing Meadows and probably overcame some of the prejudices I had carried unknowingly about people with psychological problems or otherwise.

"I cleaned your house," Mom told me when I walked into her house. "You might as well go live there again. I was okay while you were gone and I'll be okay now."

I opened my mouth to speak, but she shook her head," Aaron, no questions. I need my space and you need yours. You go right on home right after supper. I didn't remember just which day you were coming but I kind of remembered it was to be either today or tomorrow, so I made you some rivval soup. Why don't you cut up the onions to sprinkle on top while I melt the butter?"

So, without any discussion, I moved back to my own home.

"What do you think?" I asked Lady as I hand fed her some oats. "What now? I feel as though I am right on the edge of something and I don't know what it is. Then I come back here, and you are still here, just the same. It's nice to know some things don't change." The stars twinkled overhead, and I burrowed my beard into my homemade denim jacket, trying to cut the chilly autumn air. Winter was on the way.

"Aaron!" I heard Jamil's voice simultaneously as his car skidded to a stop in front of my shop. I had closed the shop door for it was chilly and rainy outside.

I put down my sandpaper and almost ran to the door.

"Aaron, it is so good to see you! I came by one time and your place looked so desolate. I wanted to check at your parents' farm to see if you were there, but that place was filled with people. So, now I know why for I got your letter yesterday! Oh, Aaron, I'm so sorry about your dad." He reached for me and then grabbed me and hugged me fiercely. Tears stung my eyelids and I hugged him back. We gripped each other and then I pulled away.

"Now listen to my good news! Your table is in the top five for the contest. They are asking you to bring your table and they will insure it and they need to keep it until after the contest is over. I am so pumped for you!" He smiled broadly and I smiled back.

"Thank you! I had forgotten about the contest."

"I know you wrote we are not to be together alone, but I must tell you this before I go. I'm going back to Iran. I have an uncle who is very sick, and my dad decided I am the one to go back and take care of him," Jamil told me.

"Do you want to go?" I asked.

Jamil shook his head. "No," he answered. "But you will understand when I tell you I must. For we, too are a patriarchal society and what my dad says I must do, I must do." Then he added, "I know they suspicion I am gay. A cousin of a cousin told my mom she saw me holding hands with a boy at a carnival. So, I think that made the decision."

Neither of us said anything. "I liked the sketch of you and me shaking hands. Now, I'll leave before I get you into trouble." Then he grabbed me again and we hugged. I felt his warm breath on my neck and without thinking I reached up and ran my hand through his hair.

"Send me a sketch of us hugging," Jamil told me huskily and then dashed out the door and slammed it shut behind him. I did not move but remained frozen to the spot.

I didn't reply to the form letter Jamil had left behind from the Woodworking Guild. I had no one I wanted to share my news with. I couldn't call it good news anymore for the good was gone out of it. I missed Jamil a lot, but what made it worse was the thought that I would probably never see him again.

I tried to throw myself into my work, my life and my Amish ways as much as I could. I gritted my teeth when the depression wanted to come and bark at my dreams and growl at me while life marched on towards winter.

I already had my firewood cut to heat the house and my shop for the coming cold days, but it was good weather to go up on the hill behind the farm and begin cutting for next year. Seasoned firewood gives over twice as much heat as green wood and burned cleanly without the sap.

I used the chainsaw and cut down diseased or crowded trees as my dad had taught me. I cut up dead wood into firewood lengths and stacked it so it could begin to dry. The big chunks I set on end and used my long-handled ax to split the wood into smaller pieces. I cut maple and hickory and ash, oak, and even poplar and pine for the softwoods were the best to start fires and to get a hot fire going. I threw off my jacket and swung the ax and watched as the blade sank into the wood and the pieces fell apart. Over and over again, day after day, I went into the woods and worked hard so I could go to bed at night and fall asleep exhausted from the hard work.

I still got up at night and was awake for hours. Sometimes I went out into the frosty air and roamed around on my little place. I wanted to sketch but I didn't dare to put my pencil to the paper. I prayed. Not with words as much as just with unexplained groans and felt my insides boiling with unspoken longings.

But I still wrote in my diary. More and more I was writing poetry. Not the ordered and cadenced poetry I used to write, now my poems were just as unordered as my thoughts. One night, I penned,

*Black out the silver moon*

*Stop the shining sun*

*Cover the words of gold*

*Don't let the rivers run.*

*Freeze the ancient words*

*Cut off the liquid notes*

*Close the pithy books*

*Block the many quotes.*

*Count no more the hours*

*Reverse the alphabet*

*Erase the classic art*

*Ground the soaring jet.*

*Let the earth alone*

*Go out into the space*

*Live among the stars*

*Far from the human race.*

*My heart is not mine*

*My life is but dead*

*My voice is now silent Nor echoes in my head.*

# CHAPTER THIRTEEN

"Were you with the man who does your photography by yourself?" Bishop Henry asked bluntly.

"Jamil stopped in to give me the response about a piece of furniture I had made," I told the preachers. "Yes, we were by ourselves for about 5 minutes."

"Did you do anything together?" Monie asked quickly.

"We talked. I had written a letter to him telling what had happened to Dad, and he wanted to offer his sympathies." This meeting was just like the other one, in the same room as the other meeting had been, except now my dad was not here. The air seemed chilly this time and it wasn't just because of the colder weather outside.

"No touching? No holding hands or kissing, or… or stuff like that?" Henry asked, his eyes staring into mine.

"He hugged me and told me he was sorry about my dad. No, I must say it like it was. We hugged each other. We are friends. Oh, and we hugged again when he told me goodbye. You see, Jamil is going back to Iran. His dad was told by someone a cousin had seen him and another guy hold hands, so his dad told him to go back and take care of a sick uncle. Oh, and when I was at Healing Meadows, Freeman arranged one day for me to attend a seminar given by a Mr. Waldorp to help gay people learn to see how disgusting it is to be gay. There were about 25 men and boys there. I made friends with a man, his name is Alex. After the lecture was over, Alex suggested he take me back to Healing Meadows as it was on his way. Once he touched my hand. Another time his arm rested on my leg when he was getting information from his glove compartment." A dam had burst inside me. My words came out, calm and unemotional, as though I were reading a manual on how to assemble kit furniture.

"It felt good to hug Jamil. Like we had a good connection. I felt his sympathy for my loss and yes, I felt something more. I'm not sure how to describe it, but maybe something like if you have an itch somewhere and you can't reach it yourself so someone else scratches the itch for you," I gave a little laugh. "No, that is a terrible comparison. It was just so meaningful to feel someone holding me and letting me know that he loved me. And when Alex and I talked, it was so real as well. A genuine connection. Neither of us were under a strain of being afraid of saying something that would be offensive or be misunderstood. We were honest with each other, talking about some of our questions and frustrations. I liked that."

The preachers said nothing while I talked but their eyes darted all over the place. Even Dan must have been amazed at my bluntness and he kept looking at me as though I was losing my mind. Poor Monie kept opening and closing his mouth like a parched rooster, looking for all the world like he had swallowed too many dry corn kernels and couldn't crow at all, not even manage a croak.

"I'm not trying to shock you and I'm not wanting to be disrespectful. I know you asked me not to be with any English man by myself and to live at home with my parents and I think you did that with a pure motive. I don't think you were or are trying intentionally to be mean and controlling. However, I also think you are continually 'barking up the wrong tree' as we say. For you the raccoon up in the tree is sex. Yes, sex between two men.

"May I suggest for me the bigger coon up in a different tree is the longing gay men have for companionship that is not found in a woman, the closeness and sharing a gay man only wants in another

132

man and the desire to live with a man who connects with you, not like a woman but like a man.

"You think being gay means having a kind of sex you don't understand. Something unnatural. I have never had sex with a man, so I don't know what that is. You men are all married, and I assume you have had sex and know the feelings that can be aroused…"

"Enough!" Bishop Henry raised his hand and his voice. "Aaron, surely you are not thinking clearly and the words you say are not even your words. It is as though another spirit is speaking through you! The Bible warns about familiar spirits which means evil spirits. I don't want to blame you wrongly. God forgive me if I do, but I cannot imagine where you are getting all this talk about sex and your feelings for another man." I could hear how grieved he was.

"Not enough," I told him firmly, yet with respect. "I battle depression and darkness like I have never experienced before so you must hear me out. I must tell you what I am going through or else you will not know who I am. I am no longer afraid of what you will do to me for if I continue to be quiet, I might lose my mind. So, please I beg of you, listen."

Quiet and gentle Lewie spoke up, "Please Bishop Henry, let Aaron speak. He is not saying this in rebellion, but he is talking from his heart. Surely we are men enough to hear him." He turned to me, "Aaron maybe you can be a little less frank about certain delicate matters?"

I nodded, took a deep breath and continued. "Thank you, Lewie. "I'll try…"

After taking a moment to collect my thoughts, I began again.

"I'm, I'm not sorry what I said but I could probably have worded it better. One of the questions I have is this. If this desire to have a close friend, a companion, someone to share the joys and sorrows of life with is a man is so wrong, so unnatural, such an abomination to God and to the church, why are some of us born gay?"

Monie squawked, literally but then closed his beak, I mean mouth.

"Can any of you think for one moment, there was a time in my life when I chose to be gay? Do you think one day I was like, 'Hmm, I'm going to choose to like men rather than women? I'm going to desire to have a man like King David had in the Bible, with his friend Jonathan? I'm deciding this, knowing it is not acceptable among the Amish, it will cause pain to my family, hurt the church and make people very uncomfortable when they are around me? Of course, you know that would never happen. Just the opposite. You must be able to imagine how often I wished I were what other people call 'normal'. Would want the intimacy from a woman instead of from a man.

"Some people think we are gay because of an overbearing mother, a weak father or a rough and mean father, or someone molested us when we were small. I come from a good family, I got along with my brothers, well sometimes Levi and I did have our scrapes but I don't have a trauma that made me gay. I'm born gay." I heard my voice crack and stopped talking. I felt so tired. So alone and yet, I was not sorry for what I had said. My tiredness and loneliness was actually eclipsed by the feeling of freedom that washed over me. I felt curiously like a new man. A tired man but a new one. Or at least different.

"Well, young man you certainly surprised me," old Preacher Dan said simply. "I didn't know you had so many words inside of you. Like Henry said, it was alarming at first because that's not how we know you, all full of talk and questions.

"I think what's happening here is you think too much. You try to figure out your life and the bigger questions of life. You are not God. We know His thoughts are higher than ours and His ways are past finding out." He was quoting Bible verses in German. "You need to relax and enjoy the life God gave you.

"You have your furniture you make, the work at your place and I see the efforts you make to connect with the regular Amish people. I just said to my wife the other day when I see you visiting with your Aunt Katie when she comes with your folks to our church, you are a kind man. Aaron there is not as much wrong with you as you think."

"But surely you can't believe a man can have the same feeling for another man as I have for my wife. Even without being intimate in bed, it is NOT the same. Even if we didn't have the Bible," and Monie shook his head vigorously and his sparse red beard swayed like a rooster's wattles, "it is like God said, not natural."

"The Apostle Paul said that, not Jesus," I interjected.

"The Word of God is the Word of God! All of it!" Monie inhaled and his eyes widened. "You sound like a heretic."

"I'm beginning to think if we read and talked and concentrated more on the words of Jesus than we do on the words of the apostles and of Paul and of the Old Testament, we would be more like Jesus. Paul was a wonderful man of God, it's true, but he was not divine, nor was he without mistakes. I'm not much of a Biblical scholar but I feel he taught some things not in total agreement with what Jesus taught."

"I think we have had enough talk for one evening," Bishop Henry said, standing up. "It is clear we are not agreeing with Aaron on some grave matters and we must take some time as preachers to discuss this. We must pray about this matter."

The others nodded in agreement.

"Aaron, you may give us space." I stood up to leave, and on the way out, I passed my parents', no, my mom's bedroom door. It was open a crack.

I'm sure I surprised Deacon Louie the very next evening - after an almost sleepless night and a very unproductive day - when I walked into his barn as he was hand milking his three family cows. My deacon was sitting on a little wooden milking stool, the metal pail between his knees, his strong hands alternately pulling and releasing the cow's teats as he expertly directed the milk into the almost full bucket. Louie owned a carpentry business and employed a dozen or so Amish men and they built barns and sheds as well as an occasional house for the English. Yet as most Amish do, he kept several cows and they used the milk to feed his growing family and churned any excess cream into butter to sell at the market. I could hear one of his sons upstairs whistling a tune and forkfuls of loose hay kept coming down through a hatch in the ceiling and piling up.

"Aaron," Louie smiled. "It's okay to have questions." He stripped several last streams into the froth of the milk and then gave a pat on the side of the cow as he stood up, pulling the milk stool with him in his left hand and holding the full bucket in his right.

"Dad, Dad!" The voices of two young children came in through the open door from the outside and Verna and Ammon came running in. "Look what we found! Kitties!" The children dashed up to their father, each with a small spitting kitten cupped inside their own small hands.

"Don't hold them so tight," Mose had dropped down the hay hole to see what the commotion was. "They'll scratch you," he laughed.

Then they all three saw me and smiled shyly in my direction.

"Were there anymore?" I asked.

"I hope not," Mose said with a laugh. "We already have too many cats."

"We only saw two," Verna babbled. "We didn't know Dainty had kittens."

"I knew," Mose told his younger siblings. "Dainty came around several days ago and was lying down in front of me and meowing and rolling onto her back like mama cats do when they have their babies. But she also kept them hidden for she didn't want old TomBoy to eat the newborns."

"Oh, that's terrible!" Verna cried, "He wouldn't do that would he Dad?"

Louie explained the way of cats to the two young children and as he stood there in the barn, milk pail in hand and having all the time he needed to do what Amish fathers have done for generations, I was once more so thankful for the ways we have been taught. Families come first, right after God and the church.

"Now take them back to their nest and let Dainty have her babies," Louie directed. Then he looked at me and smiled, "Maybe Aaron needs some cats to keep the mice out of his granary."

I must have grimaced as I said, "I do have mice! Getting worse since the weather is cooling off. Hmmm, I'll have to think about that. But it will be awhile before these two will be catching mice."

137

"If they turn out to be half as good mousers as their mother, they will do well," Mose took the bucket of milk from his dad. "I'll take it in and strain it." The children all left.

"Well, Aaron how was your day?" Louie asked tucking his homemade chambray shirt inside his trouser waist and pushing a drifting suspender back up onto his shoulder.

"Is it wrong, Louie to have questions like this? Am I allowing the devil to lead me astray? I don't want to go away from God. However, I know if I don't ask some of these questions, I will go nuts!" This time I did not speak calmly but like hail bouncing onto the pavement, my words dropped from my mouth.

"Here, sit on this hay bale," Louie said and we sat down and faced each other. "Aaron, questions aren't wrong. I do believe they often lead us to answers and sometimes those answers may not be what we would like them to be, but we at least get some answers."

I asked him how we know which verses in the Bible to obey and which ones we could ignore. I asked him why we spent so much time listening to preaching about how God was angry with the wicked in the Old Testament and why God wanted his people to kill their enemies. How could God punish people for being bad and yet be merciful. I asked him why Jesus didn't go around in his lifetime, killing his enemies and punishing those who opposed him. Why, if Jesus was God, did he always extend mercy and forgiveness to people who came to him seeking help and healing and answers? If Jesus is God, why do the two seem so different? And I asked him why we made rules from the teachings from the apostles in the New Testament and didn't literally obey the teachings of Jesus. Why did Jesus give hard sayings like, "If your hand offends you, cut it off," "If your eye offends you, gouge it out and throw it away from you" and yet we didn't take that literally but we take literally the teachings from Paul and the Apostles and make them into rules. Why were

138

there not more people "selling all and giving to the poor" and going out and following Jesus and teaching others by example how to live simply and with little. "How can many Amish be very wealthy, have huge bank accounts, save their money and yes, to the world we look like we live simply and frugally, but you and I both know there are Amish millionaires."

"Aaron, Aaron," Louie said kindly. "Trace back to where these questions come from." It was dark now inside the barn and the farm animals were pulling on the hay and I could hear the familiar sound of the cows chewing.

"Because I have these feelings for men and not for women." My words came out low and painful.

"Yes," Aaron said. "You are trying to understand too much. I think you had these feelings bottled up inside of you and because you kept them inside, which can be good as we Amish know for it is not seen as good to wear our thoughts on the outside, then when you began putting those thoughts into words, it made you have more questions. This makes you think and question almost everything you have ever been taught by our parents and by the Amish traditions."

He continued and I could hear a tone of steel in his words. "This questioning takes many a young man and too often our young women out into the world among the English and they think in their rumspringa days they now have freedom. But we also see they taste of the world and the devil and he often deceives them and then turns and bites them when life doesn't work out well for them. What do they do? They come back home to the Amish again and ask for forgiveness. I have seen the unrest that often comes back with them. However, if they continue to be obedient to the rules and tell the devil to leave them and ask God to take them back in, they can do it. But some have sinned so deeply, they are plagued with thoughts of whether they can be forgiven.

139

"I know you never did rumspringa, and I am glad you didn't. But it is as now you have a different kind of rumspringa. You must cut it off from you."

I cowered inwardly at his words. I was at fault for asking my questions. It was not seemly to ask such things. I could hear Louie was not comfortable with my thoughts and was warning me to be satisfied with life as we have had it for generations. Why had I come? What had I thought would happen? I didn't know this Louie. I had been sure I could talk with him and make him understand what I was going through.

Then I understood. My questions had rattled him. Some of my words had led his mind to some of his own unanswered questions. I had seen this before among the Amish. If we begin to question our traditions, we have a tendency to get scared and retreat back to the "old ways".

I stood up and left without a word. My laced-up work boots felt like they had doubled their weight and when I untied Lady from the hitching rack and climbed into the topless buggy, it was as though my heart had doubled in weight as well.

"I cannot help how I feel about having a man for a companion, I know I didn't choose it and I believe God created me this way, so there is nothing I know to do about it. I tried changing and it didn't work. I don't believe God made a mistake when he made me and other gay people, so I am not a mistake."

This was the third meeting with the preachers. Even after Bishop Henry had spent more than thirty minutes reading from the Bible how wrong it was for men to have sex with other men. How God created male and female, and how Jesus spoke about a man leaving his parents and living with his wife, when I was asked for my position on this matter, I pretty well said the same thing I had said before.

Sentencing was swift. I would be excommunicated and shunned from the Amish for the restoration of my eternal soul and would remain outside the Amish church fellowship until such a time as I repented from my false belief. I would be delivered up to Satan in the hopes he would torment me about my lifestyle into a place where they could have hope and expect I would see the error of my ways and return to the church of my fathers. At the end of the hour-long meeting, Bishop Henry pulled out his little black prayer book, selected a German prayer and we all knelt backwards, our arms on the seat of the chairs and facing away from each other. I put my head on top of my folded arms and tried to remember to breathe slowly. In and out. Take a slow deep breath. Over and over again until this meeting would be over.

The next Sunday, after the three-hour long church services held at a neighboring farm, Henry made an announcement. "We have before us a church matter, so we ask all the children and the visitors who are here and not of our church persuasion and any adults who are not members, to please give us privacy by going outside."

After the last ones had filed out and closed the doors behind them, Henry simply said, "It is with great sorrow we have found Aaron Peachy to have followed a false teaching condemned by the Bible and has refused to recant and repent from the error of his way. We will not go into detail, but we preachers all feel we must excommunicate and shun him for putting aside what the Bible teaches and following the deceptive teachings of the world."

There were more words, both from him and from the other three preachers. Thankfully, all were brief, even Monie's, for the Amish truly take excommunication seriously. Louie never once looked at me as he merely said, "I agree with the decision of the church and uphold our teachings and hope the young brother will repent and see the error of his ways." He bowed his head and looked at the floor.

Hell-fires were for the disobedient and heretics. I was now a condemned man. I would be considered as such until the day I repented. I wondered if I should repent from thinking.

Or was I to repent from asking questions?

I got up and left right after Henry finished speaking. The adult audience sat with heads bowed and no one looked at me. Outside, the children had started playing and the several visitors standing in a small knot on the lawn were making small talk under a sullen sun trying to push the thin gray clouds away. Some of the young men who had not been baptized yet and therefore were not members were sitting inside a top buggy trying to stay out of the chilly wind.

I went into the shed, untied Lady from the tie-up and backed her from between the other horses and then turned her and led her to my buggy. With one hand, I lifted the buggy shafts and Lady twirled herself under the raised shafts and into place. I fastened her harness to the shafts, climbed into my buggy and drove out the lane, away from the rows of black buggies lined up in neat rows, away from the normal activities of the Amish getting ready for the mid-day meal of fellowship and good food after the long services and away from the only life I had ever known.

Shunned. Different. False beliefs. Weird. Gay.

The rest of Sunday, I spent by myself.

I wanted to work on a new piece of furniture I had sketched, but of course I did not. It was Sunday, the Lord's Day.

I sketched. The interior of the farmhouse could have been any Amish farmhouse. The roller shades half drawn down on the windows, the walls bare of pictures and pretty much bare of

142

everything except a wall pendulum clock I carefully outlined with a pencil. A clock that needed winding every seven days. Battery-run clocks have been the choice of most Amish women for decades now, but I drew one with a pendulum. There are some things that should never change and for me one of these things were clocks. Battery clocks make a weird monotonous tick as the minute hand moves relentlessly around the numbers whereas pendulum clocks talk as they measure time and the hands point outwards away from the center, away into the future and send you off into adventures with a cheery and busy "Tick, Tock" to keep you from flying away too far, lest you cannot return.

Then, I drew a quick sketch of a Bishop, standing in the arched doorway between the living room, filled in the white space with a few detailed drawings of old men and then made quick strokes of Amish haircuts depicting the scores of similar looking males behind them., The other half of the picture was the kitchen where the front row of women were facing the men and these women I drew with wrinkles and rimless glasses, their hair covered with caps and then I sketched rows and rows of women sitting behind the front row. It was easy, for each one looked almost identical to the others, caps on neatly combed hair, little dots for the eyes that were looking into the living room.

I got a red color pencil and made a curved mark above the head of one of the men. Then I got an orange color pencil and lined the red with orange. Next yellow. Green. Blue. Purple. Now, everyone had something to look at. Something colorful. I opened my diary.

Shunned!!!! Then I wrote the date. September 30, 2019. I took a black pencil and slashed at the page with seven black slashes. I breathed heavily and after I had calmed my racing heart, I washed the entire page with pale yet glowing colors of a rainbow.

I hardly ever drew in my diary. "Write what you feel, not what you do or did," Bruce had told me. So, I wrote:

*Fight the dark*

*Storm the wind*

*Push away the cold*

*The night will pass*

*And the morning come*

*Hold in your heart*

*The memory of the warming sun.*

# Chapter Fourteen

"I wanted to stop by and let you know your table is finished." I had found Cousin Andy in the back of the barn, finishing mucking out a calf pen. The mixture of straw and manure had caked into layers and would make a great organic fertilizer for the fields next spring, however the rank barn smell was cloying inside the small space of the pen.

"Oh yes," Cousin Andy said, and he stuck the long-handled fork into the area still needing to be cleaned. "That table, I'm sure, is well made," he said a little slowly and then kicked at some straw in the pen.

I waited.

"You have it with you?" He finally asked.

"Yes, I do. I borrowed Dad's spring wagon and I can assemble it here. I brought some of my hand tools along." I followed him out of the barn to where Lady was hitched to the tie-up rack next to the buggy shed. I pulled back the packing blanket so he could see the top.

"Franie was saying something the other day about it. You have the bill for the table?" He studied the handwritten bill of sale I had made. "Let me go in and talk to her," Andy said without looking at me.

While he was gone, I looked around the huge farmstead. Cousin Andy kept the home farm looking good, although I didn't expect that anyone outside the community would know just how valuable his one hundred thirty acres had become. Since it was around 11:00

145

a.m., Andy and Franie's older children were all in school just down the road and I saw the faces of a few of the younger ones pressed against the storm door after Andy had gone inside. I had passed the school on my way here and watched with interest at the game of kickball in process. Recess time had always been a favorite time for me when I attended a similar school. Grades One through Eight had all been in one room where I attended, but later on when the enrollment increased, my old school had been divided into two rooms, one teacher for grades one through four and another teacher had grades five through eight. Most Amish children drop out of school after the state required eighth grade was completed and after that join their parents and older siblings on the farm or in some kind of trade, as I had done.

I heard the door slam and Cousin Andy came towards me. "Here is the money," he handed me a fat envelope and I knew he was paying me in cash.

"So, is it okay to drive the spring wagon closer to the house? If you help me lift the top and get it inside, I can do the rest if you need to get back to work."

"Umm, that's okay," Cousin Andy said looking at me with a sober expression. "We can't take the table from you. You are in the ban."

So, word had spread into the other church districts as well. I had, of course, been aware of the shunning placed on me. However, I had hoped Cousin Andy had not heard about it and I could deliver the table before he had gotten the notice.

"That's true," I said pulling the money from an inside pocket on my jacket and trying to hand it back to him.

Andy shook his head, "No, I can't take the money. It's yours."

"Oh no!" I protested, "I can't take the money if you won't take the table! Here," and I tried to give it back again. "I won't feel right about that!"

Andy looked straight at me and said sternly, "You should have thought about that before you left the Amish. You know we can't accept anything from someone who is in the ban."

"This makes no sense," I argued. "You pay me then refuse to take the table. Then, you won't take the money back because I am in the ban: and once you gave the money you say now it's mine and the church won't let you take anything from me! Oh, I see, you thought this way I will feel bad and somehow that will make me repent. Why did you say 'left the Amish'? I didn't leave the Amish." I nodded towards my waiting horse and the wagon. "I'm not driving a car and I haven't changed out of my Amish clothes."

"It would be better if you had," Andy replied. "Then everyone would know you have left the faith and you wouldn't be so deceptive about the abomination you are in. Think of it, Aaron, what we as parents have to try to explain to our children why you are in the ban. It's even too shameful to talk about! It will confuse the youth as well. I know we Amish often have to deal with the disobedient youth who rumspringa but most of them come back and join the church, but this is far worse for those, like you, who have been baptized and have promised to stay obedient to the rules and traditions of the church to disobey and be put in the ban. Think of eternity, Aaron. Hell fires burn forever and ever and any of the pleasures of this world are not to be compared to the torment of hell that awaits the disobedient."

I shook my head, "I am in the ban, and not because I left the Amish community. I am in the ban because I am open about how I feel about same sex attraction. Something that has always been a part of me since I was a young boy, but I hid it. Once again, like I told the preachers, I have not acted on those feelings but I don't want to pretend I am someone who I'm not."

"Drawing sexy pictures of two men is not acting on it?" Andy asked cocking his head to one side.

"It wasn't erotic. The two men were fully clothed, the one resting his head on the chest of the other. Maybe I shouldn't have sketched that but really, if I think about it, I am glad I did. It helped me come out about my feelings." I paused then plunged ahead. "Was it erotic for the Apostle John to lay his head on the chest of Jesus at the last supper? We can't read that Jesus said, "Don't do that, that's not acceptable and may give people the wrong idea." Yet now I am put in the ban and shunned because I drew a picture of something very similar to what Jesus did?"

"Go," Andy said loudly and pointed to my rig. "I will not stand here and hear you speak blasphemy about the things written in the Bible. How dare you compare something holy the apostles and Jesus did together just before the suffering of the Christ and with what you are doing? You are not welcome here anymore until you repent, and I will need to know you have proven yourself for a long time before I would ever welcome you here."

I shrugged and untied Lady and steered her out the lane, the table still on the back and the money still in my pocket. I wasn't upset, or sad, or hardly aware of any emotion. It was as though I were a man erased. Without a community.

On an impulse, when I went past Deacon Louie's farm, I pulled on the right line leading to Lady's bridle and went in the lane. I saw Louie walking towards the house, and I realized it was close to the "mittaug" (mid-day) meal.

"Whoah," I pulled back on the reins as Louie came towards me. At least he looked as pleasant as he always did and that was a relief for me, for I felt I could use a friend right now.

We exchanged greetings and then without preamble, I told him what had just happened. "So, now what do I do? I realize I shouldn't have tried to quickly deliver the table, hoping Andy didn't know I was in the ban, but I did. Not that I will have trouble selling it for the people in the Philadelphia studio will take it, but I think I wanted to stay in touch with my people."

"You will have to decide," Louie said quietly. "I'm sure this is not easy for you, but I can't advise you. That would not be right since you are in the ban. Aaron, this is not easy for me to turn you away, but you know we cannot be friends as we were before you were excommunicated. I will always care for you and hope you can see the error of your ways and be delivered from the deception you are in. But I cannot be involved with this."

I sat on my buggy seat, stunned by the impact of his words. Of course, I should have known it would be this way. I had taken part of shunning and withdrawing from those who had been banned from the Amish. A cousin on my mom's side had left his Amish wife and gone "out into the world" and began living with his girlfriend. There had been a time when Cousin Jake had come to my parents' farm before I had moved away and I don't remember what he had wanted but I do remember having tried to hold him at arm's length, hoping he would leave. Now I was "outside".

"Okay, I should have known," I told Louie and slapped the reins on Lady's back to get her to move on.

"Oh wait," Louie said. "Mose reminded me the other evening you might have been interested in a cat. Would you want to take her?"

A cat. I wanted to laugh. Louie couldn't be my friend anymore but he wanted to give me a cat.

"It's okay if you don't,"the deacon said with a wan smile.

"I'll take her," I said recklessly.

Ten minutes later I was headed home, a very upset half-grown cat in a cardboard box, hissing and giving anguished meows every once in a while from the floorboards between my feet where I had placed her box to keep her from bouncing around and on my lap, a styrofoam tray with mashed potatoes, fried chicken and mixed vegetables plus a piece of homemade cake in a paper napkin.

"Thought you might be hungry," Esther had smiled at me, but I could see the sadness in her eyes.

Yes, you can eat while driving a horse down the road. Lady must have sensed we were going back home, so it was easy to wrap the reins around my waist and eat the delicious homemade Amish food.

"Well, at least your former owners were not as frosty as Cousin Andy was," I addressed the cardboard box. The cat was finally quiet. "Maybe it wouldn't have hurt as much if they would not have been so kind. Mind you, they didn't want to 'fellowship' with me but to see how they still cared for me, that's what makes it hard."

Then, I shut up because it is difficult to eat and talk while you are crying, even if your horse knows the way home. I dashed the tears from my eyes and continued eating.

By the time I finished the good, but fattening food, I felt better. Then I had to laugh. I had left this morning with a table. Now I was going back home with the same table, plus the cash, and a cat, and with food. I should have felt rich.

This is the ban. The Amish have perfected shunning down to an art. The community can give gifts and money to the shunned. But they cannot take anything from us that are in the ban. They can give us food, but we can't sit at the same table with them and eat and they can never take food from us. Some of the stricter sects will not even accept anything from our hands, like a book, or something of theirs we may have picked up to look at but will wait until we have placed it on a table or on the ground and then they can handle it. It is the feeling that, if they are kind to us, give us gifts of food or in other ways help us, it is an act to make us keenly aware there is a line between us they will not cross, it will make us banned folks feel so bad it will help us try to get back into the community.

The interesting thing about this it often works! So tightly knit is the family and community, anyone shunned feels like a man without a country, a human without a planet or maybe a planet without a galaxy.

That was who I was. All of those.

A half-strangled noise of a very upset cat interrupted my thoughts. "Okay, soon enough we will be home and I'll let you out of your box. I'll put you in the barn and you and Lady can make friends."

I was almost home when I noticed a car in my driveway. "Hmm, I wonder who that is!" Could it be? A feeling of hope and longing shot through my being and in spite of the heavy load Lady was faithfully pulling along, I slapped the reins on her back to make her hurry. The car looked familiar. "Well, there are other people who drive a Honda," I told myself, but I couldn't stop the rush of hope that swept over me. That car WAS dark green!

I watched the driver's door open and a slender man got out and looked towards me. I couldn't help myself. "Jamil! Oh, Jamil!" I stood upright in the open buggy and called out loudly, my voice choking with emotion. Lady's ears turned towards my voice and then she picked up her trot and we headed home at a fast clip, the buggy wheels singing on the country road.

"Your table won! They called me this morning and they want to get in touch with you," Jamil told me sitting next to me on the sofa. He stroked the young cat who was nestled in his arms.

I was still trying to make sense of everything. Jamil had immediately taken to the cat and while I unhitched Lady and turned her out to the pasture, he had taken her inside my house. I didn't have the heart to tell him I was going to put the cat in the barn.

"Tell me everything," I told him now. "Everything! Why are you still here? I am confused for I thought you were gone."

Jamil's face turned serious. "My uncle passed away before I could even fly back to my home country. So, my dad told me I would have to wait. So maybe it wasn't just because he was afraid I was getting "corrupted" by the guys and opportunities here. Sorry, that sounded disrespectful towards my dad." He turned his attention back to the cat, who was now kneading Jamal's legs and purring loudly. Jamil ran his brown fingers through her short fur.

"She's really pretty," I said and reached over to touch her head. The cat arched her head as cats do to show their appreciation and let me rub her between her ears. I admired the mixture of orange and gray hair scattered throughout her dark gray coat. I had not often seen a tortoise colored cat before, but I liked her.

"What about us being here alone?" Jamil suddenly remembered. "You were told by your elders not to be alone with another man, right?"

"I'm already excommunicated," I told him. "I know it will not make a difference on my status right now, so I'm alright with you being here." I continued rubbing my new cat.

"I'm going to have to name you," I said. "I've never had a pet cat since I lived here. What name would you give her?"

"Hah hah," Jamil laughed. "Something easy. Nothing fancy."

We easily drifted into a dialogue about cats and their nature. "I like dogs as well," Jamil told me. "With cats, I'm never sure, for some I like and others I'm not so fond of." He gave a little chuckle.

"I never gave it much thought," I replied. "Horses have always been my favorite animal and it seems I was always too busy with my work and upkeep of this place to think about getting a pet. It was not really characteristic of me to agree so readily today when my deacon, no, make that former deacon, reminded me about his son offering this animal to me." I rumpled the affectionate cat's fur.

"You have gone through a lot in the last few days," he said soberly. "And I understand if you don't want to talk about it. By the way, where is that table? That's the first thing I thought of when I realized I'm not going back. I want to help you take it to Harrisburg. We can get a rental truck and I'll drive you there."

The cat had jumped off Jamil's lap and was walking around my house, sniffing about the chair legs and exploring her new surroundings, her tail raised straight up and waving back and forth slightly. "Looks like kitty is at ease. I'll leave her in here as we go out. I don't want her to run off." I looked at her, "Paisley," I decided. "You have a paisley pattern. You like your name?"

"You will get attached I can see," Jamil laughed. "Paisley is a good name."

We got up and went outside to the storage area next to the shop. I uncovered my table and Jamil walked around it. "Let me call them tomorrow and arrange for delivery. Yes?" he asked, his dark eyes shining with excitement. "I really want to have this happen. I think it will mean a boost in your career."

"I don't want to get my hopes up too much. I had pretty well lost all enthusiasm after you told me you were leaving the U.S. Now it feels as though I have something to take my mind… off what's going on."

I heard a car approaching my place and then slow down and turn into my lane. I went to the door of the shed and looked out. "Trevor," I said half under my breath.

"Is it someone you know?" Jamil had followed me to the door.

"I met him one time. Maybe about a month or so ago. Former Amish and he had heard I was in trouble with the church." I waited for Trevor to park his car.

"Hi there, Aaron," Trevor said. "Looks like I'm not the only visitor today!" He smiled broadly at Jamal.

"This is my friend Jamil," I introduced the two.

"When I asked Mom about you, she told me you were put in the ban by the preachers and I'm like, 'Oh heck!' and decided to come over here. But I didn't tell Mom, because she probably would have thought I was coming over here to seduce you. You know, one thing has been very interesting to me since I left home. The Amish continually try hard to keep sex out of their conversation and control who has sex and how and when but I'm thinking, they obsess so much about sex and want to know who is having sex with whom, and how do men have sex with men and can women even have sex with women and it's like, why are they so curious about all that?

154

Shouldn't they just ignore everything about sex and stop obsessing? I remember this one married man told me when I was still at home, 'I just can't imagine a man having sex with a man! I mean, how would they do it?' and I told him maybe he should try it and then he wouldn't have to imagine it.

"I thought he would be horrified at me, but he just kind of laughed in a funny way. Later, that same man was sitting next to me at our church dinner on a Sunday and I felt him rub his thigh against mine. Of course there was a tablecloth hanging off the edge of the table and no one else could see it. I was like, wow, what is he up to? But of course, I knew. So, I just let him and then he put his hand on my leg and started sliding it towards my crotch. By that time, the preacher said we were finished eating and everyone bowed their heads in silent prayer like we used to do. But this Johnny man didn't let the prayer time stop his journey towards my dick. I think he liked that I was hard for he rubbed it a little and then we all got up to leave after the prayer. He just winked at me." Trevor laughed loudly. "Does that make you uncomfortable, Aaron? You are blushing."

"Brr, it's chilly out here," I said. "Let's go to the house."

"How do you and Jamal know each other?" Trevor asked when we got inside. "Are you two a couple?"

Jamil looked at me with a slight grin. "We are friends. I photograph his furniture and help him send information to the furniture galleries in Philadelphia."

I was glad for Jamil's response. I think I may have been too flustered by all the information Trevor had flung out to us to be able to know how to reply to this ex-Amish boy who seemed to have been on the fast track into something I barely knew existed.

155

"Do you like each other? I mean, sexually? Do you have chemistry? You know that man Johnny who touched my leg and dick, I really was not attracted to him at all. I didn't know anything about having chemistry. I guess I was just a horny young man and almost any man could have gotten the same response from me. Well, I'm not sure if our Bishop could have. He's so round and fat I bet he can't even find his dick beneath all the folds of his belly." Trevor grimaced and shook his head. "But you two. I bet you could be a couple. Maybe try and see if you like each other."

"I respect Jamil very much and I like him a lot," I told Trevor after I had found my voice. "I'm not sure what it means to be a couple but I'm not trying to figure that out right now. Yes, I'm attracted to him as a companion. He's one of the nicest young men I have ever met."

Jamil looked at me calmly and smiled slightly. "I feel the same way about you, Aaron. You were the first one I thought about when I found out I wasn't going back to Iran after all and I was so happy I could come here and see you again."

"What's this?" Trevor asked curiously and Jamil told him about the aborted plans to return to his native country.

"Ahh, so you have a boyfriend," Trevor said. "Your cousin's cousin saw you holding hands with him. At that fair. or wherever you were."

Jamil shook his head. "No, I don't have a boyfriend. I do like Mohann and when we spent the day together, we felt comfortable holding hands. As good friends. I think I would have held his hand even if he would have been straight."

I felt strangely relieved for I think subconsciously I, too had been wondering about the episode of Jamil and his friend holding hands.

"In fact, in middle Eastern countries, it has not been unusual for people of the same gender to hold hands and to show affection. But now, since there is so much more attention about gay people, our countries are beginning to forbid signs of affection between people of the same gender, especially males."

"Well, I wanted to stop in and see how you were," Trevor said. "But I'm going to leave and get back to the city before too late. And Aaron, if you ever want to come and hang out with me, let me know. I could show you the scene," and he flung his hand dramatically in an arch. "I'd have your eyes bugging out. Bring Jamil," Trevor nodded towards my friend. "It would be fun to have both of you there."

Jamil smiled his thanks and I followed Trevor outside.

"Hope your trip back to the city goes well," I told him. "Thanks for the offer but I wouldn't even know how to get in contact with you."

"Oh, that's right," Trevor laughed. "Well, if you get a paper and pencil I'll give you my phone number. You should get a cell phone now."

I rejoined Jamil. He was sitting cross legged on the floor, playing with Paisley. He looked up at me as I came inside and smiled, then looked at Paisley again.

"Well, Trevor is quite the guy and says anything he thinks about," I said almost apologetically.

Jamil laughed a little and nodded, "He does." Then he added, "I wish I was more like that. I find it difficult to speak about those things I feel deeply about. I think because I have been hiding my true feelings for so long, I find it hard to be open and honest."

"You liked Trevor being blunt and asking those questions?" I was surprised.

"At first, it was shocking to me but then I began liking it for we didn't need to wonder what he was thinking, he just said it." Jamil looked at me seriously.

Jamil's words seemed to slowly drift through the distance between us and pass me by and go into the corners of my house. I looked at the young man on the floor, playing with Paisley and I was curiously aware of every small detail of this moment. The late evening sun streaming into my house, the light illuminating the profile of my friend, his face tilted to look me straight into my eyes, while with his right hand, making twirls of motion kept Paisley busily darting after his nimble hand. My clock ticked companionably and for that moment, just everything seemed right. Just the two of us, together.

Jamil left soon afterwards, but his presence was with me all evening and after I went to bed, it was as though I still sensed him being with me. I moved my right hand towards the empty space beside me and then let it rest on the cotton sheet. I flexed my fingers, and then relaxed my hand. But a chain of thoughts moved through my brain, link by link, the one thought intertwined and linked to the next thought, smoothly and effortlessly.

# CHAPTER FIFTEEN

"Eat some more. I wonder how you are doing, Aaron," Mom said as she put more of her delicious meatloaf on my plate. "Just tonight I said to myself, 'Aaron might stop in for dinner,' and then when I heard your steps coming up on the porch, I thought, sure enough there he is and here you are."

"Thank you, Mom. Not too much, I'll get fat," I protested as I always did when Mom wanted me to eat more.

"No worries about that," Mom shook her head emphatically. "You never eat enough to get fat."

I was sitting at the one end of the dining room table. One plate, one spoon and one fork. A table set for one. For me.

"How are you doing, Mom? Are you sure you are okay living here by yourself?" I think my own status of being an outcast made me more aware of anyone else who was lonely or grieving.

"I miss Dad every day," Mom said and opening the wood stove door, she poked another piece of firewood inside. She clanged the metal door shut and then pulled the tea kettle to the front of the stove to get the water boiling. "But then I make my spearmint tea, settle myself down and just try to think of all the good that is in my life. My thoughts get all jumbly but I keep thanking God for what I have. But Aaron, I just don't know why it is you must be so different. I mean, you are a good boy, always have been, never causing trouble like Levi and so handy and everything. Why must you now be so, so different? Why can't you just get a girl and marry her and put an end to all this gemache ( mess )?"

159

I got up from the table, gathered my plate and silverware together and carried them to the sink.

"No, no," Mom objected, "let me do that. You know, I'm probably not supposed to even let you carry the plate to the sink. Ach! This is too much," and she used the back of her hand to wipe away her tears.

Biting back the words I wanted to say, I went over to my mother and wrapped my arms around her. I pulled her head against my chest and rested my bearded chin on top of the small amount of hair that wasn't covered by her cap. I felt her chest heave as she tried to control her emotions and for a moment, she relaxed in my arms.

The knob on the front door jiggled and as soon as Mom heard the door creaking open, she pushed herself away from me and smoothed her apron.

"Here's the mail," Levi called out as he entered the house. "Brr, it's getting so chilly outside. Do you have…" and his voice trailed away as he walked into the kitchen. "Aaron, I didn't know you were here." He looked at me and then back at our mom. "You still come here, even after you are banned?" His voice showed the disapproval.

I didn't have to answer for Mom marched up to her youngest son and said firmly, "And he always will come here, banned or not! Aaron is as much my son as you and Jake are and I will not turn him away, no matter what he is or does. A mother is hardly a mother who turns her son away."

"Don't make trouble, Levi," I said to my brother. "I am not the one who snooped in someone else's house and unleashed the violent storm that has swept into my life. Our lives. I came here and Mom gave me supper and we were talking, then I hugged her for I love my mother. I don't keep secrets anymore and I live openly and freely." Then I added, even though I had some misgivings about doing so, "If I were you, I'd encourage you to do the same. Like maybe let the other Amish know about the cell phone you have hidden somewhere and how you use it to listen in on the ex-Amish blogs that are exploding among the many who once were Amish and still want to stay connected with each other."

I got my jacket, slipped my arms inside the sleeves and then fastened the hooks and eyes and put my hat on. Levi stood rooted to the floor, his eyes darting from me to mom's face. None of us said another word as I left my mom's house. Then I closed the front door behind me and walked out into the night.

I didn't go home. It was a short walk to the phone booth down by the corner gas station and I felt in my jacket pocket for the piece of paper. No one was making an evening call, so I stepped into the booth and closed the door behind me. I dialed the number on the paper. I could hear the phone ring.

I looked through the glass sides of the phone booth. A woman was filling her car with gas. A farmer drove up in his pickup truck and went into the store. The phone continued to ring. "I am not available, but if…." I hung up the receiver and stared at the dial. I sighed and turned to leave.

The phone rang. The shrill bell startled me and I swung around to face the pay phone. Why would anyone call a pay phone? Must be someone got a number mixed up. I pushed on the folding door to leave. But the phone kept on ringing. And ringing. I reached out and touched the receiver. On an impulse, I lifted it and listened. There was no dial tone, no voice, just a quiet nothing.

"Aaron?"

It was Alex.

"Hello," I said. "Hello," I repeated myself.

"Aaron, it's Alex. Did you try to call me? I didn't recognize the phone number on my caller ID, so I didn't answer and then when no one left a voice mail, I thought it might have been you and decided to call back. Where are you?"

"I'm at a pay phone. Close by my house. I decided to call you. Like you said. I hope it's okay."

"Yes, yes, of course, Aaron. I'm glad you called. How are you doing?" His voice was warm and welcoming.

"I'm okay," I began than I took a deep breath and said, "not too well, actually. I'm having a really tough time. I feel so alone and cut off from my family and my community. Just a lot of things are going on. I was at my mom's house this evening and, well it was tough. I need, I guess I need a friend."

"Do you want me to come over? I was just relaxing at home, watching a movie on Netflix, but I can come over if you want me to." Alex said quickly.

"No," I replied, "it's already getting late and it would be another hour probably before you would be here and then you'd have to drive back yet. No, thanks but it helps just to talk with you on the phone."

"Come this weekend and spend several days with me,"

Alex invited. "I don't have anything I need to do that can't be changed. The leaves are getting so colorful and we can drive up to Blue Knob and take a hike. The weather should be perfect for that. Then we can talk and hopefully get your mind off your troubles. I'd love to have you come, Aaron. I kept wondering how you are doing and often wished I could just call you up and talk with you. I should have written a letter or something but I'm not very good at writing letters." Alex laughed and I smiled as I remembered his friendly face when we had met at the conference.

"I don't know…" I began slowly, my mind racing with the idea of spending time with Alex. "Okay, I'll come," I said quickly before I could reason myself out of why I shouldn't.

"Cool," Alex chuckled. "I like you, Aaron. I think I see a new you. Tell you what, I'll come and pick you up early Saturday morning and we will take our time driving along the country roads and enjoying the autumn colors. We won't be in a hurry, just you and I and we will get better acquainted. Pack some clothes and stay overnight and I can take you home on Sunday afternoon or evening sometime. It's a date," and Alex laughed his contagious laughter.

"Wow, that means a lot of driving. I'll pay you for the gas and time."

"That's the least of my worries. You can pay for my lunch or something. Okay, let's plan on it."

After we had decided on a time, I said, "Alex, thank you. This means a lot to me."

"I'm glad you called. And I'm glad I called you. I look forward to seeing you again, Aaron. Very much. I need a, a friend like you."

On the way back to my home, I passed Mom's house. All was dark and I hoped Mom was sleeping. When I entered my house, Paisley got up from her spot by the wood stove and stretched and opened her mouth in a gigantic yawn. "Aww, Paisley, were you waiting up for me?"

Like cats do, Paisley rubbed against my legs as I put firewood in the stove and banked the fire for the night. I have had to learn how to redo a lot of household chores with an attentive cat demanding a lot of my attention. Thankfully, Paisley had adapted well being inside my house and because she had been a barn cat when I got her, she did not need a litter box inside, for during the day she spent a lot of time outside and when she needed to pee, she went to the door and asked to be let out. "Come here, you little pesty pest," I said when I had finished with the stove. I held out my arms and Paisley scrambled up my sturdy denim pant legs and I gathered my cat in my arms and went up the steps to the loft, Paisley purring her motorboat purr.

I undressed and drew back the covers and slid into bed. Paisley was already on her blanket, her purring a constant reminder of her happiness. I blew out the kerosene flame and lay on my back, staring into the darkness. My mind went back to my conversation with Alex. As eager as I was to see him and spend time together, I also felt prickles of apprehension walk down my spine. This would be new territory for me. Spending time with someone English for several days. And a night. I shifted in my bed and turned onto my side. I wondered how many bedrooms he had in his house.

"Would you like to watch a movie?"

Alex's house was a comfortable ranch-style house in a residential area of Hollidaysburg. We were in the living room, where a cheerful wood fire crackled in the fireplace. I knew there was another heat source besides the fireplace for the entire house was warm and cozy. "Hmm," I replied, "I've never watched a movie so I'm not sure how to answer that. What movie were you thinking about watching?"

Spending the entire day with Alex had made me comfortable with this friendly outgoing man. We had talked, hiked, eaten a big late lunch together in at a roadside diner, looked at colorful leaves and talked some more. Now I was entirely at ease, tired from the day's activities and yet I felt slightly keyed up, as though I were expecting something more.

"I watched a movie once I think you might like," Alex said. "It's called 'Latter Days' and it's about a guy from Los Angeles who is the typical gay twink and enjoys life as it is handed to him. Well, these Mormon guys move into his building and he gets acquainted with one of them. The entire story is about these two boys, both gay and yet with such different views of life. I can't give you more about the movie or it will be a spoiler."

"A movie," I echoed. "Like I've told you, I'm not sure what I can do and what I can't do. I mean, I'm still Amish. At least in my own mind. I've been outed by the congregation and the community, but not for what I did but for who I am. Now, even for myself, I'm not sure if I should try to keep the rules of the Amish, or am I now free to do whatever I want to? Does that make sense?"

Alex leaned forward, his blue eyes looking directly into mine. "I know only a little of what you are experiencing. Remember when we were at the rehab meeting? There were some things I didn't want to talk about? You see, I went through a faith crisis. After I came out about being gay, it made such a big impact on my family's life, my church's life and for myself personally, I wasn't even sure what I believed anymore." He scooted to the edge of his chair, grabbed the poker and punched at the logs. A shower of sparks shot upwards and seemed to match Alex's mood.

"I felt so conflicted about what I had been taught about being gay and what I was experiencing in my own body. There was a time when I felt I didn't believe in God anymore. Why would God give us rules against being gay and yet make us attracted sexually to other guys? It seemed to be a direct contradiction to himself." Alex put the poker into the fireplace tool stand and leaned back.

"I know that feeling," I told him. "When I talked to Brian about it, he gave me some words I feel have helped me more than anything else. He said he only follows the teachings and life of Jesus because as God's son, he is the only one who knows the heart of God and can reveal it to us. Brian said none of the prophets or teachers other than Jesus has a true concept of who God is, so we don't need to try to fit the entire Bible into the concept religion uses to make rules for their followers."

"I think your Brian must be a wise man," Alex said then he got up abruptly. "Let's make some popcorn. Come along to the kitchen."

I followed Alex to the kitchen. His jeans fit him perfectly and he had removed his flannel shirt and was wearing a short-sleeved tee shirt. "How do you make popcorn?"

He turned to look at me and I blushed as I looked away from his body to concentrate on what he was saying.

"Oh, ah, I have a stove top popper," I told him. "I have a propane gas burner so I use that because I often don't fire up the wood cook stove unless I decide to cook something. But I really like popcorn. So, how do you make it?"

"Like this," Alex opened a cupboard door and pulled out an electric hot air popper. "Can you get the butter out of the fridge please?"

"And, what shall we have to drink?" Alex opened another cupboard. "I have some ginger ale, beer, and wine. I should have gotten some cider since its fall. Do you make cider in your community?"

"We do. Some families have their own small cider presses and then there is Bontrager's Cider Mill where they do hundreds of bushels of apples during the season. That place smells so good, sweet and cider-y and then as time goes on, kind of like fermented cider." I explained to Alex how we also canned cider to keep it from becoming alcoholic.

"But that's when it's good," Alex laughed. "Here, taste some of this chardonnay. It's made in a small vineyard in eastern Pennsylvania and its quite good."

"Another taboo," I told him with a wry grin. "I just wish I knew what I should do or not do. If I were on regular proving for something I had done against the Amish, I would know not to do it again so I could be taken back in. But this way, I can't be taken back in unless I deny who I really truly am. Inside of myself. "

"Aaron, stop it," Alex said with a grin and yet I could tell he was serious. "Your life should not be a series of "don't" and "no" and "thou shalt not". Find out what you want. What you believe. Make your choices for the life you are meant to live.

"I know I am still a Christian. I cannot not believe in God. I know, that is a convoluted statement, but you know what I mean. I do have faith in God. I do believe Jesus is the most perfect man that ever lived, and he wants to give us power to live with love and be kind to each other. But I also know I will not be able to live by what other people decide is right for me and let them determine how I should live my life." Alex turned the popcorn popper on, and the loud whir of the machine filled the kitchen.

I looked at the wine Alex had poured into the wine glass.

The slightly amber liquid caught the light from the ceiling and bent it into a reflection of the kitchen. The popcorn began popping and I picked up the glass of wine and looked inside.

Alex smiled and lifted his glass towards mine. At first, I didn't know what he wanted, but then I remembered from books I had read and clinked my glass against his. "Cheers!" He said loudly and took a drink.

The first sip was mellow and smooth and when I swallowed, the wine stung my throat slightly but went down with ease. Wine, made from grapes. Crushed grapes and then the juice was strained and fermented. Jesus had made wine at a wedding. Good wine.

"Okay, I'll begin the movie and see what you think," Alex said as we went back into the living room with the popcorn and wine.

Later, much later, I wondered what I did think. One of the first scenes jarred me so much, I almost choked on my wine. I know my face got red and I felt a rush of apprehension flood my body until I was clenching my hands and more than once I turned away from the screen and paid a lot of attention to the popcorn. Then, as the movie progressed, I got caught up in the story line and felt I could watch it more objectively. I also remember Alex poured more wine into my glass and at one point he went out to the kitchen and returned with some cheese and crackers.

"You like the wine?" I had tried to focus on Alex's face and found it alarmingly slip away into the shadows. "You are getting very sleepy," I remember him saying. "Want to go to bed?"

I must have nodded and Alex got up and I tried several times before I managed to get to my feet and then only after Alex reached out and helped me up. I do remember going into a bedroom after I had used the bathroom.

Then the rest of the happenings blended into a series of some very faint memories of Alex helping me out of my clothes, helping me lie down in bed and I'm not sure but I think he may have laid down beside me and I have a distinct impression of his arm encircling my head and my head resting against his chest.

168

Now when I look back on that evening, I know I must have gotten drunk. I think I had three or four glasses of wine. I hadn't known I should have only sipped on the alcoholic liquid and waited to see how it would affect me. And as far as the movie, after a while I hadn't been able to concentrate at all and lost the story line completely.

Then there was the part of Alex helping me into bed. Undressing me, tucking me in like a big baby and how long had he lain next to me, holding me against his body?

As much as I tried, I could not remember everything that had happened. I do remember Alex helping me undress, laughing with me as he undid my Amish pants and pulling them off and unbuttoning my shirt. Then how he lay beside me.

The next morning, when I woke up, I was still a little groggy and my eyes felt heavy. I had stretched myself in bed and as I became totally aware of where I was and at least some about the evening before, I was aware I was completely naked. I even lifted the covers and looked. Then I sat up and looked for my clothes.

Alex had draped my pants over the back of an upholstered chair and my shirt was on a clothes hanger on a hook by the door. My shoes and socks were neatly placed beside the chair. My eyes scanned the room and then I saw my underwear folded neatly on the seat of the chair.

I tried to remember if I had taken my underwear off. At home, especially in the summer, I often slept naked but I had no recollection of how much Alex had undressed me the evening before. Had he been under the covers with me when he had cradled me against him? I didn't know.

Alex made breakfast for me. He seemed as nice and friendly as ever and neither of us mentioned about what had happened the evening before except Alex said he guessed he should have warned me how much wine can affect someone who hadn't been used to drinking.

He took me home and our conversation was relaxed and we even had periods of comfortable silence as we drove out of the city and into the countryside. After the hour long drive he stopped his car in my driveway and I put my hand on the door latch of the car and then turned to face him but he had already unbuckled his seat belt and was getting out of the car. I took my bag and stepped outside. Paisley came running from the barn and I knew she was probably indignant about her night outside.

"Here," I put three twenty-dollar bills into his hand. "Thank you for everything. I really enjoyed my time with you. I feel bad you had all this driving to do on your weekend."

Alex tried to brush my hand away but I quickly slid my hand with the money into his pants' pocket and he did not pull away. "You don't need to pay me anything, Aaron," he said huskily. He leaned towards me and I slowly slid my hand out of his pocket.

We had stood there, face to face and I felt my face grow warm. "I really, really, like you, Aaron," Alex said, and he took his arms and wrapped them around me.

At first, I had stood rooted to the spot and then I acted on my impulse and hugged him to me fiercely. Every nerve in my body came alive with such intensity I felt tears prickle the inside of my eyelids. I clenched my teeth and breathed heavily and then with a supreme effort, I took my arms and gently pushed Alex away from me.

I tried to say something, but I couldn't. My voice would not work and so I just grinned at Alex as much as I could and turned and scooped up Paisley who had been winding herself in and out of our legs, meowing loudly and purring between her yowls.

I stood and watched Alex's car disappear into the late autumn landscape and then a shaky sigh escaped me, and I took my love-starved cat into my house.

# CHAPTER SIXTEEN

"**H**ey! I love your outfit!" The boy who yelled at me so I could hear above the loud music smiled broadly and reached out and snapped my suspenders. "You look like the Amish! Where did you get it?"

"His mother made it!" Trevor yelled and grabbed the young man by the waist. "You like it? I can get you an outfit like that for Halloween!"

"Ohhhh, yeah!" he laughed and then turned to me again. "What's your name, handsome sexy Amish? I'm Ryan."

"Aaron," I said and then yelled louder again as the music exploded into even a greater volume, "Aaron!"

Just then, the music stopped, and I became aware of my voice filling the air for a brief moment and then the noise started up again.

"Hi Aaron," Ryan yelled. "I like you! You look really handsome. I've never seen you here before. Where do you live?"

But before I could answer, a big bear of a man came up behind Ryan, took his massive arms and picked up Ryan as though he weighed nothing and twirled him around and began kissing him on the mouth. With a squeal of delight Ryan wrapped his skinny arms and legs around the man and as they kissed, they seemed oblivious to anyone else. I looked around in the murky interior of the place where Trevor had taken me, and saw mostly men, many of them dancing with wild abandon and only a few sitting at tables or on stools but what drew my attention the most was the open display of affection they showed for each other. I gulped another drink from my glass, ginger ale only, I had insisted to Trevor.

My head throbbed from the wild and loud music, but I felt my feet twitch in response to the beat of the drums of the music. I wondered how it would be to go out on the floor and dance like the rest of them. I watched their feet, their legs and their bodies as they twisted in response to the music. None of them danced in synchronization with anyone else but moved to their own interpretation of what they felt. Trevor had met someone he obviously knew, and they were dancing arm in arm and more than once they kissed each other.

A tall, slender black man had come in through the front door and I studied him intently. Slender and sleek, his bare arms were like carved mahogany, muscles rippling with every move, and he was wearing white jeans and a black shirt, unbuttoned half-way down his chest. A gold metal chain lay against the skin of his neck and I thought he could be an Egyptian prince or at least nobility. He looked my way and smiled a dazzling smile at me. Not brazen or rude, just a warm, friendly smile showing how confident he felt with himself.

I think I smiled back at him, for after he ordered at the counter, he turned towards me with two glasses. "Hi, I'm Musgati! Call me Gati, like my friends do." He handed one of the drinks to me. "Cheers!"

I took the glass and looked at it. "Hi Gati, I don't want to be rude, but what is it? I'm not drinking alcohol tonight. Oh, I'm Aaron."

Gati reached out and took the glass from my hand and set it on a shelf next to the wall. "Then I'll save it for later because it sure does have alcohol," he leaned close to my ear so I could hear him

173

speak. An exotic smell of spices and even a hint of leather came from his cologne and I hoped my own unscented deodorant was working.

"So, Aaron, what brings you here? Are you by yourself?" Gati studied me for a moment, his eyes scanning my face and then taking in my homemade shirt, suspenders and pants.

"I came with Trevor," and I nodded towards where he was still entwined with the other guy on the dance floor.

"You want a refill of what you have in your glass? What is it?" And he took my glass from my hand.

"Ginger ale," I said, leaning close again so he could hear me above the pulsing music.

Gati nodded and put a hand on my shoulder. "Let me get a refill then we'll go over to the other end where it's quieter. Here, can you bring the other glass?" and he turned with a feline grace and went to the bar. I followed him and admired his boots, narrow and black with side inserts of elastic.

He wore his hair like a cap of shiny curls, several dropping on his neck, full of life and vitality.

"Quieter here, yes?" We sat at a wooden table and even though the music followed us, it was noticeably easier to talk.

"Thank you for the ginger ale," I told him. "This is my first time to a, to a place like this. Trevor persuaded me to come and I wasn't sure what to expect."

"First time to a gay bar?" Gati asked with another dazzling smile. And even though I figured he knew how handsome he was, there was not an ounce of haughty superiority about him. "What do you think?"

I looked around the dim room, the dancing figures, the strobe lights stabbing the darkness and said, "I don't think I know what to think. The men and boys are so uninhibited and free and I like that, but they seem to just kiss anyone they want to and say whatever comes to them. No one seems to care much about what other people think about them. But they all seem very friendly towards me. The music is so loud I find it hard to collect my thoughts. I do like the beat, though," I grinned and drummed my fingers on the tabletop.

Gati threw back his head and laughed, loudly and with abandon. "You are amazing," he said. "What a refreshing find! Where do you come from?"

I told him and he shook his head, "Never heard of Belleville. I'm from New Orleans and visiting family in Philadelphia. Soooo, you think the guys are friendly? Any of them too friendly? Like they are hitting on you?"

I felt myself get hot and was glad the darkness hid my blush. "I don't know," I said candidly. "So many of them come up and want to talk and they look at me all over and I feel as though they are wanting something and I'm not sure what they want."

"Oh, they want something all right," Gati said with a grin. "When did you come out?"

"Just tonight," I said and then I realized what he was asking. "No, I mean I came out here tonight but I was actually found out about three months ago. I'm Amish."

Gati looked at my clothes and nodded, "I figured maybe. Or former Amish. I used to live in Georgia before I went south to the coast and there were scads of Mennonites there, including car Amish."

175

"So Aaron, have you ever hooked up with a guy?" Then when he saw me hesitate to answer he followed it with, "Have you ever had sex with a man?"

Although his direct question made it easy for me feel comfortable with him, I still hesitated. Then I shook my head, "No."

"Hmmm, that is rare. How old are you?"

"I'm 33."

"Would you like to have sex with me? Are you a top or a bottom?" Gati's dark eyes were not threatening at all, just curious.

I took another drink of ginger ale. "I don't know how to answer either question," I told him honestly. "I am attracted to you but I am not ready to have sex with anyone because I don't feel I, I am ready. My conscience would bother me, I'm sure. And top? Or bottom? I'm not exactly sure what that all means but like I said, I am gay because I know I'm attracted strongly to men but I also know I'm not ready, not ready for all of this." I waved my hand to include the scene around me. "I'm overwhelmed."

The entire evening suddenly wanted to close in on me. I looked around for Trevor, but I couldn't see him in the dim light. I got up from my chair.

Gati watched me intently. He stood up and took my elbow. "Do you want to go outside?" He asked kindly. "I can see this is a bit much for you."

All I could do at that moment was nod my head. "Did you bring in a jacket? Or coat?"

"I left it in Trevor's car," I told him.

We stepped outside into the frigid air of a Pennsylvania winter night. The wave of cold air that hit me felt good, even though I shivered.

"Did you see Trevor on the way out?" Gati asked as I looked around for his car in the parking lot.

I shook my head.

"Here," Gati said, "my car is right over here. Let's sit inside out of the cold."

It was all I could do not to scream as I felt the cold and darkness sweep over my spirit as well as my body. Everything inside of me wanted some kind of release from the nightmarish ordeal I was in. Like the black dogs in the night, I felt surrounded by new and strange emotions and I wondered if I would collapse. I looked at Gati and I felt a strange rush of emotions race through me. How could I trust this good looking, suave man who had taken an interest in me? Why had I come with Trevor, who surely knew what he was doing when he had persuaded me to accompany him here and where was he now? All I wanted to do was turn back the wheels of time and be a simple Amish man again, secure in who I was, secure with my family, my church and what I believed God wanted me to do. Now, here I was, staring down on the icy parking lot, cold and miserable, standing beside a man who had just invited me to sit with him in his car.

"Are you okay?" Gati asked and I could hear the concern in his voice.

"No," I shook my head. "I feel all troubled inside." I felt I had to voice my fears.

"You are experiencing a lot," Gati said. "There is no way I can say I understand, for I don't. But I can try to help you find your friend so you can get out of this cold if you want me to. Is he driving?"

"I think so," I said. "He told me he won't get drunk because we have to drive back yet tonight."

"My offer is still open," Gati said and I realized I had not answered him.

"Yes," I said. "I don't want to go back inside. I'll sit with you in your car if you still are inviting me to."

Gati's car was of course cold when we got in, but he started the motor and it warmed up almost immediately. I felt the seat beneath me warm up and it felt so good. "Sorry," I said into the interior of the car and above the faint whir of the heater. "I don't want to be a trouble to you. Thank you for, for I don't know what to say, but I feel somehow you rescued me from something. At least from the cold," and I chuckled just a little.

"It's all good," Gati said. "Look, if you want to talk, feel free to talk. But if you just want quietness, I understand that, too. You don't need to try to explain anything. It's all good," he repeated.

I nodded my head. I didn't know what I wanted. Did I want to talk? What would I say?

"The other evening, I was sitting by myself, thinking about all the changes I have gone through. I felt words pulse inside of me, felt I needed to express to myself what I should do, so I wrote this," and I pulled my little notebook out of my pocket.

*"Build your house on a rock but walk on shifting sand*

*We have feet to go to places strange and new*

*Dare to explore where there is no place of return*

*Where worlds collide and leave your plans askew.*

*Don't give up the dreams that lure you on*

*Learn to ignore the broken moments of the past*

*What does not break us gives us greater scope*

*The hourglass drains and golden memories last.*

*Dare to walk out and explore the new."*

I read the lines out loud and felt the same emotions return when I had written those words. I had to go forward. I knew I could not return to what I had thought was the safe place on the rock.

"You wrote that," Gati said and it was not a question. "That is beautiful and says more in a few lines than many could say in an hour-long speech. You have the heart of a poet. There is something special about you. Pure and clean.

"I have words for you, Aaron. Don't push yourself too hard. Let things happen to you, but don't let anyone push you before you are ready. This gift you have is not for yourself alone, but also for others. Hey, is that your friend?"

I looked and saw Trevor outside, scanning the parking lot.

I opened the door and stood up. "Hey, Trevor!"

Gati got out of the car and came over and shook my hand. "It was nice to meet you, Aaron. I am only here until tomorrow and then I return to New Orleans. But I'm so glad we met. You are amazing."

He smiled at me and I saw his eyes were wet with unshed tears. He reached for me and we hugged briefly. Trevor honked the horn of his car and I turned and walked over the dirty, frozen snow to the car.

"Hey, what were you guys doing?" Trevor asked once he had pulled onto the interstate heading east. "Were you kissing and making out in there?"

"No," I said. "Just talking."

"Well, you could have made out with a lot of the guys there tonight. They liked you. You were fresh meat." Then he laughed and I hoped he was not drunk for he slurred his words just a bit.

But I was lost in my own thoughts and even after Trevor turned on the radio and blasted music from the speakers, I thought back on the evening.

"Glad you came?" Trevor asked but I didn't answer.

In spite of the loud music, in spite of the boldness of most of the guys there, and in spite of the moment of crazy emotions I had experienced, I was glad I had learned an important lesson about myself. I could be me, even in the middle of a place where I felt strange, an alien and it was okay, there were probably some people who would still "get" me, in spite of my different take on life. I also knew I did not have to try to make myself into a man I wasn't. I realized now, I had felt some pressure to become like Trevor, learning quickly the way of the English so I could fit in somewhere.

For that, I could thank Gati. Polished, educated, refined and so handsome and worldly, and in an environment where I had never thought I could really connect with anyone, yet he and I had connected. "…the hourglass drains but golden memories last."

"Now here's some of my fried chicken and what you don't eat today, you can eat tomorrow," Aunt Katie threw back one end of her black shawl and put a plastic container on my tabletop. Then she removed her black bonnet and put it beside the container. "I said to myself, now Aaron is not going to church anymore and maybe only

180

to his mother's place, and I think he could use some of his Aunt Katie's fried chicken. So, when I came over to see your mother, I told her she can't have any of the chicken because she still cooks for herself, even if she is by herself now, with your father gone and all. Of course, she knew I was joking. Ach, all the sad things you and your mother have been going through."

"Sit down, Aunt Katie. Rest awhile and tell me about what is happening in your life." I drew a chair out for her. "Or would you rather sit on the sofa? It's softer."

"I will sit on the sofa," my aunt replied. "Ach now, what comes here?"

Paisley came down the steps from the loft. She was almost full grown now, her body sleek and perfectly groomed. 'It's Paisley. Cousin Louie's Mose gave her to me. I guess he thought I should have company and Paisley has fit right into my life. Or maybe I have fit into her life but any way you look at it, it seems to be a perfect fit."

"Well I remember Bishop Abner often preached about people's inordinate affection for animals. Then someone gave him a little boxer puppy for his birthday, and he was so fond of Pepper he used to talk about him so much, how people should be more like their pets, loyal and affectionate, forgiving and easy to forget." She reached her hand out toward my cat and Paisley went forward to sniff at the extended fingers.

"I'd think we could learn to love more," I replied reflectively. "I know I could take more love the last while. Paisley does her share, don't you?" I asked as my cat headed my way and rubbed against my legs.

"Well, I did want to talk to you about that," Aunt Katie said, leaning back against the sofa cushions. "Now tell me, Aaron, do you think men can love men as a man loves a woman? Or as it is said, women love women as a wife can love her husband? Me, I've never had a husband and I can't say anything with authority on that matter."

"Love is love," I replied settling myself beside my aunt. "If there is love between two living creatures, I think it can be celebrated. Definitely different kinds of love but I think I can safely say I love my cat." Paisley was on my lap, pushing her arched back against my hand as I stroked her lustrous fur.

Aunt Katie laughed. "I think so! And she obviously loves you!"

"Would you like to be married to a man? Maybe I shouldn't ask, but ever since I heard about how you are, I've been curious." My aunt was known for being frank and she was as true to form with me as she could be.

"I think that question is maybe good for me to think about," I told her. "Right now I am still trying to think how I can reconcile the way I am with how the Amish church feels I can be. As it is never been a choice for me, now that the Amish know how I am does not make me a different person than I always have been. People have just found out something about me they didn't know before."

"Something that can be fixed, or can't be?" My aunt's question was direct. "I hear there are places to go and get counseling or therapy."

My mind went back to the day I had spent listening to Mr. Waldorp. I know he was not the perfect example to use for conversion therapy purposes but I couldn't help but think of his day-long rant against being gay. "I don't know, Aunt Katie, but if there is a way of being changed, I don't know about it. I have read there are people who claim they have been changed but I also know many of them later acknowledge they really are not changed but have changed their behavior."

"What do you say? Would you like to be married to another man? I hear there are now many states that allow gays to marry." Aunt Katie was not going to be deterred from her original question.

"Who would I marry?" I dodged the question. Yet, I immediately thought about Alex. "I don't know of any other Amish men who are gay. Or stayed Amish when they acknowledged they were gay." I thought of Trevor but knew I was not attracted to him at all.

"Of course you couldn't marry anyone Amish," Aunt Katie chuckled. "Amish don't do gay."

"You are saying if I am gay, I can't stay Amish?" I questioned.

With a firm shake of her white capped head, my aunt said

"Absolutely not!"

"But gay is not what you do, but who you are!" I almost shouted. "I'm not doing anything I didn't do when I was with the church. Well, I've gone places I didn't go when I was a member of the church, but nothing about my behavior. For me, being gay is how I was created by God and who I am, not by what I am doing."

"Aaron so I am thinking you should just answer 'Yes' when I ask if you would like to be married to a man. I'm not saying I approve but that is not the point. You need to know what you want." She folded her arms across her bosom and looked at me with a direct gaze.

"First, I want to become more settled where I am headed in life. Right now, I don't feel like I belong to the Amish anymore. Not that

183

it was my choice, but I was put out because of something I didn't choose."

"Oh, stop it!" Aunt Katie snorted. "You keep repeating yourself. I think you need to know what you want, not what you don't want. If you want to be married to a man, then you need to let yourself think about it."

"Someone would think you want me to marry a man," I said pretending to be shocked.

Aunt Katie shrugged. "I just know it is good for you to know what you want. It keeps you from getting so mixed up. Are you sleeping at night?"

Glad to change the subject, I said eagerly, "Yes! It is so unusual! I work hard during the day and now, when I go to bed, I sleep all night! So amazing." Then I stroked my cat again, "Maybe it's because Paisley sleeps on my bed. I'm not alone anymore."

"Inordinate affection," Aunt Katie joked. "Sleeping with the cat," then she chuckled at her own joke. "I have to be going. It will get dark before I get home if I dawdle too long over here."

I gave my aged aunt a hug before she went back to my mom's house to drive her horse and buggy back to her own place. She squeezed me to herself and I could smell the faint odor of the homemade soap she used to do her laundry. I loved my Aunt Katie.

# CHAPTER SEVENTEEN

"You make me feel so comfortable," Alex murmured as he drew me close to himself. We were on the sofa in his house, and Alex had switched on his TV, a documentary about the threatened environment in the Arctic Circle, but really, my environment wasn't threatened at all. I put my arm around Alex's neck and drew his head against mine.

Falling in love with Alex was not something I chose to do. But every time we were together, I again realized how much this older man meant to me. He was understanding, kind and seemingly without an agenda. "Let's just let happen what will happen," he had told me the first time we had both acknowledged our affection for each other.

"I feel comfortable with you," I said in return, taking my finger and outlining Alex's nose and mouth. When my finger reached his mouth, he opened his lips and gently bit my finger.

"I never ever thought I would be able to experience this," I told him now, feeling his shaved stubble with the back of my hand. "I used to wonder how it would be to just touch a man. Without being rebuffed or feeling weird about it. Now it's the most natural thing in the world and yet the most wonderful and awesome experience. I just can't get enough of you," I said as I kissed his neck.

We embraced passionately on the couch and I felt a desire to be completely consumed by this man and to give him everything I could give him. "I love you so much," I whispered hoarsely as our hungry mouths explored each other.

"I love you, too, Aaron," Alex said, nibbling my ear and causing immense shivers of pleasure surge through my body. "I think I loved you the first day we met."

"Really?" I asked pulling away from him so I could look into his eyes. "How could you have? A bewildered Amish man, dressed in homemade clothes and so stumbling and new to being among the English? I know I'm not acclimated yet among the world, but I must have been like a man from outer space entering your world."

"Come here," Alex laughed his infectious laugh. "You have to understand your wide-eyed innocence is a big part of why I like you. Do you know how many calloused guys are in the gay circles? Never underestimate your lack of experience to a lack of attraction. Keep what you have as long as you can. Too soon, it may disappear."

I shook my head, "I hope not. What I saw the night I went out with Trevor was scintillating and yet something inside of me reacted negatively towards the open display of sexual attraction I saw there that night."

Alex kissed my hand and drew me to himself again. "But the really cool aspect of you is you are not afraid of showing affection, even in public. When we go out together, I love the way you reach for my hand, and you don't mind if anyone sees you or not. Your affection is genuine and comes from the deep place in your heart. I love that about you."

For a moment, I could not speak. To hear these words from this wonderful man moved me deeply. The morning melted into a seemingly timeless place in my universe.

Even though I wasn't sure just how I had reached this place, whenever I look back to the transition from feeling bound by the rules of the Amish and gradually allowing myself to explore and even reach outside of the accepted ways of dressing and living as the Amish do, there was not a defining moment but rather a slow departure. I think the first Amish rule I violated was accepting the flip phone from Alex. "So that I can reach you and we can talk every day," he had said with a twinkle in his blue, blue eyes.

Yes, I had to tell myself, I was not violating the rules because there were no rules. If I was put out of the Amish church, then that meant I was no longer bound by their rules. And even though there were times I had questioned my decision of not keeping the rules, I always came back to the same thought. I could not go back to the Amish unless I change who I am, and I did not think it was possible to change the way I was born. We talked every day on the phone, often in the evening when we were both in bed.

"I wish you wouldn't have to go back home," Alex tousled my hair with his right hand, his left hand gently running down over my chest. "Why don't you just stay and go home tomorrow?"

"And how would I do that?" I asked, my practical-self speaking. "You have to go to work and I don't have a car."

"How about Uber?" Alex asked with a laugh. "It would be expensive but I could share the cost with you."

"Oh, Alex," I sighed and drew his right hand to my lips to press my mouth against it, "I would really enjoy that. But I also know the longer time I spend with you, the harder it is for me to keep myself from having sex with you. I want to so much, but you know..." My voice trailed away into sigh.

"It's okay, honey," Alex murmured pulling my head to rest on his chest. "We will work through this and someday soon, I hope we can be free to do whatever we want to. My divorce should be final next month and maybe by that time you can come to peace in your heart with what God wants for us. Yes, it is hard to wait, but as I've said before, that is just another aspect I really love about you. You have core values and that makes you who you are."

"I feel so safe with you," I told his chest. "You make me feel secure and loved like I've never felt before."

That is the way it was, every time we were together. So much intimate times of holding each other and kissing and we both feeling the desire to have sex, and yet I always not yielding to the desires I was feeling. "We are not married," I would tell Alex over and over again. "Maybe we shouldn't be kissing and touching. I guess that's why the Amish teach so strongly a dating couple shouldn't have any physical contact with each other before they are married. They must have the same intense feeling for each other we feel for each other! I never imagined how strong that attraction can be. Sometimes, I feel as though I'm drunk and don't even have control over my feelings."

Alex would always be able to assure me it was okay, and he was willing to wait. "I understand how strong your teachings controlled you and I also know the value of letting you understand what you are comfortable with. So, I will wait."

Alex took me home. We talked some on the way back but mostly we just held hands and although I tried not to think about it, I felt a heavy mood want to settle over me because I knew the time of parting would always be hard. "I love you so much," I said choking back my tears.

Alex moved his fingers between my fingers and increased the pressure of his grip. "Thank you for that, love."

"Have you loved any man before you loved me?" I asked hesitantly. Alex had not shared a lot about his previous experience with men.

Alex turned the radio knob and the jazz music faded into a lower volume. " I think I have," he said slowly. "Even when I was married to Evelyn. You know, there were times I was not faithful to her. First, I wanted to find out if I truly am gay and I thought well, let's find out. So, I downloaded an app and made a connection with a guy. We got together at his place and yep, I knew without a doubt I am gay. That's when I went through all the questioning my faith in God, wondering how this could be, and not wanting to end my marriage. It was then I met Tom."

The tires of the car whizzed over the freeway surface. I stroked Alex's arm. "Well, I don't really care because now we have met each other and our love is so strong, what you did before is over, right?"

"Yes," Alex said hastily. "Tom and I weren't right for each other. It was soon obvious because Tom was so much in the closet and was always afraid someone would find out he was gay. It wasn't as though he had been married, for he was single all his life and I found out he had been secretly seeing guys ever since he was in his 20's. Even though I wasn't out, I didn't want to be with a guy who still wasn't comfortable being himself. I was wanting to be more open. Anyway, I did love him." Then he said a little slowly, "But I don't know if I fell in love with him. To be in love with someone is different than to love someone, I think."

I nodded. That made sense.

I loved being in love. Even though I had mentioned the sense of loss and pain every time Alex and I parted, I was still buoyed up by our love for each other, all day long and in the night whenever I woke up, Alex was the first person I thought of. I found myself smiling whenever I thought of him and I think I must have smiled almost constantly.

The parting was as usual. Alex came into my house and we stood for long minutes, wrapped in each other's arms, our bodies pressed tightly against each other. "You literally take my breath away," I had texted Alex one time after he had left.

The intense desire to totally give myself into Alex's welcoming body was so strong sometimes my mouth would dry out, my eyes wanted to glaze over, and my clothes seemed way too tight. Yet, there was that "Stop" in my mind that would make me push myself away from Alex's amorous and roving hands and finally disentangle myself from his arms.

"Wow," Alex said now as he finally straightened up and ran his hand through his hair. "Okay… until next time," and he bent forward to kiss me once more.

After he had left, I held Paisley on my lap and tried to collect my thoughts. Would I feel free to have some kind of commitment ceremony with Alex after his divorce was final? Even though I knew Alex was getting a divorce, for the Amish, there is no divorce. Marriage is for life and no matter how incompatible the couple might be, the church always insisted on the marriage to stay intact. It could even become so incompatible that the two would no longer sleep in the same bed. But they still were expected to stay married. So, not only to be coupled with Alex was a hurdle in my Amish conscience but also that he would be divorced.

Maybe the non-Amish could never quite understand how strong the teachings we have been raised with stay branded in our minds. Using the fear of hell as a strong deterrent to crossing the lines of non-Amish has proven quite effective for years for most Amish. However, there is still the strong teaching about such subjects that will not go away overnight.

I stroked Paisley's fur and her purring response was comforted my troubled thoughts. "I will go back and talk to Brian," I told my cat. "For a while I've wanted to share with him what has been going on in my life and tomorrow I'll call and make an appointment." I missed my therapist. I drew my diary towards me. "Write what you feel, not what you do." Brian's voice echoed in my head.

## Poetry

*Poetry is sparkling diamonds, shining among the gravel.*

*It's damming up floods into distilled sentences*

*A poem is born when moisture is frozen into snowflakes.*

*It's the fragrance of a rose rising to delight our senses.*

*Poetry is the love of two hearts melting into one*

*It's the gaze of silver moons and of blazing stars.*

*Poetry brings to life the hot sands of the desert*

*It streaks among the planets of Venus and of Mars.*

*Poetry is kittens, mountains, oceans and seas.*

*It opens locked doors, releases the caged birds*

*Poetry is thoughts, emotions and all of the above*

*Plus, poetry is the clever use of all ordinary words*

"You look so different," Brian told me as soon as we were seated in his study. "More alive and yes, if may say so, less Amish."

I laughed. "Well, I stopped wearing suspenders. And I bought this shirt instead of wearing the shirts my mom made for me. Oh, and I now have a cell phone. Alex gave me this so we could talk in the evenings."

"Alex?" Brian said with a smile. "Tell me more."

So I told him how I had gone to Mr. Waldorp's daylong seminar and how Alex had been there. "We connected." Then, as I told him about being put out of the Amish church and about the difficulty of losing my father and the subsequent dead-end street of staying with my Amish community, Brian was most sympathetic.

"I had no idea," he said as I struggled to contain my emotions. "I used to wonder how you were doing and how you were coping with life but wow, that really was a huge and momentous time in your life."

I told him about the loneliness and during that time about reaching out to Alex. My mood must have lightened as I talked about my times with this wonderful man.

"Are you boyfriends?" Bruce wanted to know.

"Umm, yes, I guess," I stammered. "How does one know? We love each other. Very much."

"Yeah, you may not have gone through anything formal or made a declaration, but do you talk about spending a future together? There is a difference between planning to live together or just being good friends. In love, as you say you are." Brian probed.

"Alex's divorce will be final next month. I think then we will talk more about our future. I'm still struggling with how we can be

192

together as men and then, I was always taught it is wrong to divorce and here I am in love with a divorced man! That's one of the reasons I came to see you."

"Those are truly legitimate questions for you to have,"

Brian nodded. "I assume you've had sex together?"

I must have blushed at the direct question, for Bruce said, "Maybe I've assumed wrong?"

"No sex," I told him. "I am not ready for I think we should wait until we are married. Or have some kind of commitment ceremony. I have been doing a lot of reading and praying about this and I'm thinking marriage is not what most of us think it is. The very word 'marriage' means combining. Blending. Voluntary commitments. Since I believe in separation of church and state, I don't think God is looking at the state to approve of a marriage, more he is looking at the people agreeing to a union. So, I don't even know if I want a state marriage. Because most reasons people want a state marriage is to have tax benefits, survival rights and a status in the community. I would like to get married but not by the state."

Brian laughed. "Whoah! You have put a lot of thought into this, but I must say, I mostly agree with your viewpoint. But back to you and Alex. What do you anticipate your life together will look like in, let's say, five years? You two living in the same house, sharing the same bed, and living a life where you are equal partners in your union, or marriage?"

I nodded eagerly. "Yes! That's what I want. He has two daughters, but they are adults and we, Alex and I, could have our own family. We haven't talked about children but I'm sure we could adopt. The state had become quite lenient towards same sex marriages being considered for adoption."

"Well, Aaron, I'm impressed by the advances you have made in researching and learning. I know you didn't leave the Amish on your own, but I must say it has helped change you into a better-informed man." Bruce put his fingertips together as he thought a bit.

"No sex. What does Alex say about that?"

"I know that it is hard for him. We kiss and hug and then I always stop him if he wants to go further. We sleep together but we always wear our underwear. I have told him how much it means to me that he understands and is patient. He laughs and tells me he thinks it will be worth the wait but yeah, it's not easy. Love brings a lot of complications for us." I glanced out the window and watched the wind whip the bare maple branches towards the east and a few snowflakes went streaking through the early afternoon sky.

"I would say your relationship is very uncommon," Brian said slowly. "But I do appreciate your caution and your convictions. You are a strong man and true to your principles. I'm sure Alex knows that."

"Yes, I've never met anyone like Alex. I have had emotions and feelings so deep for him that I didn't even know they existed. Here I am, in my 30's and I feel as though I'm a teenager, discovering love and romance at such a late age. But I love it!" I smiled at my therapist.

"I'm so happy for you," Brian smiled. "My son is not having a very easy time navigating being gay. There is so much we all have to learn about life and sexuality and we now have so much information on our desktops. By the way, do you now have a computer?"

I shook my head. "Not yet. I've been thinking about getting one but when I think of changing too quickly, I get scared. What if

I can't handle all of this? I can't go back because that bridge is burned. I'm not even sure getting pushed into a different life will be better for me however I don't seem to have a choice. You see, I get so lonely. After I quit going to church and going to community gatherings, it was as though I were a stranger in the night. I still go see my mother but even going to either of my brothers' places is a strain. So many of the Amish that leave the church usually go to a car-Amish or Mennonite church, but I also know none of those churches would welcome me. So, on Sundays, I spend time at home alone. At least I did until I began spending weekends with Alex. He has opened a door into my loneliness, and I will forever be grateful for that."

"I can see that," Brian said. "That you have met a man whom you have fallen in love with so quickly after you came out is truly wonderful. Your experience with the other ex-Amish guy, Trevor you said his name is, also shows you the road many newly out gay boys and men get exposed to. Follow the directions of your conscience and let God guide you with his wisdom. So, you are totally comfortable with the idea of two men or two women being married? Or committed, as you say?"

"I don't like the word 'committed'," I said rolling my eyes, "it sounds as though we are signing into a mental institution or something."

Brian laughed heartily. "Well, let's use marriage. Even if it's your interpretation of marriage."

"The best I can describe my feelings is this. We are all planned and designed by God. Hair color, height, right or left-handed, and with what sexual orientation we have. I used to think gay people needed 'fixing' and we are like someone born with a cleft palate, or maybe one leg shorter than the other one, and that we could use doctors to help us become "whole". But I don't feel like that

195

anymore. So, back to your question, am I totally comfortable for Alex and I to get married? If it is just between the two of us, yes. That's what I have told Alex. Whenever I think of all the questions and even more shunning and being ostracized completely by the Amish and Mennonite communities, I recoil. But it's not all about the communities that don't like us. I'm hoping we can make other gay and straight friends who will accept us as we are. So, we can have our own accepting community. Does that make sense?" I asked.

Bruce smiled, "It makes lots of sense. Plus, it is idealistic which is not wrong. You already know the value of community and I do believe wherever you go, you will contribute to whatever community you belong in a very positive way. You carry your gifts with you."

"To think I first came to you because I couldn't sleep. Now, I fall asleep almost immediately and hardly ever wake up at night. If I do, my first thoughts are about Alex. Sometimes I feel a little guilty about that for I don't want him to be my idol. But I just love him so much!" I let out a long sigh as I ran out of breath.

"During all this wonderful experience, don't forget to stay in touch with yourself," Bruce said with a smile. "Reflect often on the man you are, and on the gifts God has given to you. As fun as it is to be on cloud 9, and I have no idea where that phrase comes from, remember to keep your feet on the ground and your head uncluttered."

That evening, I called Jamal. We hadn't seen each other since the day trip we had taken to transport my table to the Pennsylvania Woodworker's State Show, but we occasionally talked on the phone. It was a new experience for me to connect on a regular basis with anyone with the ease the cell phone gave me and I liked it.

"Hi Aaron, how's life?" Jamal's voice was warm and friendly.

"Going really, really well," I told him. "I got the check for the table last week and the guy who bought it wants to come down sometime and see my shop. I'll try to let you know when he comes, and you can come out and meet him as well. You have helped me so much in my business ventures. I'm busier than ever since having the runner up entry in the show."

"I still think you should have gotten the blue ribbon," Jamal said loyally. "Your table was the best made entry." "Well, the design of the winning table was very innovative," I said. "I feel I have a lot of pointers to learn about design for my own pieces. How is life going for you?"

"I'm doing okay," Jamal said. "Busy traveling to take photographs. I never thought I would be a wedding photographer, but my cousin got married and he chose me to be his photographer. Now, I'm getting swamped with requests. Some of them as far away as Oregon! And California! Taking pictures as weddings is a big business."

"Maybe you can take pictures at my wedding," I said hesitantly but with a grin.

"Whaaattt!!! You and Alex are talking about getting married!" Jamal's voice faded out, then he added, "Oh my gosh, yes! I just didn't know you were at that stage!"

"Well, not really a wedding but an exchange of vows and yes, a reception for our friends. It will be very small on my side. But Alex's divorce becomes final next month, and we keep thinking soon after that." I felt excited to share this with my good friend.

"What does your family say? And the rest of the Amish?"

"Well," said slowly, "they don't know it. Yet."

"Oh wow," Jamal was quiet for awhile. "That's going to be a shock to them, I'm sure."

"Oh well, " I replied. "They put me out, so what do they expect? I can't let them rule my life anymore."

"True," my friend replied, "but family is family."

"Not if you are Amish. And gay," I said quickly, and I felt a bitter taste in my mouth.

After my phone conversation with Jamal, I tried to call Alex but all I got was his voice mail. I felt loneliness engulf me, and for a brief moment I thought about going to my mom's house. But the wind was now sending icy sleet against the window and I could occasionally feel my small house shake as the storm gained strength.

"Paisley, Paisley," I murmured as I gathered my cat up in my arms. Her soft fur brushed against my cheek as I moved my face down towards her warm body. She purred contentedly as I picked up my pen.

## Love Is...

*Love is one candle, blown in the wind Flickering bravely to stay alight Love is one candle.*

*Love is one scarlet leaf refusing to let go A radiant spot of color on a gray misty day. Love is one scarlet leaf.*

*Love is one remembered word held close Echoing over and over in the memory. Love is one remembered word.*

*Love is one star shining in the black of night Opening the skies to see heaven come through Love is one star shining.*

*Love is one evergreen tree growing on the mountain top Letting the wind blow and shape the trunk. Love is one evergreen tree.*

*Love is one gift inside multi-colored wrappings Never revealed until it is opened. Love is one gift.*

# CHAPTER EIGHTEEN

"**I**s Jake not keeping up with replenishing your woodpile?" I looked at the large pieces of firewood in the wood box next to my mom's cookstove. "Some of those pieces should be split. I can take them back out and…"

"No, no!" Mom objected. "You don't need to. I would like to have more small pieces, but Jake is busy with his own household and I can make do. I just have to remember to put the big pieces on before I need a hot fire. Anyways, you know you are not supposed to do anything for me. It has been this way for generations in the Amish community. Those in the ban are not allowed to help those in the church."

I made a noise that must have echoed the way I felt for mom glared at me for a moment, then said, "Bishop Dan asked me last Sunday about you. Asked if you had gotten a car yet. I think they all are thinking it may just be soon you will stop being Amish. Now tell me why he didn't ask if you had decided to stay Amish? Why was he thinking you would leave and be English? Like he was thinking the ban doesn't work with you? So maybe he does know it's not your choice? Now I'm not saying I agree with you. Nor can I say I understand how you can be the way you are. But when it really comes down to it, how many people can understand people they are not the same as? Ach, I know my ramblings make no sense, but when it comes to splitting up families, how can that be what the Bible teaches? Life seems to be full of questions."

"At least you acknowledge the questions," I told my mother. "So many people don't even allow themselves to ask questions. You know we are not encouraged to think for ourselves. I remember when I was young some of the young people were together and one of the boys said something about the strict Amish not being allowed to family reunions because they were too much like parties but they could go to weddings and everyone laughed. Then I asked why we were allowed to have zippers on our jackets but not for our pants and later the young minister who was with us told me I should not have said that because those kinds of questions create unrest among the youth. If we are not supposed to ask questions, is it any wonder that so many things are secret and hidden among our people? On the outside it looks good and suddenly something happens and we realize things have not been going so well after all."

Mom threw up her hands and I could tell she was agitated. "Ach! I know I shouldn't say anything, but it's like that Monie," then she clapped her hand over her mouth and shook her half apron as if to get rid of invisible dirt. "All these years, with those young girls coming in to help poor Bertha when she had another baby, and now it's come out he's been indecent! Sneaked into their rooms at night and told them to be quiet and if they told anyone they would be in trouble."

"Mom! Please stop!" I covered my ears. My mind was whirling in circles. Monie! I had never had much respect for him however I never suspected anything like this.

"The last one was a feisty girl. I think it was Far-Away Jake's granddaughter. Red hair she has, all curly and bouncy and when Monie tried to do his hanky-panky with her, she up and boxed him where it hurt. Next day, she told Bertha and said she was not staying in their home one more night. Sent word to her parents, she did."

I could tell Mom was ready for someone to talk with. Her words tumbled out faster and faster. "And you would think Bishop Dan would have done something about that, but he came and talked to that little red haired girl's parents, she was only 15 mind you, and told them that it was all taken care of. Monie sent word he was sorry. Sorry! Oh, sorry, was he? And Dan thought it was over? You know the Amish want to take care of our own problems and not let the outside know about it. But the girl's dad and mom went to the other parents of the girls that had worked for Monie and yep, they said it happened to them, too but they were scared to say anything because he told them it would mean trouble for them if they did."

"Oh my!" I was too curious to stay quiet, "What happened to Monie?"

"It all came out," Mom said with a quick shake of her head. "No one knows for sure, but some of us think it was that red-haired girl, I don't remember her name, that kept on talking and suddenly the officers from the county came out and talked to Monie. At first, he refused to speak, but they warned him if he didn't cooperate and if his guilt is proven, it will be a lot worse for him. He asked for Bishop Dan to come and be with him while he talked, and they granted it for him. Now, he is awaiting trial in several weeks and his two oldest girls have been sent to live with relatives."

Mom continued on with more details but I didn't really want to know more. This was enough. Monie would forever be considered fallen. The Amish want to always put on a good face to each other and when someone is "found out" that reputation dissolves and hardly ever re-appears. I felt so sorry for the young Amish girls, working at a place where they probably had felt safe and secure, among their own people. And then came the sexual assaults and the consequent warnings to stay quiet from the very man who perpetrated the deeds. And yet those girls did not have any adults they felt safe to confide in? That was the terrible part, and yet, how well I knew that feeling. I would never have felt comfortable to talk about my same sex attractions during my teen years or even into my adult years.

"Why am I even telling you this?" Mom said and sat down in her rocking chair. "I guess it is because Dad isn't here and sometimes I don't know who to talk with. I often think how it would have been if I would have had a girl. A daughter would probably have listened to everything a mother has to say."

I chuckled, "Mom, you used to say, if you didn't have a girl, at least you have Aaron."

"Oh poof!" Mom managed a smile. "You know what I meant. I meant you listened just as good as a girl." Then she said suddenly, "You know when I was young, we would never have dared talk about these things. My parents kept even more quiet about intimate things than we do. I was an adult before I found out Cousin John's Susie wasn't my first cousin but my second cousin. Cousin John and Amelia kept it quiet as long as they could and I still don't even know just how it came out she was actually my second cousin." Mom clucked her tongue and shook her head. "Turned out Susie was the result of a brother and sister who shared the same bed more than they should have and since it was winter when the sister found out about it, her mother just kept her at home except on Sundays and then all bundled up and there was a big snowstorm and no one went to church for several weeks and the women just stayed home and then there was Amelia with a newborn. Of course, the other Amish women clucked and fussed about not knowing she was expecting and they hadn't thought Amelia could still have a child, but there the poor little thing was. Raised like their own daughter they did. I know the dad of the baby was already gone from the home, went to another community, married and had a family. The poor little girl child was so sickly and maybe a little slow in her head, but life went on. Still alive last I heard and cares for her old parents. Well, they were really her grandparents but I don't know if she even knows that."

"So here I am, cast out of church for something I can't help," I said and as I heard my words, I realized they sounded bitter. Were bitter.

That evening, I made the decision. I would get a car. I was not going to try to remain Amish any longer. It was not an easy choice to make but I needed to move on with my life and being Amish was no longer an option for me.

# CHAPTER NINETEEN

"**C**ome in!" I greeted Alex with a big hug and drew him into my house. "Wow, I'm so glad to see you. How were the roads? Hopefully not too bad. When you texted me ten minutes ago to let me know you were almost here, I thought well good. At least the roads must not be bad. Here, let me take your jacket and hang it here by the wood stove. It will be all warm for you later. You sure you won't stay overnight?"

Alex handed me his jacket and although he smiled, I immediately knew something was different about him. Still friendly, but not as sparkly as he usually was. "Are you tired?" I asked him. "Come sit down. I made some roasted red pepper soup for you and toasted Swiss cheese on Mom's homemade bread. I don't have any wine but I did make tea. Or would you rather have coffee?" "Tea is fine! Aaron, you didn't need to do all this. Remember I told you I won't stay long because I need to get back tonight so I can go to work tomorrow." Alex sat down on the couch and Paisley came over and rubbed against his leg. Alex reached down and stroked her back.

I got the tray and put the food on it and then carried it to the couch and pulled a small table I had made in front of the couch and set the tray down. I poured the tea. The steam rose from the fragrant liquid and everything should have been just right.

"May I come over for a while this evening?" Alex had called me around 3:00 p.m. that afternoon. I had been in the shop when I heard my phone ring.

So here he was, driving on the winter roads for more than an hour to come see me. "Try some soup," I urged him settling down beside him. I handed him a cup and a spoon.

"Delicious," he said as he sipped the soup from the spoon. His eyes looked into mine over the cup and he swallowed. Then he set the cup down. He reached for my hand, but then drew his hand back. "I want to tell you Aaron, why I came. I should have insisted you don't make anything to eat, because I'm not hungry. And I'm afraid you won't be hungry either after I have told you."

My heart plummeted faster than a meteorite streaking across the night sky. "Alex?" I managed to say.

"I so hate to hurt you. I'm so sorry," Alex said and tears pooled in the corners of his incredibly deep blue eyes. This time he did take my left hand in his right hand. His fingers pressed hard against mine. "I had sex with a guy on Monday."

"Oh."

The fire crackled in the wood stove and the wall clock ticked normally on the wall. It was a still night with no wind and the stillness from outside crept into my house. The silence grew louder and I could hear my own breathing.

"You did?" I couldn't think of anything else to say.

"Yes. I'm sorry."

I nodded my head a little. I wanted to say something, but I had no words.

"I know this is a shock for you," Alex said, his voice choked with emotion. "I didn't want to hurt you but I also knew I had to tell you because I love you too much to deceive you. You may have questions and want to talk about it now or you may just want me to leave and be by yourself as you process this. I will do whatever you want. I don't want to hurt you more than I have."

"Do you want to tell me about it?" I heard myself asking and my voice sounded just like normal. But it was as though it was not my voice.

"It doesn't make you angry?" Alex said in his usual caring way. He reached out and touched my face with his hand.

I did not respond at first but then I sighed and said, "Not angry. But sad."

Alex withdrew his hand. "It was with a guy I had been seeing off and on before I met you. At first, we'd just go out for drinks and during the dark times when I was questioning my faith and if I even believed in God anymore, we had sex. Not frequently but several times. Then after I went through my dark times and came out the other side, I stopped seeing Jimmy and told him I was not going to have sex anymore. We stopped seeing each other, and then I met you. You never asked about my past and I always thought I would tell you before we coupled but I didn't even know if you suspected or not. We never talked about it. I think we should have, and I should have told you. But this week, after you had been with me for the weekend, I was feeling lonely and on Monday night, Jimmy called out of the blue and asked me to go out with him for a drink. I told him okay."

There was an awkward pause, as I waited for Alex to continue.

"He told me then, that he had never gotten over me and wanted to see if I was interested in dating him. I told him I am dating someone and told him about you."

I wet my lips and then took a drink from the mug of tea. The hot tea scorched my throat and my tongue but I swallowed the hot liquid anyway. I felt I needed to feel a different pain than what I was experiencing from Alex's revelation. My mind was detached from who I was. At least, who I thought I had been.

"I don't know what to say," I said when I could speak.

"It doesn't seem real. Like it happened to someone else, not us. You are still here, right beside me. It does not seem like you are any different than before." I put my hand on his leg to make sure he was real. His leg felt the same.

"He had picked me up and when we went to my house to take me home, I invited him in for another drink. We got drunk and then we had sex on the couch. He fell asleep on the couch and I went to bed. Sometime in the night he went home. I haven't spoken to him since."

This was Wednesday. On Monday, Alex had sex with Jimmy. Alex was my boyfriend. I was Alex's boyfriend.

I don't know why but when life throws curves at me, I try to break everything down into hard facts. Perhaps so I can cope with the impact it makes on my emotions.

I looked at Alex. He was staring intently at the floor. Then he felt my look and looked at me. I could see the sorrow in his eyes and as he studied my face, he looked raw and vulnerable. Yet, the strength I always felt in his gaze was somehow still there.

"Do you want to talk about it? Or would it be better if I would leave? I know it hurts and you have every right to be angry and tell me you don't want to see me again, but Aaron, say something, please." He took my hands, "Talk to me."

I felt his fingers in mine. The same fingers, the same hands I have felt over and over. In my hands and on my hair and all over my body. Wonderful hands conveying deep feelings and arousing

208

physical and sexual desires I had not known I possessed. Yet, these were also the same hands that had been all over Jimmy's body. Jimmy's probably naked body.

I turned his hands palms up and studied them. The deep creases were still the same. I took my forefinger and traced over the creases. Then, I took his fingers and closed them and then I cupped his hands with mine and held them.

"Do you still want Jimmy?"

Alex looked at me. "I don't. I want you if you will still have me. If you can forgive me. I love you, Aaron."

Usually, I was the one who cried easily. I was the one who had to restrain the rain pouring out of my eyes at unexpected moments of sorrow or of joy. Alex had more than once teased me lovingly about the storehouses of tears I had and used napkins to dry my eyes and kiss the eyelids still salty with tears.

As I held Alex in my arms as he sobbed on my shoulder, I knew my time would come later. Maybe all by myself when the rawness of what had happened would hit me over and over again. When in my vivid imagination I would see Alex and Jimmy in each other's arms, having sex. I knew myself well enough to know I would struggle immensely with what had happened and ask myself countless times why, why, why?

But all I knew right now was Alex needed me. Needed me to let him know he was still the same Alex. Yes, a man who had "slipped" and done something he deeply regretted. I also felt how much he hurt because how much he knew he had hurt me. For some unknown reason, that made me love him even more.

The wood in the stove continued to burn, the clock continued to tick, and the soup and cheese sandwiches got cold and the tea was no longer hot. Paisley must have gone up to the loft, because I did not see her downstairs and yet, I kept on holding Alex in my arms, stroking his back with my free hand, holding his hand with my other one.

"I better go, Aaron," he finally said rising from the couch. I got his jacket, helped him slip his arms into the sleeves and then I zipped up the zipper. I walked him to the door, and he turned towards me. This time, I did cry. Not a lot, but some. He held me, kissed me on my mouth and said huskily, "I love you so much".

I woke up several times that night and the black dogs of the night wanted to come in on me, but I just turned to my other side, re-created our hug on the couch or our hug before he left and went right back to sleep.

The next morning, I woke up and immediately the scene from last evening swept over me like a wave of despair. I began weeping, clutching the quilt with both hands and moaning. I turned on my stomach and stuffed my pillow into my mouth as hot tears streamed onto the sheets. When I felt something warm on my neck, I turned my head and Paisley's big eyes were staring at me in the dim light of the morning. She had taken her paw and touched my neck. I reached out and began stroking her fur and she settled next to me and began purring. Gradually my tears subsided and yet, I continued petting and stroking my cat.

"I have no community," I told Brian. "I had Alex and I talk to Jamil on the phone and my mom. Oh, and Aunt Katie. Other than that, I hardly see anyone. Now with what happened between Alex and me, I am more alone than ever." I felt my voice crack and stared at my shoes.

"What happened between you and Alex?" Brian asked. I lifted my eyes to look at him. "I told you. He had sex with Jimmy." Why was he asking this?

Brian smiled. "This may seem strange to you, but I still ask, what happened between you two? That your boyfriend had sex with another man is not the answer for my question."

"How can I trust someone who says he loves me and yet has sex with someone else? Does that seem strange to you?" I was getting slightly aggravated.

"Hold that question and we will try to get back to that." Brian scribbled on his pad. "There is nothing wrong with your question, but I would like for you to look squarely at my question and see what answer comes to you. Did you tell Alex you do not want to continue to date him? Did you break up? Did he say do not call him anymore? Just what happened between you and Alex?"

"Nothing. I held him after he told me he was sorry. We just sat on the sofa for a long time, saying nothing. Then, he left. So, in a sense nothing happened."

"Did you call him today?"

I shook my head. "I didn't know what to say. So, no I didn't call."

"Text?"

Another shake of my head.

"What do you want to do? How do you feel?" Brian asked.

"I want it not to have happened." I shook my head violently and said, "I just freaking wish it had never happened! Everything was going so well! We were so close and we often talked about someday living together after we had the commitment ceremony. We were so much in love! Now, I am haunted by mental images of Alex and Jimmy lying in each other's arms, kissing and having sex. I thought we were saving ourselves for each other! I thought Alex loved me as much as I loved him! One time he told me since we began dating if any other guy tries to flirt with him, he always makes sure not to encourage them because he doesn't want anyone else but me. So now how could he do this to me? To us? How can he change from wanting only me to having sex with Jimmy? I have tried today to push it away, but it is like a knife has plunged into my heart and cut a piece right out of it."

"Your first real true love," Brian said. "When you love someone as much as you love Alex, you will hurt if you feel your love has been spurned. Or threatened. That is only natural. It's not a choice you make to be hurt, you are mentally and physically hurt. There is no cure for that."

"My life is a shambles," I mumbled. "Banned by the church, shunned by my friends and family, now betrayed by my boyfriend. What purpose do I have for living?"

"Aaron, I care enough about you that it also hurts me to see what has happened to you. To see you agonize with the blow to your affections and love for Alex hits me deeply. A part of me wants to tell you to move away to another community, start life over again. But I also know that would not really be an answer for the deep hurt inside of you. You can be distracted but you can't run away. You need to face it."

I nodded. "I thought of running off somewhere else as well. But I have no idea where I would go. None of my Amish or Mennonite relatives would want me to come be with them. Or they would try to heal me."

"So, Aaron, I'm going to do something difficult. But it may help. Tell me again how you felt when you were holding Alex. What went through your head?"

I remembered how Alex had sobbed onto my shoulder, his body limp in mine as I wrapped my arms around him. "I felt needed. Wanted, too. I was deeply hurt and yet, I didn't cry because I needed to support Alex in his sorrow and remorse. So, I put my own feelings aside so I could hold and support him."

Brian nodded. "That's what I thought you told me. I wanted you to hear yourself say that again. To have you realize how you could lay aside your own feelings for the sake of the man you loved. So, I want you to do it again. Now."

I was bewildered. "How? Alex isn't here. Will you be the proxy for Alex? Do you want me to hold you?"

Brian roared with laughter. "No, no. No roleplay." But then he said seriously, "You will listen to me while I outline what you may have overlooked.

"So, you and Alex have been dating now for what, two three months? Yes, I thought so. During that time, you have hugged and kissed, lay in each other's arms, slept together… Now wait! I know you said you never undressed… and you became closer and closer to each other. Aaron, you tell me you never had sex, right? But you know Alex did. Of course, with his wife for years and years and then after their separation with other men. Then he met you and he concentrated on his relationship with you. You kissed him, you hugged him and by the way it sounds your hands explored his body a lot. He did the same with you. I don't need to ask if you got sexually aroused. I'm sure you did. As did Alex, right?"

I nodded. "I knew he did. So much so that at times I pulled away from him because I did not feel comfortable with how desperate his needs were getting."

"People are wired differently. Since you haven't ever had sex with anyone, your sex drive may not have evolved to as high a level as someone who has been sexually active. So, picture Alex, loving you so much and being so intimate physically and yet being stopped by you whenever he was aroused to a very high pitch. Think of how he must have felt after you left. Whenever he thought about being with you again. He left, wanting you so much and yet knowing you were not ready. I am thinking he may have felt sometimes you may just give in, for he probably imagined that you wanted sex as much as he did but figured you must be a stronger man. I am not putting words in your mouth but trying to help you look at it from how he may have felt. Does this make sense?" Brian asked earnestly.

I sat for a minute, silently digesting what Brian had just said, before continuing.

When I was finally able to speak, I began, "Of course, it was hard for me, too. There were times I wanted to tell him we shouldn't spend so much time in each other's arms with our bodies touching, but I wanted it, too. I have this gigantic hunger to be loved. To be held." I paused. "So, are you suggesting maybe it was my fault Alex had sex with Jimmy? That somehow I aroused him so much he just finally gave in?"

Brian shook his head. "We use the word, fault, as though that is a reason, an excuse. Mistakes are not faults. I know you didn't intentionally arouse Alex's sex drive, but it just happened because of what you did. To say it would be your fault is to make you feel guilty. No fault. No guilt. We are not looking for answers. We are looking how to cope, to learn, to adjust and to move forward."

214

"Why are you saying this?" I asked him. "How is this helping? So that I have pity on Alex and say that I am okay with what he did?"

"Aaron, my goal is not to try to help you. My goal is to assist you in coping with what happened and know how you can go forward. So, tell me, do you want to see Alex again? Do you want to call it quits? It's over for you two?"

"No, no! I can't imagine my life without Alex. But I can't get over what he did. Oh, I don't know what I want." Then I corrected myself. "I want to have him hold me. To hold him. I miss him so much."

"What do you plan to do for community?" Brian asked, abruptly changing the subject. "You need people in your life. We all do. Have you considered attending another church for instance?"

I lifted my eyes off my shoes to look at my therapist.

"I've thought about it, but I don't know where to start."

"I don't want to try to persuade you, but you would be welcome to come to our church. We also host a small group gathering here in our home every two weeks on Sunday afternoons. We get together and talk about what we've been doing and try to encourage each other. It's nothing formal. However, most of us are couples with children but you are more than welcome to come. You may want to try to visit some of the churches in the area, or since you now have a car, you could travel to a city church. Look around. It doesn't have to be a church but you do need people in your life. Maybe you could learn how to dance." Brian grinned at me.

"Dance?" I echoed and tilted my head back and rolled my eyes. "Amish don't dance and I can only imagine what a spectacle I would make trying to dance."

215

"Ah, hah!" Brian said triumphantly. "You have thought about it. That's why you could take dance lessons. To learn how! Listen to music. With your range of interests continuing to broaden, you have a lot of opportunity to meet other non-Amish people in the community. "

"Thanks, but right now I have no interest in broadening my interests. I want Alex back again." I puffed out my lips in a huge sigh.

"Well, from what I gather, you never lost him. I'm not hearing how he pushed you away." Then he said, "You know, for many people in a relationship, they can overlook a lot of slips or mistakes. But if it is sexual, that usually means it's over. Let's look at it another way. What if it doesn't end the relationship? What if the relationship actually survives and becomes stronger? What if the slip is not so huge that it ruins the relationship, but in some manner opens up discussions and windows into each other's lives that are good? Yes, Alex was stupid. Got drunk enough to lose his resolutions to wait for you and had sex with Jimmy. You can't undo that. But you can do something about it. You can tell yourself you love Alex enough you want to stay with him and walk through this hardship together. Or you can call it quits. I'm thinking it is still up to you." Brian was blunt but I knew he was sincere. And what he said made sense. Finally.

# CHAPTER TWENTY

"**A**lex? It's Aaron."

"Hi Aaron."

I tried to think of something to say. "Have you been busy?"

"I have. We are going through last year's records in the office and so I've been staying late trying to get everything caught up to get our tax work finished. How's your day, or how have your days been?" Alex's voice sounded tired.

"Not too good. I've been trying to stay busy but it seems I can't get much done." I don't think my voice sounded any less tired.

Again, there was a silence. "I was thinking, if it's okay with you, I'd like to maybe take a week or two to process the feelings I'm having. I resumed my sessions with Brian and I know I need to process some things I have been unwilling to face, and this doesn't really have to do with what happened between us, but more some personal issues I need to face. Oh heck, that doesn't make sense, even to me. I'm sorry. I'm rather an emotional wreck right now."

"Aaron, I'm the one who should say 'sorry'. I'm the one who ruined everything between us." Alex said soberly.

"No, not ruined everything! Don't say that! Ruined means we have nothing and we both know we do have something. Something I don't want to lose. Maybe rebuild at a different level but not ruined." Now the words spilled out of me. "Alex, I know I put you into some real predicaments when we hugged and kissed and lay side by side in bed, hugging and making love. I wanted your love

217

so much and I felt so needy so I was trying to get from you everything I could except for actual sex, and it opened up a way for me to see more into the depth of who I am. Anyway, I want you to know I am not blaming you or wanting to stop seeing you. But I feel I have to take some time and examine some areas of growth that I need before we see each other again. That is, if you want to continue to see me. Perhaps you need someone closer to your age. Someone less emotional and needy than I am."

"I'm not looking for anyone else," Alex said quickly. "I am also needing to evaluate what happened and take full responsibility for what I did and how that not only affected you but also how it reflects on the person I've become. I'd love to see you again soon however, I respect your request for time."

"Thank you," and my voice choked up.

"Have you been sleeping, Aaron?" Alex asked and I could hear concern in his voice.

"Not much. The first night I slept alright but after that, I keep waking up. But that gives me time to write. And sketch."

"Send me some of your writings. If you want to."

"How can I? I just have a flip phone. That reminds me I have to find another way of charging my phone. My solar panel has barely been working the last several days because it's been so cloudy for so long. It's kind of depressing." I checked the battery and saw it was way down.

"Ok, I won't keep you," Alex said. "Thanks for calling and is it okay if I still call you or do you want no contact?"

"Call me," I answered. "I want to know how you are doing. And I, I need you. Please."

"There is such a huge chasm between the Amish and the English," I told Brian. "That time I went with Trevor to the gay bar, it hit me with full force. The music was loud, and I had no idea of who was singing and mostly didn't understand any of the words. My knowledge of movies and TV is non-existent. I barely even know who the famous actors and celebrities are. I'm like from another planet. A foreigner. In my own country. I feel lost. I can't go back and be accepted by the Amish. Really, I no longer want too. I'm beginning to see more and more the inconsistencies of my people and no longer want to be a part of that. However, to go forward into the English world is a journey of gigantic changes. I bought a car and I am studying to get my license. Signed up with a driving school and all the other students are young. I'm the only Amish guy, of course."

Brian smiled. "I hear you. There should be an acclimation course for integrating ex-Amish into the English world, I guess."

"How about an acclimation course for integrating gay ex-Amish guys into a gay English world? That is the leap I am trying to take. Like I said, many Amish who leave, especially my age and older, hardly ever just go right out into the world, as we say, but climb the ladder of going to more progressive churches, like car Amish and then Mennonites, etc. There is almost always a community to plug into. I have none."

"Have you ever considered how many English people never have had community?" Brian asked. "You talk about what you lost, and to be true, if we lose something we grieve more than if we never had it, yet as I sit here listening to you talk about not having community, this world today is filled with migrating and moving populations in search of career and jobs and if they ever did have community, they also lose it when they move. How do you think they cope?"

"Good question. I guess if they move for school or a job, they interact with other people they are with daily," I suggested.

"Some definitely do. I am thinking, you might be surprised how many people also are very lonely. I've talked with people who barely have two or three people they interact with. Maybe they work from home or in environments where there is not a lot of co-worker interaction. So, I have a suggestion. Make community happen. Intentionally interact with people. You have a house and live by yourself, right? Invite people to come and spend an evening with you. Cook for them and maybe have a game night. Plus, I would suggest you don't just invite people you know really well. Issue invitations to anyone you can think of." Brian smiled at me.

"Would you come?" I smiled back at him.

Brian laughed. "Well, you really took my advice to heart. Um…, yes, I would. I'd bring my wife. We've lived among the Amish all our lives and we have yet to set foot inside an Amish home. Not that you are Amish anymore, but you know it would be fun."

"I'd invite Alex," I said.

"Are you guys still talking? Seeing each other?" Brian asked.

"Talking, yes. Seeing each other, no not yet. I asked for several weeks of respite so I can process some of my own feelings. I'm still mulling over a lot of things we talked about the last time I was here. Not sure I'm making progress. It's as though I'm frozen in place. My mind still goes around in endless circles with hardly any different bunny trails. I'm not sure why I can't lift myself out of the doldrums," I said ruefully.

"How much time do you spend in meditation? Quieting yourself and shutting out the world and learning to listen to what your heart and mind are telling you? We as Christians are taught the value of daily Bible reading and prayer, and yet I don't think we set enough time apart to just be quiet. Not read, not pray just sit and silence the voices in our head so we can hear the voice in our hearts. You may want to get a book on meditation and practice some steps in quieting your soul." Brian raised his eyebrows questioningly as he cocked his head slightly sideways.

"Sounds New Age-y," I matched Brian's eyebrows by raising my own. "We've always been warned against mysticism and told it's connected to the occult."

Brian shook his head, "No, I'm not promoting any Eastern religions. Meditation is quieting ourselves. Isn't there mention made in the Bible about God speaking to us in a 'quiet, small voice?' I do believe we so often fill our own voids with prayers of petitions and yes, even thanksgivings. However, I am thinking if we make ourselves still, God can speak to us and we can hear truths we would not otherwise think of or hear."

"I want you to help me plan a dinner," I told Alex that evening. I told him about Brian's suggestion of creating community and how I began thinking how important it is for me to have connections. "I was thinking of a Saturday afternoon early dinner, since it is still winter, and if you could come early and help me get ready, I'd appreciate that."

Alex didn't reply right away. "Okay," he responded. "I think I can arrange that." Then after a period of silence he asked, "Don't you want to meet up and talk about... well, about stuff before the dinner? Just wondering what you are thinking. Maybe we need to talk some things over first."

"I'm not adverse to sometime discussing what has happened. But I am thinking it would be good just to be together again and spend time with each other in the company of others. Sometimes I feel we are so geared to talking everything out that we don't allow natural processes and interactions to just develop organically. Is that okay?" I questioned.

"Aaron you continue to amaze me," Alex exclaimed, and I could almost see his eyes sparkle again. "Your thought processes and ideas are original and fresh. It is what makes you so... so..."

"Strange?" I suggested. "Different? Amish?"

"Whoah," Alex laughed. "Yes and no. I think I'd use words like *refreshing* and *original*. Yes, *original* probably is the most succinct word to use. One of a kind."

Our conversation drifted into some of the particulars of planning for the event. I felt relieved and more comfortable with our interaction on the phone than I had felt for days. I felt hope surge through me as I thought about being with Alex and how I could begin to be rational about moving into a connection again.

"I guess we could call it the United Nations," Cecilia, Brian's wife, laughed. "Aaron, you sure did pick a good cross culture of people."

It was true. I grinned at Jamil, who had brought his friend, Mahmud. He looked about eighteen years old, and also had the same handsome smile, dark skin and black hair that was even curlier than Jamil's.

"Well, I represent the white women class," Kate Whiler, our postmistress laughed. "When Aaron invited me to a 'dinner at my house for my friends' I felt honored to have been invited. I knew Aaron ever since he was a little blond haired boy, coming to the post office to drop off a package or to pick up an order. Now here he is, a young man with obvious talent," and she waved her hand to indicate the interior of my house. "I go past here often, and today, I get to see the interior. Very nice, Aaron."

"Und I am the Amish white woman, "Aunt Katie laughed. "I have probably known Aaron the longest and changed his diaper when he was just a newborn baby. His mother is my sister and I helped out whenever Vernie had her boys."

I looked across the room to where my aunt was sitting comfortably next to Mrs. Whiler. I could barely believe she was here. Like I've said earlier, her church district is even stricter than the one I used to attend but perhaps that was why it worked to have her come because no one expected her to. Plus, there were plenty of people who had already learned it was not wise to tangle with my aunt. She might look Amish but inside she was a woman with a mind of her own.

"And I'm the English white man," Alex joked from his seat next to me. "I really like this group and after the delicious dinner Aaron served and the warm and friendly company of all of us, me included, I think this has been one of the most interesting dinners I've ever attended." He placed his hand briefly on my shoulder. "I thank you, Aaron for your generous hospitality and warm welcome."

There was a murmur of assent from the assembled group. I felt my cheeks flush as everyone smiled in my direction.

"If more people would reach across what we often think of as religious and racial barriers," Brian added, "we would soon recognize we all are basically in need of the same things. Food, shelter, friendships and acceptance from those who may have different customs and belief systems from our own."

"It is the true," Mahmud said quietly. "For me, it is the good of America for to see this. To learn new ideas. New customs. New friends." His teeth flashed white in a wide smile. "So amazing to have the Jamal invite me to come today. Now I can decide on if it is good to become Amish or not." He reached out and lifted my black Amish hat from the hall tree and put it on.

Again, the laughter was easy and friendly.

"And I," Trevor said with an eloquent wave of his hand, "represent white, English and gay for this group. Oh, and ex-Amish. Like Aaron, I too was raised Amish. I left before I was twenty and ran off to explore what the English life looks like. Wasn't easy, but I am not intimidated by hardships so I've learned quite a lot of things about the English. Still miss the old Amish ways sometimes, but I could never return to the primitive lifestyle. Have to stay in touch with all my contacts." He waved his smart phone about. "Actually, got to leave now as I have a hot date tonight. This is the third time we are meeting, and you know, as they say, 'Third time is the charm.'"

Yes, I had invited Trevor. It had been a little bit of a debate in my mind whether I should, and when I had voiced my hesitation to Alex, he had said, "Invite him. He may not come but you said Brian encouraged you to invite people you know, not whether you like them." And so, I invited Trevor and he had come. True, he spent a lot of time texting on his phone and yet he seemed to enjoy himself at least a little.

As the group got up to get ready to leave, Aunt Katie bundled herself up warmly in her big black shawl and pinned it together in the front with a large shawl pin. Then she put on her big black bonnet. She was wearing her sensible plain shoes and since there was no snow outside, she was not wearing her usual winter boots over her shoes.

"Miss Katie," Kate Whiler said kindly, "will you allow me to take you to wherever you are going? The roads are clear and for an older woman like me that means a lot when it comes to driving but I would be happy to take you."

"Ah, but Trevor picked me up and he said he'll take me back," Aunt Katie said. "You are kind to offer, but I will go with that young man. Even though he drives too fast."

Trevor laughed and said, "Come on, Katie my girl. I'll drive slower if you want me to."

"Excuse me but I thought Amish don't ride in cars with ex-Amish," Kate Wildner was clearly puzzled. "Isn't that a part of the shunning?"

"Well, you see Trevor was never baptized into the Amish church," Aunt Katie explained. "So, then that makes it okay for me to ride with him. Now, Aaron! That's different, because he was baptized into the Amish church and now has a car so I couldn't drive with him." But she smiled at me and I knew she has not lost an ounce of affection for me.

"It gets confusing to non-Amish," I told my postmistress. "You almost have had to be born Amish to learn all the intricate rules and don'ts."

"Ach, well, it is the ride I will get," Aunt Katie said. "Come on, young man, it will soon be dark outside."

Then it was just Alex and me. The clock ticked loudly on the wall. Alex gathered up Paisley from the floor and sat down on the sofa and held her on his lap. I sat down next to him. I wanted to hold his hands, but I waited.

"Jamil is really nice. You two have been friends for a long time?" His voice rose in question. "He seemed really comfortable in your house."

"I've known him for over three years, I guess," I told him. "I hired him to photograph my furniture and our first meetings were mostly professional. Only more recently have we connected more and more as friends."

"I see," Alex said and looked at me and smiled. He picked up Paisley and she immediately began to purr.

"I'm not the only one that likes you," I smiled at him.

Alex said nothing at first then he pushed the cat off his lap and went to get some water.

"The divorce will be final in a week," Alex told me from the kitchen. "We've agreed to sell the house and pretty well everything will be divided equally between the two of us. We have agreed to wait to put the house on the market until springtime as that should be a better time to market homes than in the winter."

"Will you handle the listing? Or your firm?" I asked.

"Our firm will, but I won't be the listing agent. I'll have Margaret list it and refer any buyers to someone else." Alex was very sober as we talked about the sale. "Twenty-eight years we have lived in that house. Sometimes, I wonder if I made a mistake in being honest about who I am. Perhaps it would have been better to stay quiet and go on pretending."

I didn't reply. My thoughts went back to the time I was still Amish, still a part of the community and yes, still gay. In a sense nothing had changed and yet in another way, everything had changed.

After an awkward pause, I blurted out: "Where will you live? After you sell the house?"

Alex shook his head, "I'm not sure. Probably rent an apartment." He looked around my home. "If I could find something like this I'd like that. Small enough to make it easy to keep up and yet large enough to be comfortable." He scanned the interior again. "The only interior door you have is to your bathroom. I like that, all open and with the bedroom on the second floor, it still gives it enough privacy."

"Do you still want to marry me?" My question came out small and subdued.

Alex looked at me. "I think I should be asking that question. You didn't do anything to ruin what we had before. So, I don't know how to answer your question until I know how you feel. Do you want to marry me?"

"I love you, Alex. What happened shook me deeply, for sure, yet I know I have still always loved you. For me, love is not a spigot where I can open and shut but love is a spring of water flowing freely and easily. Obstacles can hinder, or cause rapids in the flow of love, but it is not in my power to stop love just like that."

"Wow," Alex said huskily. "Aaron, that is beautiful. Thank you for voicing that to me." He lifted his hand and touched my face. I put my hand over his and pressed it to my cheek.

"I do love you, but I'm not sure I'm ready to go ahead and marry you. Not just yet. I'm embarrassed to say it, but it's because I'm not sure I am emotionally ready for it. I, I think I need to grow more. My emotions and feelings are still, like so close to the surface, and only covered with a thin skin of something very fragile. I don't know why I feel this way, but I'm going to try to find out." I tried to put into my words something that made sense, even to myself.

Alex dropped his hand onto Paisley's back and began stroking the purring cat. "I love you, Aaron. I don't know how I can endure this waiting any longer, however I must. I will never force your love. Whenever you are ready, I'll be waiting for you."

We both cried. The enormity of the moment was so huge it wanted to swallow us up. The blackness was growing, the dogs growling and yes, the snakes were hissing. Everything I had ever known shrank into small meaningless shapes and puddled into oily nothingness. Yet, I was aware of the man next to me. I was aware of Alex's suffering as keenly as I was of my own pain.

Alex got up to leave. He took his jacket and draped it over his arm. He stepped forward and hugged me. Hot tears coursed down my cheeks as I sobbed on his neck. I could not say anything.

# Chapter Twenty One

I stood outside Alex's door. The winter air was cold and still. I lifted my hand, extended my forefinger and touched the icy round button of his electric doorbell. I hesitated just for a split second, then I pushed it all the way in. I heard the musical jangle inside. I waited.

My car was in Alex's driveway, just outside his closed garage door. I had chosen an ordinary car for my first vehicle, a Nissan Sentra, for I was not really a car person. At least not yet. The novelty of owning and driving a car was enough for right now.

I slowly exhaled my breath into the frigid air and waited. Maybe Alex was sleeping so well he didn't hear the doorbell. I pushed it again.

I rehearsed my little speech. "Alex, I am ready to marry you. I realize I am as ready as I'll ever be. I can never know how everything will affect me, but I want to marry you. Will you marry me? Now?"

I replayed my surprise. "If you say yes, I want to make love to you. Now. I want to give myself to you completely and without reservation. I want to make you my husband and I want you to take me as your husband. Nothing should ever be between us, only love."

Over and over again I had rehearsed my little speech in my head as I had lain sleepless in my bed after Alex had left the evening before. My emotions had been so raw, so searing and I had realized I could no longer contain what I was feeling. I knew it was crazy but as soon as the thought of driving through the night to Alex's house entered my consciousness, I could not stem the force of what was building up inside of me. So powerful was the surge of love I felt as though I would burst wide open if I tried to contain it any longer.

"Marriage is the blending of two lives, two hearts, two bodies and two people who voluntarily unite as one. Therefore, you and I are married. Out spirits have blended into each others' until we do no longer know where the one begins and the other ends. So, I am totally ready to make love to you. Now."

Where was Alex? I pounded on the door. "Alex!" My voice was loud. I checked my watch. Three a.m. Of course, it was late. Or early all depend how you looked at it. Where was he? I tried the door. Locked, of course. I could try to call him on my phone but that would give away the surprise I wanted to give him. I wanted to present myself totally to him, without reservation. I pushed the doorbell again.

There was no light suddenly coming on inside Alex's house. No response to my summons. Nothing. I turned and went back to my car and climbed inside. I shut the door to keep the cold out. I started the engine. I briefly thought of blowing the horn but decided that would not be welcome in the quiet residential neighborhood where Alex lived.

The inside of the windshield fogged over and I experimented with the air flow to see if it would clear. I rubbed the steam away from the side window and looked towards the dark house. Nothing.

I leaned back against the seat and adjusted the angle of the backrest. I wasn't cold anymore. At least not on the outside but deep inside there were frigid fingers of doubt clawing at my heart. What if Alex would not respond as I was expecting? "I'll be waiting for you," he had said but perhaps, on his long, lonely ride home he had despaired and sought out Jimmy again? Would he have?

"He's not fickle," I told my suspicious brain. "He made a mistake but he's not fickle."

But the fingers of doubt did not disappear. They grew. I was simply an Amish man, not used to the ways of the English. Why would a smart, good looking man like Alex ever be satisfied with a simple man like me? We didn't have much in common, this real estate agent and me. My tastes were simple, I knew very little about his culture, his life and how could we ever make a couple? Was love enough? Would the feeling die away and we both grow into apathy?

"Geh sztrick heim."

Who was that telling me to go back home? Who had said that? It, it sounded like my dad's voice. Was I going crazy? Then I heard other voices, all of them speaking to me in Amish German. Telling me to go home. Telling me to leave, to forsake this wild trek I was on. Warning me of dire consequences and I began smelling smoke. Was I in hell? Was this what was happening to me? Was I already suffering torment and flames even while I was alive? The black dogs were there and other more sinister shapes. I wanted to scare them away, to cover my ears and put to flight all my tormentors. But I couldn't move. I tried in vain to lift my arms, to shout and to scare away the clamor of dark warnings.

Then, I saw a figure pushing aside the dogs and demons, running towards me with arms wide open. All the voices died away and the beasts turned tail and disappeared. A blast of cold air woke me up from my dream. "Aaron! Aaron, what are you doing here?"

I sat bolt upright and saw Alex's face next to mine, the cold night air swooping into the car. Alex reached out and took my hand and drew me outside. He wrapped his arms around me and kissed my neck. "How long were you out here? Why didn't you come in?"

I couldn't speak. I began shivering.

"Come. Come inside."

He closed the front door behind us, and we went into the living room. I tried to talk, to tell him I wanted to marry him. I tried to remember my rehearsed speech but all I could do was look deeply into the eyes of the man I loved. Finally, I said, "I want you. All of you. You can have all of me. I marry you."

"Oh Aaron, yes! Yes, yes, yes!"

I put my arms around Alex's waist, and he hugged my head agains his chest. I could feel his racing heart thump wildly in my ears and felt the delightfulness of his chest hair against my cheek.

Sometime much later, Alex reached out and drew up the blankets and covered our bodies as we lay snuggled together, entwined in each other's arms. We needed no words to communicate, for our kisses spoke volumes and our hands used sign language to continue our love making with each other. At one point, I turned onto my other side and Alex drew me to himself and we lay spoon fashion, his mouth on the back of my neck, his arms gathering my body up against him and his one leg between my legs and the other one on top of me. It was then I could no longer hold back the tears of happiness and love and I cried without a sound, the hot tears scorching my cheeks as they soaked into the pillow. Alex tightened his hold on me and continued to hug my body, his hand moving up and down on my arm.

"It's okay," he whispered into my ear. "I love you, Aaron. It's okay to cry. Let your tears of emotions flow freely. I am here with you. We are together. I love you!"

"I love you, Alex!" I said when the storm of tears abated. "I love you so much."

The bright light of the moon shone in through the window and bathed us with a sliver sheen. I knew I would never forget this magical night, secure in the love of the man I loved more than life. Married to each other without the need of witnesses for our love for each other was the only witness we needed. No matter what else would happen, we would always have this perfect night of our marriage to each other.

I reached out and stroked Alex's beard with my left hand. He was still sleeping, his head only inches from my face. I didn't want to wake him but I couldn't resist touching him gently. He moved his face slightly towards me and opened his eyes. "Good morning, Beautiful!" he smiled.

"Good morning," I echoed. I leaned over and kissed him. I marveled at how perfectly natural this was.

# CHAPTER TWENTY-TWO

"Aaron, it's the most natural thing in the world," Brian told me seriously. "Think of the years of literature and classic books written about love. Romantic novels still outsell all other genres of books. So, we do hunt for fulfillment in finding the right person. It's a deep inner desire that is natural and has been perpetrated for generations and generations."

I heard Brian's words, as even though I could make sense of what he was saying, it was as though the words hit my ears and then fell around my feet, hollow and empty, crashing into shards.

"But why did he allow me so fully into his heart, and into his life, and yes into his bed if he already knew then he was not 'ready to take you on' as he said?" Even as I asked the same question for what seemed the hundredth time, I couldn't stop from asking one more time.

"Why did he say he loved me so much? Why did he say with his voice, and with his body, and with his eyes and every other way he could during the entire night and day we spent together? I do not understand how he could do that!" My voice was hard, devoid of emotion. I had no more tears to cry, no more deep, inner wails erupting from the dark and cave-like spaces inside my heart in the middle of the night, leaving me drenched with sweat.

"All I have left from that time is my pillow, wet with tears.

Every night. That's it. Tears on my pillow."

Brian said nothing for a while. "How many people have you shared this with? Have you talked about it with anyone?"

I shook my head. "For the last four days I have avoided everyone. Not answered any calls, not left the house except to drive around the dark roads at night staring into the tunnel my headlights from my car illuminate."

"You haven't shared it with any of the people you had at your house that evening? Sia? Your Aunt Katie? Trevor?" Brian questioned again.

"What shall I tell them? 'Hey! Guess what? Alex and I spent the remainder of Saturday night at his house and had sex for the first time! Then, we fell asleep and the next morning, we had more sex. Coffee and toast in bed, more sex, then more sex and all the time we made love, I thought how wonderful it was to have this man love me like this. We spent the entire day at his house, most of the time in bed, making love and talking about how wonderful this was, until late that evening when I returned home to feed my horse and take care of my cat, then decided to call Alex before I went to bed, and then he told me it was all over. He wasn't ready to take me into his life. Shall I tell them he said he realized he had let his emotions out of control when I showed up at his house, looking so lost and lonely? Shall I tell them how, when he was telling me this on the phone, I could barely keep from screaming? Shall I tell someone how it was as though my heart had turned into a stone and how I could barely say anything when he asked me questions? How can I tell other people about this? I can barely tell myself, or you about this nightmare." My words came out in bursts of emotionless sentences. I realized as I replayed my story to Brian, probably for the tenth time or so, it was as though I was trying to find some kind of pain to find out if I were still a human with any kind of feelings left.

"Yes."

I lifted my eyes to look into Brian's face.

"Yes, you need to find someone you can tell this to," Brian repeated. "You need to. You don't have to, but it will be for your good."

"I don't want to," I finally managed to whimper. I was surprised by my own voice. I thought I had no tears left, no emotions to change my voice, my words and yet, as I answered Brian, I heard my voice break.

As hot tears fell yet once again and ran into my beard, I didn't even try to keep them back. I was so shattered that I could still feel so deeply and knew immediately I would still be able to hurt even more.

It was quiet in Brian's study. I heard the furnace blower turn on and realized the sun had set outside and even though winter was fading into Spring, nights were still cold. I wiped my tears from my eyes with the back of my hand and looked at Brian.

Brian's eyes were wet with tears as he waited for my storm to abate. "I"m so sorry," he finally said. I nodded my head to show my appreciation.

"Of all the people I met that evening at your place," he continued, "I would recommend you talk to Trevor."

"Trevor?" I jerked my head back, staring at my therapist. "Whatever for? He and I are as different as night and day! All we have in common is we are both ex-Amish. And both gay. How could he know how I feel?"

His mouth turned up at the corners just a bit and he smiled a small smile. "Well, that's my suggestion. Of course, I can't make you do it. You can choose someone else. Or no one at all but as your therapist I highly recommend it."

"And you need not to tell me the reason why," I said cryptically.

236

Brian chuckled. "Nope, I don't. Just because that is what I am trained to do."

We talked some more, but I don't remember much of the rest of the evening. "Come here," Brian said when I got up to leave after our session. He opened his arms and I walked into his hug. He embraced me briefly then slapped me playfully on my back. "There, you are recharged. Talk. Share. Listen. Hug."

I nodded my head. Although I didn't think it was possible, I actually felt lighter. Yes, the pain was still as deep and heavy as before, yet for some unexplainable reason, something was different.

"You will hit bottom time and again," Brian told me as I put on my jacket. "When that happens, walk into your pain. Allow yourself to feel as deeply as you feel like. Don't try to hunt up more hurts, but instead, allow all your thoughts to run through your mind. Until there are no more."

"Will it get better?" I couldn't help but asking.

Brian shrugged his shoulders. "What do you want me to say? Pithy words? Do you want a bunch of clichés like we often hear people saying to someone in pain? I'm not here to tell you your future. I'm here to walk with you through what you are experiencing."

"It has to get better or I don't know if I want to live anymore." My voice had turned cold again. I opened the door and the chilly air slapped my face. I walked out into the dark.

"Door's open. Come in." Trevor's text blinked on my phone. I reached out and tried the doorknob. It yielded and I opened the windowless door and stepped inside. The front hall was tiny and dark. I removed my boots and went towards a closed door where light shone around the perimeter. I knocked on the door.

The music inside drowned out my knock so I turned the knob and opened the door. Trevor was on his sofa, his arm around a shirtless man, probably in his 40's. "Hi Aaron!" Trevor yelled and then reached for the remote and the music died into a muted clang. "This is Flin. Flin, my friend Aaron."

Flin smiled in my direction and took another drink from a dark brown bottle he was holding. His biceps bulged as he lifted the drink to his mouth.

"Have a seat," Trevor nodded. "Want something to drink? Check out what's in my frig. Make yourself comfortable."

The kitchen was small and relatively empty. Several dirty dishes were piled in the sink, but the counters were mostly bare. I opened the refrigerator door and looked inside. Several cans of beer, a half empty bottle of red wine and some cranberry juice in a jug was all I could see for drinks. I pulled the cranberry juice out, found a clean glass and poured the red liquid into the glass. When I returned the jug to its shelf in the refrigerator, I looked at the red wine and then took the bottle and poured a generous amount into my glass. I didn't know if would be good or not but felt reckless enough to experiment.

When I returned with my drink, Flin had put his shirt on and was zipping up his jacket. "Hey Aaron, nice to meet you. Trev, until next time," and then he walked out into the hall. I heard the front door slam.

"What's up, Aaron?" Trevor asked. "Come, sit down. What brings you out tonight?"

I talked and Trevor listened. I told him how Alex and I had met, about our attraction to each other, the agony when Alex told me about having sex with Jimmy, then my night trip to Alex's house and our night and day of bliss. I was able to actually tell him about the breakup without shedding a single tear and wondered once again if I was changing into a hardened shell of the man I used to be.

"Oh man, I feel for you," Trevor said. "Welcome to the heartbreak club."

"So, this is it?" I asked taking a drink from my glass. "You give your heart to someone and find out what it is to love more than you thought possible only to get it thrown away because the man you gave your heart to decides he's not ready to handle what comes along with you?"

Trevor lit up a cigarette and offered me one. I politely refused. He took a "drag" of his cigarette and shrugged. "Too often. My first love lasted three months and then I found out Dan was still sneaking around and seeing his regular fuck buddies. Told me he loved only me and the others were just 'fun stuff' and I needed to get over my romantic ideals. I got over my ideals all right. I think it was about the second year of my coming out I decided if I can't win them, I'd join them."

"Is Flin your boyfriend?" I asked nodding my head towards the door.

There was an awkward pause while Trevor finished his cigarette.

"I don't think so," he replied after several minutes, reaching for his beer bottle. "We've known each other for over half a year and he comes over here somewhat randomly. Especially when he has an argument with his roommate. Since the arguments are frequent, he comes over often. I don't really mind because I like him. Just not sure if I would want him for a boyfriend. We'll see." He shrugged.

"And I thought gay guys were mostly looking for partners. For something permanent," I tried to put into words I was feeling.

"I'm sure you are finding out there is not one 'gay way' or as so many people call it, 'gay lifestyle.' Think of it, Aaron, we Amish knew only a man and a woman getting married, having a family and staying together for a lifetime. The English community was vastly different. How?" Trevor leaned forward towards me.

"Divorce and remarriage. Sex without marriage. Split families." I answered.

"Exactly. It's more like the difference between Amish and English is a greater chasm than the difference between gay and straight. There are as many different views of what relationships are in each world as there are varieties of dogs. Because you and I and a number of other gay guys were raised in religious circles, this is so foreign to us. We knew it existed, but it was not in our world. Not directly." Trevor told me. I looked at him with new eyes. I had never heard him express his feeling like this.

"There are guys who want a monogamous relationship. And a few who want to have sex only after they are partnered or married. But Aaron, think about it, how many straight couples in the English world wait until after they are married to have sex? Even among the Evangelical churches, I would guess more than half of all couples getting married have had sex before they exchanged their vows. This is the world we live in."

I pondered his words. "But Alex is, or was, a Baptist minister. He was having sex before he met me. And then with Jimmy."

Another shrug from Trevor. "I've seen it often. Especially among religious guys. They come out of the closet and begin experiencing the freedom of expressing themselves as now being gay instead of closeted straight guys. This freedom extends into experimenting with guys and having sex just because they can. The first time I had sex with my neighbor boy, I didn't even feel guilty afterwards." Trevor laughed. "We were taught so strictly against boys and girls having sex before marriage, but no one gave us gays the same teaching.

"So, for me, it wasn't a feeling of guilt afterwards but for a long time I still thought it was wrong for guys to have sex with girls if they weren't married! It was crazy! Perhaps if we would have been given the same teachings about not having sex with each other we might have had a bigger wall against easily having sex before marriage. By the way, how did you reconcile having sex with Alex? You weren't married!" Trevor looked at me with mock disapproval.

"I had wrestled with that for a long time," I told him. I looked at my glass, empty now. "I came to the conclusion marriage is between two people who loved each other and entered into a relationship voluntarily. Like Isaac had for Rebekah in the Old Testament. I knew Alex loved me, well at least I thought he did. No! I know he did. So, I decided we were married in our hearts. That's why I gave myself completely to him that night. And the next day. I gave him everything, Trevor, everything. Then the next day, it was all over. Is all over."

"I'm so sorry," Trevor said and lay his hand on my shoulder. "It hurts. No greater hurt in this world. Some get it at a breakup and others at a death. Either hurts more than anything else in the world. Always did, always will. Sucks like crazy."

We bonded that evening more than ever before. We talked about the loss of community as we had known it. We talked about our personal lives and Trevor told me he still felt at a loss what career he wanted to have. His work as a waiter seemed empty and without a future for him and yet he did not know how to plan for the future. Even though I had my woodworking business and was successful enough, I told him about how I felt constricted, even in my own home and surrounded by the Amish.

I had another glass of wine, this time without the cranberry juice. It got late and Trevor's roommate Suellen came in, said Hi and went to her room.

"Stay the night," Trevor said. "You can't drive. Too much wine."

So, I slept on the couch.

The next day, I drove home through the first blush of springtime green. I usually immensely enjoyed this time of the year, but now I seemed like another person, a different Aaron. No longer Amish, shunned by most of all my family and community, failed at connecting with the first love of my life and hurting so deeply inside I wondered if I could ever recover. I felt more alone than I have ever felt before. Cut off from going back into the Amish community, cut off from my connection with Alex and having only a handful of people in my life.

Paisley greeted me with affection and Lady snorted and came running when I pulled into my driveway. I picked up my purring cat and carried her with me to scoop oats into Lady's box.

I really didn't need Lady anymore, but I was reluctant to sell her. As fond as I had been of Prince, I had also learned to really like my new horse. She was such a graceful creature and I knew she loved to be harnessed and be used for errands. So, I had never stopped hitching her up to my buggy, mostly the topless one when the weather was nice, and taking her out. On an impulse, I hitched her up after she had munched her oats and I steered her towards Jack's Mountain. There was a dirt road I liked, winding through the coves and little ravines at the foot of the mountain and I wanted to lose myself in something familiar, something traditional. Lady's hoofbeats beat out a staccato rhythm until we left the blacktop and then her trotting was muffled by the gravel road.

The Valley lay before me as I rounded a bend and I looked at the patchwork of fields surrounding the big farmsteads, punctuated by the tall rising silos. The landscape has remained almost unchanged ever since I could remember. I breathed in deeply and for an hour or so, I was able to banish most of the malaise that had gripped me for the last several days. I felt Amish again.

Well, almost.

# CHAPTER TWENTY-THREE

"Set him a table, once," Aunt Katie said to my mom. "Just because he's in the ban doesn't mean he can't eat."

"Patience," I laughed, chucking my aunt under her chin. "You know your sister would never let anyone go hungry, in the ban or not. It is never easy for me to eat at a separate table when I come home, but I'm getting used to it."

"Ach well, Aaron," Mom said as she took a small square tablecloth and covered the table in the corner of the kitchen, "if you were still Amish, I would not have to set a separate table. But it makes no difference, I am still your mom and you are still my son. That will never change!" She set the everyday china plate on the table with a clatter. "I don't know how long it will take for us to get used to having this difference but even so, nothing has changed in our love."

"Mom!" I said with surprise, "I love to hear you talk like this! Love is the strongest emotion and goes places far beyond any man-made rules. It's interesting how we can talk about love so easily anymore. I never remember talking about love when I was young or growing up."

"Times change," Aunt Katie said firmly. "Even among the Amish. So many people think we traditional people don't change, but of course, we do. Cell phones are easy to hide. Our church just put a man, not to mention names, on proving because he was found out having a television in his shop. Hid it inside a box but someone must've spotted it. It will take him at least six months to prove himself to the bishop, a year if he doesn't seem to be truly repentant."

Mom came over to my table, carrying the cast iron skillet in a potholder. "Dandelion greens. I got Levi's Ammon to gather me a poke full and I washed the leaves and made them for the gravy."

I quickly served myself some mashed potatoes and spread them out into a receptacle for the delicious specialty I never got tired of. I looked at my loaded plate. Fried chicken, a leg and a thigh for Mom knew I liked the brown meat of a chicken, mashed potatoes topped with a gravy loaded with dandelion greens and a generous helping of applesauce was the most typical Amish meal I could think of.

I bowed my head for silent prayer as I had always done and then began to eat. The front door was open for the spring evening was warm and balmy. I knew the farmers would soon be making the first cutting of hay for the rains had been plentiful and the meadows were brimming with clover, Timothy grass and an assortment of other grasses that made the best hay for the farm animals. I heard the song of the wood thrush coming from the grove of trees up the slope of the mountain.

"Are you staying with Mom overnight?" I asked, directing my question to my aunt.

"If I can sleep," Aunt Katie said ruefully. "I've been having a difficult time lately with the sciatica pains. Wakes me up at night, it does. I guess I need a stronger medication. I dread going to the doctor again but if the pain doesn't abate, I must."

"Now Katie," Mom said briskly, "I just got word of a new herbal extract from Australia that is just for pain! I read in "The Budget" how so many people are being helped. Let me look for it," Mom picked up the newspaper circulated among most of the Amish communities and scanned the columns. "Oh, my Mosie Jakie passed away. He has been ailing for years. I think he must have been close to 100 already. Oh, yes here it says, ninety-eight. So poorly for so long he was."

"Don't get carried away," Aunt Katie said bluntly. "You were looking for the magical potion for my pain. Probably just a hoax. Isn't it interesting how we Amish are still suckers for something new all the time. Let there be a new doctor or a new healing method and there are van loads of Amish loading themselves into rented vans with drivers and filling the waiting rooms." Aunt Katie snorted, but looked with interest at the advertisement Mom was showing her.

"Remember when that doctor in Ohio was doing iridology?" I asked. "Took his 'special' light and shone into his patient's eyes and decided where their ailments stemmed from? It wasn't until after about a year when enough people had gone to him and shared their experiences, they realized he was giving them all the exact same pill. Some enterprising person sent one of the pills to a laboratory and it came back with some obscure herbs, but mostly a powerful herb to treat parasites? I remember hearing Norman Vesta saying, 'They all have the worms! Everyone that came to him for a cure was given a worming medicine.' Must be Amish food causes worms. Mom, are you sure you picked all the worms off the dandelion greens?"

"Ach, Aaron," Mom scolded as Aunt Katie snorted with laughter. I heard footsteps approaching and my brother Levi's form appeared. He came inside, nodded to Aunt Katie, then looked at my half-filled plate. His eyes traveled to the dining room table where Mom and Aunt Katie were seated.

"It's okay, Levi," Aunt Katie said. "Aaron isn't eating with us. See, his table is at least a foot away from ours. Oh, we can still visit though because, see we are facing him and that way we can still talk."

Levi frowned at Aunt Katie's lighthearted teasing. "Are you staying, Aunt Katie? Your horse is still tied up at the hitching rack. It's getting dark already."

"Ach my," Aunt Katie said with a sigh. "I'm getting old. I forgot about old Pat. She's probably tired, too. Yes, I'm staying, Levi. Can you let her out in the pasture for the night?"

Levi nodded, looked briefly in my direction, then turned to leave.

"I wish I could come see your children," I said to his retreating back. "I miss them."

Levi stopped but didn't turn to face me. "Once you get rid of the car and return to the Amish, you can come over. Not before."

"How about if I get rid of the car, wear nothing but Amish clothes, let my hair grow long again but I'm still gay, will I be able to come even then?" I'm not even sure what made me ask that however I realized I was getting much bolder about who I am than ever before.

"Sin is still sin," Levi said. "Turn back to God and cleanse yourself," and with those words he marched outside.

"And Levi is still Levi," Aunt Katie said loudly. "Learn to be kinder and you will not be so miserable."

"He's always been so," Mom said sadly. "The older he gets the more he is like Uncle Fred. Stubborn and not willing to change for anything. Remember, Katie how Fred would insist on all the women in his family wearing the bonnets, no matter how warm the weather?

I remember once when their Anna came in from outside, her black bonnet pushed way back from her young warm flushed face and Uncle Fred started scolding her for pushing her bonnet back. She was just trying to get some little breeze to cool her face, but no, Uncle Fred wouldn't have it."

"Let's see," Mom said reflectively, "Anna married Far Away Aaron's boy, didn't she? She was just young when she got married. Has nine children I think Amelia said."

I finished my meal and got up from the table. The evening light shone in through the curtain-less window and I looked at my mom and Aunt Katie's profiles facing each other. Both were wearing the white Amish caps, both had faces lined with wrinkles and yet, there was something very peaceful about their auras, even as they continued gossiping about who married whom and relative matters.

That evening, I picked up my sketch pencil for the first time in a long while and began to draw. Much later, I held up the sketch pad and looked at the two Amish ladies. Yes, these two women were about the only bridge I had back to my Amish heritage. The rest of the community shunned me almost completely. I felt as though an era was passing away from my life. I now felt as though I were English. I stared at my drawing. What made the Amish, Amish? Only by birth? Heritage? Were my people really different genetically from the English? Almost 98% of all Amish can trace their roots back to Germany. Have we been isolated so long we actually think differently, act differently and are wired differently than the English? Was that why I was having such a difficult time getting over what had ended between Alex and me? Had Alex felt this so strongly he that he did not want to try to have a relationship with someone so different? I sighed and went to bed. Maybe I would never know. Was there anyone out there I could really connect with and could I ever hope to find a lover, a husband?

I studied my sketch again. The sideboard had a solid wood top, resting on a network of galvanized pipes I was going to paint a glossy white but all the couplings and corners providing a visual frame for five wooden drawers, each at a different level from the others and when viewed from the front, I wanted to have the drawers appear to be floating. I was using birch because I liked the lighter connection of blonde wood and white iron to provide a contemporary look.

The iron framework was already complete, and I was waiting to make an appointment to have it sprayed at a body shop to get a high glossy white and meanwhile I was working on the drawers. An echo of the traditional dovetail joinery for the drawers, instead of having a blind dovetails for the sides of the drawers, I used a blind dovetail for the front. Each drawer front had the handmade dovetails, framed on the sides with an edging of wood. I was still undecided about what hardware to use for the pulls.

As I sanded the twenty-four inch slab of birch I was using for the top, I inhaled deeply. Outside, spring was in full swing, the morning dew disappearing under the warm sun. I could see Lady in the pasture, cropping the mixed grass of her meadow. Framed by the doorway, it was spring at it's finest. I reached for my smartphone and turned the camera on. I had rapidly learned to use the digital features and was expanding my experiments with photographing ideas and scenes from my everyday life.

My phone vibrated while I was focusing on the hillside picture and Jamil's name appeared.

"Hello!" I heard his friendly voice. "How's your day my friend?"

"Doing well," I answered. "I was just taking a picture through my wood working door of my horse in her paddock. The morning light is perfect!"

"Ahh, you will soon not be needing me to take your photos," he laughed. "Since you got your smart phone you will be learning all the tricks of the trade."

"Don't worry," I returned with a chuckle. "My pictures are not the quality of professionalism you do with your work." I sat on my wooden stool. "That's why I left a message. I want you to come and take pictures of my current project as I am working on it." I described the sideboard I was working on.

"Great! Sounds amazing. Can you send some pics right now? I mean of what you have done?" My description must not have been very adequate.

"I keep forgetting about sharing pictures," I laughed. "Sure, hang on."

I snapped several pictures and forwarded them to him. I head the metallic swoosh of them leaving.

"Got them," Jamil said. "Let me put you on speaker."

There was silence for a while. "Aaron, this is absolutely spectacular! Such a departure from what you've done before. When can I come?"

"Thanks, pal," I replied. "Anytime."

"I've got a few things to wrap up here and then I'm on my way. Let's see, I can be there by 11:00. Is that good?"

I mentally went over my schedule. "Perfect. I would love to have you come. Let's do lunch!"

"Aaron, you sound just like… like an English-er!" Jamil's delighted laugh came over the phone.

"You've never been here before?" Jamil asked as he sat down across from me at Tabletop Diner. "This place has been here for years and always gets a great rating from reviewers."

"Amish do go out to eat but usually not up here on the ridge," I reminded him. "Thanks for recommending it. Do you eat here often?"

Jamil pulled out the menu and opened it. "I do. I don't even need to look at the menu for this is about the only place I eat hamburgers. Their cheese and onion ring burgers are my favorite. I try to eat healthy food however I splurge when it comes to Tabletop Burgers. I warn you. If you get a burger, you will need a lot of napkins for the juices have a tendency to run down your arm to your elbows!"

"Then they must be good," I laughed. "I'm going to have one on that recommendation alone."

We placed our orders. Jamil opened his camera and began flipping through the pictures he had taken of the sideboard. "If I lighten the iron pipes to a white, you will be able to see how your completed table should look. At least with the two drawers you already finished. Or if you want, I can copy and paste the finished drawers into the empty spaces where the drawers will be." He flipped the camera so I could see the sideboard with the metal grid in white.

"I like that," I said. "Just wait until the sideboard is finished. I kind of like this look of 'under construction' picture. What do you think?"

Jamil looked at his picture again. "You are right. To see it evolve is good. I'll make a duplicate picture and reverse the changes I made. I visualize a progression of the sideboard in sketch mode and then the finished piece focused in the bulletin."

"I'm thinking of making a limited number of this one. Signing each one and numbering them. Like artists do with limited editions of wall art. I also want to have a certificate of authenticity of each one with a registry. Then anyone who has one can always request an update on the website to make sure they are not buying a reproduction. Is that a good idea?" I asked.

Jamil didn't answer right away as the waiter brought our meals. We thanked him and I looked at the mouthwatering sandwich. "How can I open my mouth wide enough to put that monster in my mouth?"

Jamil laughed and picked up his burger. "Your idea about the registry is great. The more popular your work becomes, the bigger the threat of someone trying to ride in on the coat tails of your success."

I didn't reply because my mouth was full of burger. I nodded my head in bliss as the beef patty hit my taste buds. I gave Jamil a thumbs up sign with my free hand.

"One of the gallery owners in Philadelphia informed me of someone who had made a replica of one of the coffee tables he had in his shop. A customer had taken a picture of it in another store and brought it in to see if it was yours. I guess I should be flattered, right?" I laughed.

Then we were silent as we ate our burgers. The cafe was crowded, and I guessed the spring weather had already brought the tourists into our area from the cities.

"How are you doing?" Jamil asked, wiping his mouth with a napkin. "Is it getting any better?"

"Is getting used to being numb, better?" I asked pushing my empty plate away from me. "If it is, then I'm definitely better. I was able to throw myself deeper into my work, busy myself with gardening and in general making my life as full as possible. Almost nothing socially, though."

Jamil nodded. His dark eyes looked intently into mine. "Do you want to go on a hike? Walk away some of these calories?"

We paid our bill and left the cafe. The gravel parking lot was crowded. "There is a trail head about a mile along the ridge road," Jamil told me as we climbed into my car. "We can park there and take an easy hike through the woods to a lookout."

It took us only 30 minutes to reach the lookout point.

"There's my place!" I pointed it out to Jamal. "Isn't it funny? Lived here all my life and hardly ever came up here to explore. Mostly if I went on hikes it was around our home farm. Now that I have wheels, it is so easy to slip away and explore in my own area."

"Just why do the Amish not have cars?" Jamil asked as we sat on a boulder. The valley stretched out at our feet, the farms like sets of toy buildings set in green fields.

"When cars became available to the public in the early 1900's, the Amish most generally didn't buy them because the roads in the country were terrible. Plus, automobiles were expensive, and I doubt very many Amish had enough cash to buy one. So, initially the Amish didn't have cars because they weren't rich enough. Then, during the advent of mass production and consequently cheaper cars, the Amish began seeing the influence easy transportation had among the general populace. They eventually made rules against having cars because they were afraid the ease of getting around would assimilate the Amish into the 'world.' During this time, also, many Amish churches began restricting other modern inventions. To my ancestors, the 1900's were the beginnings of rampant inventions threatening our lifestyle." I tried condensing our complex society into a brief summary.

"It makes sense," Jamil nodded. He picked up a rock and turned it over in his hand. "We too, have been kept back from supposedly dangerous influences. Often, when I was younger, I would ask why I couldn't do something or go somewhere. I was usually told, 'It's not our tradition. Don't ask why'. I got so tired of hearing that."

I laughed out loud. "Really? That sounds exactly like my group."

Later that evening after Jamil had dropped me off at my place, I realized how my spirits had lifted. I felt energized and decided to hitch up Lady and go see Aunt Katie. I wanted companionship. I wanted to continue this burst of human interaction. I whistled for my horse and she came immediately to the barn. I rewarded her with a scoop of oats and as she munched the grain in her box, I curried her and brushed out her mane and tail. "You want to go on a spin? Take me to see Aunt Katie?" I dusted off her harness and cleaned her bridle. Then, I buckled the straps on her and led her outside to where my topless buggy was waiting.

I was already on my way when my phone rang. I dived for my phone in my pocket, keeping my right hand on the reins to guide Lady. A wave of anxiety swept over me. It was the ring tone I used for Alex's number!

"Hi Aaron," his familiar voice came clearly through. "I thought I would call you and see how you are. I miss you."

"Hi. Hi, Alex," was all I could manage to say. I pulled on the reins and slowed Lady's trot to a walk.

"What are you doing?" Alex yelled into my ear. I could hear the pulse of music in the background.

"I'm, I'm on my way to see Aunt Katie," I said loudly. "I'm driving Lady in the buggy. It's a beautiful evening."

"Oh!" Alex said loudly. "It's beautiful!" Then I could hear him burp into the phone. I heard another man's voice say something. "But not as beautiful as you are. I miss you, Aaron!" He repeated himself.

"I miss you, too," I told him honestly. "I hope you are doing well."

"Need you…" and then his voice died away.

"What did you say?" I asked. The music pounded away in the background.

"Alex is okay. I've got this." Another voice came over the phone.

"Oh, that's good," I answered. "I'm glad to hear." Then, my phone hummed as I lost connection. I looked over the fields towards the setting sun. "Whoa!" I pulled on the reins and stopped my horse. I stared at the dark screen of my phone.

My mind tried to recreate the scene. Alex, in a bar, drinking with one of his friends? His voice had sounded like it always did but he had slurred his words and it had been a weird conversation. "I miss you?" Just like that? Yes, clearly, he was drunk. Who was the man who had been with him? Jimmy?

I checked the road to make sure there was no traffic coming. "Get up!" I clucked to Lady and pulled hard on the right rein. She obediently turned and we headed back home. I didn't want to talk with anyone right then. I had been sure I had already reached the bottom of my emotional upheaval but now, after hearing Alex's voice again and even in spite of his inebriation, the words, "I miss you" had stirred up all my feelings and emotions again, plus opened up any wounds that may have begun to heal.

"Why? Why? Oh God, why?" I crammed my pillow into my mouth to stifle my cries as I tossed and turned in bed. I vacillated between feelings of bitterness and yes, even hatred for the man whom I loved, had loved so deeply and once again feeling those feelings of intense love flood me as I replayed his words over and over again. "I miss you!" What had he said after "I need you...."?

I sat up in bed. It was late, almost midnight. Paisley lifted her head and I reached towards her. She began to purr.

I toyed briefly with the idea of getting in my car and driving through the night to see Alex. The other time it had worked. That was the time when we had such a wonderful connection. The night I had given my heart and body to the man I had loved. Would it work again? Was there enough love still between us I could make him see whatever differences we had could be overcome by love?

I put my one bare foot on the floor. Then, I hesitated and lay down again. I wouldn't go. Because my vivid imagination also painted another picture. What would I do if Jimmy's car were in the driveway where mine used to be parked? What if Jimmy were in the bed with Alex, their limbs entwined together, and bodies pressed together like Alex and mine had done that blissful night and day only three weeks ago? Could I bear having my hopes dashed again?

I turned the pillow hoping to find it dry on the underneath but it was already damp from my early evening tears. I pushed the pillow away and lay my head on the sheet, exhausted and feeling the familiar despair wanting to crush my spirit.

"This is what you get" a voice seemed to say. "You thought you could find love with a man. You thought your love for Alex was strong enough to take you two into a lasting relationship. See, it's not normal. God never created two men to be a lasting couple like a man and a woman. The devil took you for a ride and now he's dumping you. Just like Alex duped you into believing he loved you. It was all a fake. Give up."

On and on the voice talked. Telling me how stupid I was. Reminding me how I could never have a normal life, would have to suffer for being gay by being by myself. I heard thoughts come into my head, thoughts like, how could I imagine anyone wanting an ex-Amish for a partner? How I was too different, too strange to ever be wanted. Faster and faster the accusations were hurled into my brain until I thought my head would explode. I lay helpless in my bed, alone and in total despair.

# CHAPTER TWENTY-FOUR

"**S**o why is a nice young man like you single?" The friendly voice of an elderly woman asked me, looking at my ringless fingers. "Are you dating? Here comes my granddaughter, Peggy with the coffee. She's single, too."

I took a deep breath. "I'm gay," I told the lady.

"Oh, then you should meet my great nephew, Blake," the gray-haired lady smiled up at me from her seat across the table from me. "He's gay, too. Such a nice man. A little shy, he is, but you could probably get him over that."

"Grandma!" Peggy set two cups of coffee down on the table. "Just because guys are gay does not mean they are looking for partners! Just like heterosexuals, not everyone is looking for dates."

"Peggy, I didn't say that," Mollie laughed. "Just that he should meet Blake." She turned to face me, "What was your name again, young man?"

"I'm Aaron," I reached across the table and shook hands with both of the women.

"Aaron, a nice Biblical name. Are you a Christian?" Mollie wanted to know.

"I am," I replied.

"I guess so or he wouldn't be here in church, right?" Peggy said brightly. "Now Aaron, where are you from? I don't think I've seen you around here before."

"I live close to Allentown," I told her. "It's a small town in the Valley close to Belleville."

"Where the Amish live," Mollie said, nodding her head. "I buy Amish butter and sometimes Amish bread. I shouldn't be buying their bread but it is soooo good. But the Amish butter, I will always buy that."

"Have another doughnut. If you are interested, we have a singles' group from church and we meet once a week for conversation and socializing. Sometimes we go to a movie or go bowling. Do you get into Harrisburg during the week?" Peggy asked, pushing a plate of doughnuts towards me.

"Hardly ever. But thanks for inviting me. It sounds interesting."

I selected a glazed cake doughnut and dunked it into my coffee. I firmly erased the thought of an earlier conversation about dunking doughnuts away from my memory.

"A dunkard!" Mollie giggled. "Like there are Dunkard Brethren churches. And Dunkard Sisters, too I reckon."

I laughed with her. "You remind me of my Aunt Katie," I told her. "I enjoy spending time with her. She never married and is my…" I lowered my voice, "…favorite aunt. Not supposed to have favorites, you know." I winked at her.

"Oh my!" Mollie chortled. "I am so glad I got to sit across the table from you. I don't always come to church since my accident, but I try to come as much as I can. I love my church family."

"Is our church much like other churches you attended?" Peggy wanted to know. "I mean, we are gay friendly and there are still many, many Christians who do not accept gay people or even want to acknowledge people are gay. I mean, who would still think that way? This is 2020 and no one needs to hide themselves in some obscure ancient era, like… the Amish for instance." She seemed to suddenly remember Mollie's reference earlier.

I heard a gong sound and Peggy got up. "Come Aunt

Mollie, coffee klatsch is over. The sermon will begin soon." Then she turned to me, "Aaron, I hope to see you some more. You are always welcome."

"Young man," Mollie said with a twinkle in her eyes, "I still think you and Blake should meet." She winked at me while Peggy tried to shush her.

"I would like that," I said firmly with a smile. "I don't know very many people here in Harrisburg and I need friends."

I followed the two women back into the sanctuary. The worship leader was already up front, strumming her guitar softly while the people reassembled. I noticed the crowd was bigger than it had been for Sunday school. I guessed some people came just for the sermon. Or maybe the coffee and doughnuts and the sermon.

"Search for a church," Brian had said. "Look beyond your own community, perhaps in a larger city. I'd recommend you Google 'Gay friendly' and see what you can find. I know it's not easy to exactly determine what kind of a church it is online, but it's worth a try."

So, I had done just that. I had taken a tutorial on how to use the web when I bought my laptop and even though I was not adept at using the search engines, I had been able to pull up a list of 'gay friendly' churches in Harrisburg.

Now, as the worship leader began singing, I stood up with the rest of the congregation as we followed the words on the huge screen in the front.

Coming to an English church had been another huge step for me. I had only been inside a non-Amish church one time and that had been to the funeral of an English neighbor when I had still been a teenager. Mrs. Bittinger had been our neighbor for as long as I could remember and she bought milk and eggs from our farm and when she got older, I used to mow her lawn and trim her bushes.

However, Oakview Methodist Church here in Harrisburg was not at all like I remembered the small country church. I looked up at the timbered ceiling soaring high above our heads and admired the stained-glass windows letting colored light inside the shadowy interior. I had seen the date the church had been constructed on a plaque outside the huge double front doors when I had entered. Built in 1889.

But as old as the church building was, I had not been prepared for the lively and energetic opening. They had a choir that sang several Spirituals which I had never heard before, and then just before the Sunday school had started, we all stood and sang "What A Friend We Have in Jesus." At first, I thought I could sing along, but the familiar tune was only sung for the first verse and then rollicked into an arrangement that I could not follow at all. The congregation had become lively, clapping their hands and swaying to the beat. Now, as the worship leader sang, the lights dimmed and her tune was contemplative and reverent. "Come Holy Spirit, I need you! Come, sweet Spirit I pray!"

In spite of the novelty of being in an entirely new environment, in spite of being so unfamiliar with everything this church was doing, I felt a calmness in my spirit. I closed my eyes and heard the words echo in my spirit. "Come with Your strength and Your power! Come, in your own gentle way."

I breathed in deeply and softly. As I exhaled, it was as if I was releasing a pressure somewhere deep in my heart. I felt my eyes sting and I swallowed with difficulty.

Then the song was over, and we sat down. The pastor got up. "Good morning!"

"Good morning!" The response was enthusiastic.

"I guess you all greeted each other over coffee and doughnuts. So, for any visitors, I'm John McClenney, the senior pastor here and I will continue on my series of messages on 'Being Relevant in Today's Society.' I assume one of our friendly ushers has already made sure you got a bulletin so you can follow along." Mr. McClenny smiled as he looked at the congregation. His black robe hid his clothes and although he had gray hair, he still looked quite young, barely in his 40's.

I followed the outline in the bulletin. I was impressed with the precise wording, the succinct homilies and interspersed with anecdotes, the sermon was never boring. I had little time to digest some of the more radical, for me, ideas he presented. However, I knew there was much here for me to think on in the days ahead. Several times I was blindsided with several statements I thought were not at all according to the Bible, but I let it slide, trying to keep up with the rapid progression of the sermon.

Then, church services were over, and we sang a final song after the benediction.

"Thank you for coming," Pastor McClenny greeted me as I followed the queue of people filing outside. He stood in the doorway, shaking hands and exchanging pleasantries with the crowd. "Feel free to come again and if you haven't already, I welcome you to fill out the 'First time visitors' sheet."

"I enjoyed the sermon," I told him as I shook his hand. "I needed to hear this."

"Thank you. I appreciate you coming. Hope to see you again."

"Aaron!"

I turned and there was Mollie, her stooped figure making her have to crane her head to look up at me. "I wanted to tell you goodbye. I hope you can come again."

"Thank you," I said and acting on my impulse, I bent over and hugged her.

"Oh my!" she laughed and hugged me back, her hands reaching around my waist. "I needed that hug! I could take a hug like that every day!"

"Me, too," I told her. "May I give you my phone number? I'd like to talk with you some more if you want to connect with me on the phone."

"Oh son," she said softly, and I saw her eyes well with tears. She smiled at me. "I'd like that. My days are long since Sidney passed away, and I have lots of time."

I gave her my business card with my name and contact information. "Now you have my name and phone number." I opened my smart phone. "May I have your number, please?"

"Of course, young man," Mollie laughed and I entered her information.

"Take pictures of the people you connect with," Jamal had told me when he had showed me how to get more use out of my smart phone. "Then put them in your contact list." "May I take a selfie with you?" I asked.

"Oh wow," Mollie laughed again. "It's not every day a good-looking young man pays so much attention to me. Why, of course!"

I dropped down on one knee beside her and took our picture. I viewed it and then showed it to her.

"You make me look good," She joked. "I like that."

"Aunt Mollie, time to go," Peggy had pulled up in front of the church in her car.

I opened the car door for her and took Mollie's arm to help her inside to the front seat of the car.

"That was a great movie," Jamil said as we exited the theater with the rest of the crowd. "I had read an online review and there was also some chatter about why it won an Oscar in Best Picture over some other contenders."

I nodded, still in a mental cloud about my reaction to the movie. "Yes," was all I said. We made our way out into the parking lot where Jamil had parked.

"Thanks for inviting me," I said. "I'm still so new to watching movies and I didn't know what to expect, but I got so totally into the story line I kept forgetting it was a movie. I mean, I felt the emotions so strongly from the characters. I don't know how to process all that."

"I grew up watching selected movies in Iran, however some of these newer movies make a really big impact on my life as well." Jamil unlocked his car. "Are you hungry? Do you want to celebrate the first day of Spring by staying up late to take an advantage of longest day of the year?"

"Yes, to question number one. Yes, to question number two." I climbed into the passenger seat.

"Hamburgers?" Jamil asked as he started the car.

"Well," I began, "we could."

Jamil laughed loudly as he began driving. "I was teasing you. No, I'm not interested in hamburgers, either. There is a really cool spot about half a mile from here that serves delicious grilled vegetables and they don't fry any of their entrees or even offer French fries. Everything is either grilled or roasted or broiled."

"Nothing raw?" I said in mock horror.

Jamil reached over and playfully slapped my leg. "Now who's a tease?"

"Takes one to know one," I replied. "That place sounds perfect. What's the name?"

Jamil shook his head, "I don't remember. Something like Roasted, or maybe it is Grilled Garden Cafe? Wait, gardens aren't grilled or roasted, are they? Anyway, I do know how to get there."

We ordered and sat outside on the patio. The last light of evening still lit the western skies and the patio was dimly lit with strings of overhead lights. Several couples were sitting in the patio area as well.

"What was one of the most outstanding parts of 'Green Book' for you?" I asked Jamil, spearing a wedge of roasted sweet potato.

Jamil cut a bite of salmon off his entree. He lifted his fork and then paused. "Remember when Tony was chauffeuring Mr. Shirley through the southern landscape and they came up on the black workers in the field? Well, that made a big impression on me. I know I resent it when people think all Muslims or Middle Eastern people are the same and lump everyone into the same mold, however I did not realize how much I subconsciously was doing that with black people. When Mr. Shirley clearly was more out of touch with the field workers than Tony was, it helped solidify how we are all different, even among our own people and yet still the same in general, all wanting the same acceptance no matter who we are."

I nodded, even with my mouth full of grilled chicken. The food was everything Jamal had said it would be.

"How about you?" Jamal wondered wiping his mouth with the white napkin. "Was there something that moved you deeply?"

I nodded, "Many, many scenes really moved me. However, for me the strongest part of the entire show was the friendship that developed between Tony and Donald Shirley. That scene when Donald thought Tony was going to leave him and then he came outside of his room and offered Tony a pay raise and other benefits if he stayed on? I admit I teared up when I saw how deeply Donald wanted Tony to stay and how he was willing to put aside his pride to almost beg Tony to stay on?" I wanted to say more, but I couldn't say anything.

Jamil reached across the table and put his hand on my arm. "It's okay, Aaron. Your emotions do you proud." He pulled his hand back but left a warm spot on my arm.

"Thank you," I said after I took a drink of water from my glass. "After that scene, I watched for the signs and words of affection between the two. I guess it culminated when Donald showed up at Tony's house. That was a great ending!"

"Do you think there are a lot of straight guys that have that kind of friendship?" Jamil asked. "I know there are great friendships, but I wonder if there are lots of one on one friendships? I tend to think there are, however when I was growing up, I never had that kind of friend. I think I was too afraid someone will wonder why I like guys so well, so I kind of shut myself off from letting any friendships develop."

"I know what you mean," I said. "I was always careful not to let my feelings show as well."

Jamil folded his napkin on his plate and leaned back in his chair. "There was one guy, after I was in my late 20's, that was different. He was very friendly, and we used to get together at a coffee shop and just talk. I think he knew I was gay and after we got to know each other very well, I told him and he just nodded and said he didn't care, he liked me as a person and it didn't matter what gender I preferred.

"Wait!" I was puzzled. "Late twenties? I thought you are in your early twenties, but you said in your late twenties you guys were friends."

"I'm thirty- one," Jamil laughed. "You thought I was in my early 20's?" Again, he laughed easily, his white teeth contrasting with his dark skin.

"Ach! I just assumed." Then I said, "Tell me more about this friend of yours. What makes you think he knew you are gay?"

Jamil exhaled softly and dropped his eyes for a moment and then he looked at me. "I'm embarrassed to say this, but one evening we were in the back yard, drinking beer and just being goofy and joking around. I said something to tease him and he jumped up from his seat and knelt on the grass beside my chair and wrapped his arms around me and said,

'You are so silly, Jamil! But I like your silliness.' We were both slightly buzzed and when I felt his arms around me, I instinctively reached for him and hugged him close to my chest and then I began playing with his hair. He didn't resist but he didn't encourage me, either. So I released him and he got back up and gave me another bottle of beer. We continued our talk and fun and he never mentioned it or made me feel awkward."

"Wow, wow, wow," I said. "That is amazing! I never thought anyone could have that kind of experience. Everything I've ever read about male affection was always gay guys being rejected by any straight guys who they had come onto."

Jamil nodded. "I'm hoping eventually it will become the normal when a gay man makes any move, whether in flirtation or just out of natural interest, if the other guy is straight, he is able to say, 'Hey, I like you, but it will never be more than a friend,' without getting freaked out and reacting in a negative way. I have actually heard that is more and more the case but mostly in the big cities I'd think, where urban folks are more interested in the person rather than what gender they are interested in."

Shouldn't you say, 'What gender you are attracted to sexually'?"

Jamil shook his head. "No. Like we've talked about before, being gay is way more than the sexual part. It's the social part as much as the sexual if we look at it realistically. I know there are many who don't agree, but I feel because the sexual part is so often at the forefront, it eclipses the natural desire of companionship from a man."

The waiter came back outside. "Is there anything else you guys need? No hurry but we will be closing in fifteen minutes."

Jamil took me home. He skillfully drove through the night and neither one of us spoke. Yet, it was not an uncomfortable silence but more a restful, companionable sharing the space inside the car without need for words.

"Thank you for coming with me," Jamil got out of the car when we reached my place and gave me a hug. I hugged him in return and said, "You are welcome. I enjoyed it very much. Let's do it again sometime. Soon."

"Absolutely," Jamil said giving me a final squeeze and then releasing me. "I'm glad we are friends." He smiled at me and even in the dark, his smile seemed to light up the night.

# CHAPTER TWENTY-FIVE

"I'm glad you came," Peggy reached out and gave me a hug. "My grandmother talked and talked about you on the way home from church. I realized in a new way how much she needed affirmations of love. 'He hugged me with such warmth!' She kept saying over and over in the car.

"She died in her sleep. I was in my room and never heard anything amiss or unusual. Like she always did, she had her warm herb tea, and looked up from her book when I passed her door and called her usual cheery 'Good night' and I imagine soon afterwards she turned off her light and went to sleep," Peggy's voice broke and a few more tears puddled in her red eyes.

I nodded and replied, "Peggy, you have my sympathies.

She made a genuine impression on me that Sunday I visited your church. So friendly and full of fun. I'm sure you will miss her. However, I know you will always have her with you in your memories."

Peggy nodded and straightened herself up and smiled through her tears. Then she looked at Jamal.

"Peggy, this is my, my friend, Jamil. He came with me so I wouldn't be by myself on the drive home tonight. Jamil, this is Peggy, Mollie's granddaughter."

Jamil bowed slightly and shook Peggy's outstretched hand and I could see her eyes search his face a moment. "Nice to meet you, Jamil. That was really nice of you to accompany Aaron on his way here."

Then she looked at me. "I found your card in her purse and at first I didn't remember who 'Aaron Peachy' was but suddenly I recalled the connection you and Grandma had so I decided to call you and so I left a message with the information for the viewing and the funeral. Thank you so much for coming."

"You are welcome. God bless you," I said as we turned to follow the line filing past the coffin.

I paused briefly to look at the still form in the silk-lined coffin. The gray hair looked soft and waved slightly just above her forehead and Mollie's face looked wrinkled and worn, however about her mouth there was somehow a look I could hardly understand. It wasn't that she was smiling, yet it was as though suddenly she could break into a chuckle and I was astonished to think it possible for someone who's life had passed away could still maintain her character.

I talked about it with Jamil on the way home. "It was as though she was somehow still there! I've never had this experience. Before, when I went to funerals, it was as though the deceased was sleeping. Or dead. Yes, many look dead." I gave a dry laugh. "Well, duh, they are dead! So they look dead. But Mollie looked alive!"

"Maybe it's because she lived. Really lived," Jamil said reflectively, looking forward through the windshield into the night, his hands holding the steering wheel.

"That's what I want," I said. "I want to really live." I sighed audibly.

Jamil nodded, "Me, too, Aaron. There are times I wonder just what I will do with my life. So, I join you in saying 'I want to really live'."

271

"When you find out what that is, let me know," I said trying to lighten our mood. "Then, perhaps we can take that journey together."

There was no reply from my companion.

Long after Jamil had dropped me off at my house and his headlights had disappeared into the darkness, I lay sleepless in my bed. "God, what is life? Why do I keep having questions and keep wanting to find out more why I am alive? Is this questing after wanting something fulfilling ever over?" My prayers were mostly questions anymore. I reached for my diary.

*"Bloody Knuckles*

*I found myself knocking on doors again last night*

*To find the purpose and meaning of who I am*

*I knocked on door after door all down the hall to find*

*The room where I could be everything I am meant to be*

*I once again came to realize with chagrin*

*I still have calluses on swollen knuckles*

*From a life long knocking on reluctant places*

*Yet incessantly I find myself knocking again.*

*When will my restless consciousness*

*Find my questing of a moral cogniscent pattern?*

*Where I end my endless quest of eternal answers*

*To once and for all end my final concentric circling thoughts?*

272

*I will continue kicking on so many doors*

*Of reconciliation and exoneration and forgiveness*

*I will appease my aching and bloody knuckles*

*Until I gasp out my very last breath*

*I have been made to keep on knocking*

*There is no answer, no magic bullet to swallow*

*The only reason the sand on the hourglass drains out*

*Is so we can upend it again and again*

*It is only when I embrace the truth*

*Of this relentless and unceasing perennial search*

*I can say to my own life and heart*

*I was made to knock incessantly on doors."*

"You want life to be perfect," Brian told me. "You wanted to come out of the closet, meet a special guy, save sex for after you get married and then live in harmony until you grow old and die."

"Is there anything wrong with wanting that?" I asked.

Brian shook his head, "No. But as in other areas of life, when something doesn't work as planned, we change course and work with what is left over. That doesn't mean life is ruined, does it?"

"It sounds so elementary when you put it into simple language," I laughed. "No, it doesn't mean life is over. Am I disappointed? Yes."

"The furniture maker. The artist. The granary restorer. The right horses. Your life was quite tidy for most of your years, right? Then you got outed and suddenly you find yourself in a tailspin. You fall in love. You have your first sexual encounter. Life was still pretty much on track. Then, Alex tells you about his affair with his former hookup. You reel in shock from that, realize your love for him is stronger than your initial negative reaction, so you give yourself wholeheartedly to him by going to him at night and you 'marry' him." Bruce used air quotes with his fingers.

I nodded. "I still don't know what to make of that. I was sure he understood because we had discussed it earlier."

Brian shook his head. "Discussed it isn't the same as agreeing. I still think he was pleasantly overwhelmed by your eager readiness for committing yourself and having sex with him. However, you don't know if he was already having questions about you two being together when you showed up that night, do you? It could be he was mulling over the fact about whether you guys are compatible. But probably swept off his feet, literally, by your eager and ready desire to get 'married'.

"However, none of that really has anything to do with the present. That is in the past. You said he called and told you he missed you and you think he was drunk and probably with someone else at the time. How do you feel about that?"

"Like I don't know him," I admitted. "I realize there are so many areas of getting to know someone I wasn't thinking about. But yeah, I think I'm disappointed he wasn't what I thought he would be. But," I said lifting my hand to stop Brian from saying anything, "I know, I know! I'm assuming things. Like wanting Alex to fit into my perfect world."

Brian laughed heartily.

I told my therapist about attending Oakview Methodist Church in Harrisburg. Brian seemed pleased I was making an effort to be a part of a community. "I'm sleeping well again," I told him. "After Alex called it off, I thought I would go back to my sleepless nights and yes, I did at first while I was grieving so deeply and I kept waking up but now, for the last several weeks, I sleep all night long. I guess I'm finally maturing."

That evening, I was working in my garden, watering the new cabbage plants I had just set out when I heard the Amish national anthem, the steady trot, trot of a horse and buggy. I thought I recognized the bay horse coming towards me. It looked like… it was my former deacon Louie's horse.

"Good evening" I greeted him as he pulled up in my driveway and pulled on both reins to stop his horse.

"Aaron," Louie nodded and he smiled a strained smile at me. "How are you this beautiful spring evening?"

"I'm doing well. Enjoying this weather so much. I just put in my tomato plants today. I think it's going to rain tonight," I said as I looked at the clouds overhead. "Did you see the sunrise this morning? I kept thinking all day it was going to rain and then the clouds would blow away again."

"Yes," Louie said. "Do you have time to talk?"

"Sure," I told him. "Tie your horse to the rack. We can sit on the chairs under the maple."

Louie was quiet as he tied his horse to the rack and followed me across the lawn to the chairs. Barn swallows darted around in the heavy evening air, catching mosquitoes and giving their distinctive chirps as they flung themselves about.

"Aaron, I'm here to see if you have repented. I have heard you now have a car and was told you no longer wear suspenders." Louis said in a sober voice.

I was wearing jeans and a belt, and my short sleeved shirt had a lay down collar so it was obvious to any Amish I had "gone high" or had become English.

"Yes, that's true," I nodded.

"Well, we know the outside reflects what is in the heart," Louie said simply. "So, I guess I don't need to ask if you feel any different on the inside? But I wanted to come and talk with you. I am grieved by what I see. Even though I had heard from others you were making changes, I didn't want to just go by what they said but do the right thing and come see for myself. And to talk with you."

"Thank you for that," I told him. "I know you care. At first, I didn't change anything for it was not my desire to leave the Amish. I liked our ways, our traditions and I really missed the community. I felt thrown out after I was excommunicated, and in my loneliness, I did reach out to the English. For even the Mennonites didn't look kindly at me so I didn't do the usual gradual going from one church to a more liberal church. I guess I took a gigantic leap and landed here."

Louie nodded. "Yes, you did. So, you have not changed anything about being a homosexual? About going against God's plan for men? By going against the Holy Bible?"

"May I ask you a question?" I looked at Louie. "Or maybe several questions."

Louie looked at me. He didn't reply.

"Do you look at the Bible as a rule book? And if so, if we don't live up to all of the rules, will we be cast into hell and not be able to make it to heaven?" I tried to remain calm as I asked the questions.

"I'm not here to discuss these matters with you," Louie skillfully avoided my questions. "You are not in a position to question what the church has decided is God's will for people."

"For if you look at the Bible as a rule book, I fear you will not make it to heaven, either. Even if we make a list of the teachings of Jesus and turn them into rules, I am pretty certain no one obeys all of them and therefore will make it to heaven."

"Then whose rules do you follow?" It was as though Louie could not refrain himself.

"I no longer look at the rules," I told him. "For I don't find rules and commandments as the teachings of Jesus. Instead, I am trying to center on the most important 'rule' if you want to call it that of loving. Loving God and loving all people. Really quite simple, isn't it?"

"I've heard that many times," Louie said gravely shaking his head. "It always comes before a great falling away from the Bible. We deceive ourselves by thinking only love matters."

I heard the steady trot of a horse coming up the road, the wheels of the buggy providing the background music of the traditional Amish transportation mode for hundreds of years. It was my brother Levi's rig for I recognized his horse before I could see who was driving. I waved at him and Levi began lifting his hand and then dropped it as he stared at us.

I realized the tranquil looking scene of two men sitting under a maple tree on two lawn chairs was anything but tranquil to him. And

I could only imagine what he was thinking as he saw the deacon sitting next to his wayward brother.

Louie left soon afterwards, and I turned and walked towards the home farm.

"Aaron, come in," Mom's voice found me before I opened the door. "I saw Louie's rig leave and so I looked towards your place and sure enough, you came around the bend by the barn. Now come right in and I'll fix you some banana soup. It was so warm today and I realized I would not get all the bananas eaten before they got soft, so I decided to bake banana bread but then I'm like, oh it's just too warm and so I decided cold banana soup would be just right. Are you hungry for banana soup?"

"Yes, Mom!" I told her. "That sounds perfect. I don't think I've made banana soup since I moved into my own place. It will make me feel like a boy again."

Mom began breaking up several pieces of her homemade bread into small pieces and put them into a bowl. I watched as she sliced two bananas and added them into the bowl. "It will need to set just a little, you know," Mom said as she got milk from the refrigerator and poured it on top of the bananas and bread. "Brings the flavor out better. But I'm sure you remember that."

"I do but I don't mind you telling me again," I smiled at my mom. "What have you been doing today?"

Mom liberally added some brown sugar to the bowl and then stirred the mixture gently. I could smell the familiar mouthwatering aroma of bananas and milk and brown sugar and I breathed in deeply.

"Worked in the flower beds this morning. Too warm already this afternoon and I got out of breath, too. I so soon get winded anymore. Guess it's my age," Mom said with a chuckle.

When she brought the soup to me and set it down in front of me, I bowed my head in silent prayer. Mom respectfully stood beside me and waited until I raised my head. "Taste it," she urged. "See if it needs more sugar."

The first bite was as delicious as I anticipated it to be. "Perfect," I told her. "Just a little too sweet, but otherwise perfect," I teased her.

"Just like Dad used to say," Mom said with a smile. "Aaron, I miss him every day. I wonder if I always will."

"Its okay to miss him," I told her. "I think our memories are kept alive longer if we allow ourselves to speak about how we feel. Too many times I have tried to keep quiet about my feelings. I think it has kept me from knowing how to make friends. But I was always hiding who I really am."

"Is that why Louie came?" Mom questioned, drying her hands on her half apron. "To see how you are feeling about, about everything?"

I continued eating for a while as I thought about her question.

"Yes," I said. "He wanted to see for himself if I was no longer dressing Amish. He told me he had heard I wasn't but wanted to come and see for himself. You know, I appreciate that. I know he genuinely cares about me even if he doesn't support who I am. But knowing he really cares does mean a lot to me."

"Guess he could see you aren't Amish anymore," Mom said waving her hand towards my clothes. "But did he want to know how you feel inside? Did he ask if you are still... still gay?"

"He asked if I changed anything about being a homosexual," I told her.

"And?" Mom asked and pulled up a chair and sat down.

"You know, I didn't really answer his question. I asked him some questions. Like if he felt the Bible is a Rule Book and did he feel if we don't keep the rules would we not make it into heaven." I finished the banana soup and placed my spoon in the empty dish. "Thank you, Mom. That was really, really good."

"Rule book," Mom said as she got up. "That's what Aunt

Katie called it when she was young. During the times many of us wondered if she was going to leave the Amish."

"Aunt Katie?" I asked incredulously. "She thought about leaving the Amish?"

"Well, she never said as much in so many words. But I know my parents were worried because Katie joined the most liberal of the Amish youth gangs and sometimes wouldn't come home until late at night. No, make that early in the morning. If I asked where she was, she would tell me it was none of my business, but yes, she called the Bible the Rule Book more than once. Then, she moved to Ohio for a while, and helped one of her friends who had gotten married to an Ohio boy. When she came back home, she seemed changed. More quiet and subdued. Less restless, you could say," Mom nodded her head.

"I didn't know that," I mused out loud. "I've always known she was a little different and more headstrong."

"I used to think that's why she never got married. Did too much thinking. Maybe too much talking for the Amish boys." Mom picked up my bowl and took it to the sink. She rinsed it and put it in the drainer. "We only got close as sisters after I married your dad.

280

She helped with you boys, like she is fond of telling you, when you were little."

I nodded. "Yes, she likes to tell people that she changed our diapers. Poopy ones, she says."

We laughed together as I mentioned my aunt's graphic description.

"Has anything changed?" My mom asked. "Do you still feel the same? Towards men?"

I nodded my head. "Yes, I'm still attracted to men. But what I want is only one man. For a while, I thought I had found that one man. Then he wasn't sure he was ready to take on a former Amish."

"I felt you were going through something," Mom said.

"But I didn't want to pry. Or be nosy. But Aaron, I cared. I felt sad for you even though I didn't know what all was going on or even though it is still not clear to me just how you can feel this way about a man. But that doesn't matter. I know you still have deep feelings and when you hurt, you hurt all over."

# BOOK II

I woke up and checked the morning light to gauge the time. It was October so the days were definitely getting shorter. Through the uncurtained window I could see the ridge of Jacks Mountain outlined faintly against the dawning sky. I closed my eyes again and felt myself sink into the mattress. I felt rested, however I was content to stay in bed awhile yet, luxuriating in having the weekend ahead of us, and even though I often had used weekends in the past to run errands or do some project on my little acreage, today I had nothing planned. So, I was ready to enjoy this moment, this Saturday morning.

Paisley must have sensed I was awake, for she raised herself up from the towel at the edge of the bed and arched her back and then stretched herself before she sat down and like me, looked out the window. I pulled my right arm from out under the bedcovers and reached towards my pet. It didn't take long for her responsive purr to reward my affection and she lowered her head so I could reach her favorite space right between her ears.

I felt a movement from the left side of me and I stopped massaging Paisley and held still. I could feel a smile lift the corners of my mouth for I knew what was going to happen next. I felt the bedcovers lift and then a hand reached out and touched my leg. I let out my breath softly and slowly and allowed the sensation of intimacy sweep over me and flood my being.

The fingers walked slowly up my leg towards my waist and I responded by moving my left hand down towards the seeking fingers and when our hands met, the dance of intertwining our fingers began. The first grasp was the pleasant touch of hand to hand. Then, as we interlaced our fingers, we made sure our fingers were fitted together perfectly. My fingers responded to the tight squeeze of the hand holding mine. Then, we lay still, side by side in our bed and I felt the moment of magic that never stopped amazing me. I heard Jamil's breathing slow down again and I knew he was falling asleep again.

I felt my eyes prickle with tears of complete and joyous satisfaction. Even though we had been married now for two months, it was as though this was our first morning together. Well, not exactly for I really think our connection was getting better, although I cannot really say how. From our first night together, I used to wake up in the middle of the night to feel Jamil's hand seeking for mine and even though it woke me up often, I was always deeply moved at the love language Jamil's touch wrote on my heart.

My mind drifted back to our early evening wedding. It had been Jamil's idea to have the ceremony and reception at my place. "You have this idyllic setting right here," Jamil had said, his practical mind seizing on what seemed obvious. "It will be small so parking won't be an issue."

We had rented a large white tent in case a late evening August thunderstorm would cancel the outside ceremony we had planned. Then, we decided to host the reception in the tent and the weather had been perfect and we had left the side curtains open until later in the evening, we had closed two sides to block out some of the night air.

I felt Jamal move slightly and then he turned onto his right side and he moved up against me in the bed. I flipped over onto my right side and we lost our handhold. Jamil slipped his right arm under my neck and cradled me against his chest. I reached up my right hand until our hands met again and we interlaced our fingers again. His left arm circled my waist and he pushed up my tee shirt and rested

283

the palm of his hand onto the bare skin of my stomach. I moved my left hand and slid it onto his hand, covering his fingers with mine.

Once more, Jamil fell asleep, his body pressing tightly against mine and I feeling overwhelmingly loved and cared for, was wide awake.

Since Jamil had moved in with me after the ceremony, we of course learned so much more about each other. The two months we had dated had given us a lot of time to get to know each other even better than we had before as friends, and now since we were joined, our journey together continued to unfold with an easy transition from my singleness. Jamil had still been living with his parents and yet, he too had to adjust to sharing a space with another person.

The wedding had been very small, especially according to Amish standards, and less than twenty people had gathered together to join our special time of union. Several of Jamil's friends, but no one from his immediate family, had attended on his side and the people who had responded to our invitation from my acquaintances were basically the same people who had attended the dinner party I had hosted last winter.

I moved my right hand carefully and placed it on top of the bedcovers, right over Jamil's heart. His breathing was still deep, his body motionless and yet his right hand was very alive in my left hand.

I marveled at all the questions that had come to me when I realized how much I had been falling in love with my friend. Even before I asked him if we could be more than friends, be boyfriends, I knew my questions were never going to be answered. I was moving out in the belief we both shared. Our love for each other had to be bigger than any of the questions

"You are Christian, I am Muslim. Well, at least by birth," Jamil had told me when we began seriously talking about our union.

Then there had been the question of finances. "Will we share our checking account? Do we keep our finances separate?" I had questioned Jamil.

"What if our families never acknowledge our union? Can you accept the fact you might never be welcome in my parents or relatives' homes?" This was his question.

"Love is bigger. If we need to have all of these questions answered and decided on before our wedding, we will be quite a bit older than we are now." This was Jamil's wisdom.

So, we had agreed to move ahead and have the ceremony. "On this one thing we agree for our ancient religions both have the story of Isaac and Rebecca," I had told Jamal. For yes, I did tell him my view of marriage, how it was not important to me to have any civil wedding, no marriage license, nothing from the government to legalize our union.

"Let's call it a wedding," Jamil had said. "I don't want to have to explain to everyone we are married, but not really married. A wedding is the celebration. We definitely will celebrate."

I had asked the pastor, Mr. Clenney if he could come and pray over our union and bless all of us. He had set up an appointment with us and after an hour, he had said, "I will be happy to come and bless your union. You guys are definitely unconventional, but so is life. Happy to be a part of your lives."

We had not done a lot of planning, just invited our guests, hired a caterer to provide food and drinks and then went wild with flowers stuck in rustic buckets, vases, pottery jugs and anything we could borrow or rent that we liked. Early on the morning of our epic day, we had spent over an hour gathering late summer wildflowers from the roadsides, from the fence rows and even foraged in the woods for greenery. The cut flowers from the wholesale florist accented the wildness of nature's largess and turned our backyard into what we wanted, a riot of natural colors and textures.

Paisley got up from her towel and jumped onto the wooden floor. She is still slender and even as a now full-grown cat, she is a queen, and she knows it. But her jump onto the floor still thumped loudly enough to make Jamil stir in his sleep. He sighed and pulled his arm out from underneath my head. Then he turned onto his back and I flipped over as well. I waited.

Sure enough, his right hand moved onto my leg as he reached out for mine and I responded. Hand in hand, fingers interlaced, we lay in bed. "Good morning," he murmured. "What time is it?"

I reached out and pushed the button on my phone.

"Seven eighteen," I replied. "But we don't need to get up. It's Saturday and if I remember correctly you don't have any appointments. I know I don't."

"Uh huh," Jamil grunted sleepily. "I'm still not awake."

I reached out and put my forefinger on Jamil's forehead, just under his hairline. I traced his profile, running my finger down to his nose, tracing over his short mustache and then as my finger reached his lips, he opened his mouth and licked the tip of my finger with his tongue. I stopped the journey of my finger and he nibbled on my pointer finger and then he exhaled and turned his face towards me.

I continued tracing his profile but by the time I had reached his chest, he had fallen asleep.

I lay back in bed. Usually, in my single days, I hardly ever just lolled about in bed. For me, waking up had always meant getting up. I felt I had things to do, an urgency to start the day.

Now, I was perfectly satisfied to stay in bed. With my husband. Lolling. So, content to lay back and do…. Well, do nothing!

I turned to face Jamil and studied his face in the light streaming into our window. My eyes absorbed every detail I could of this man I loved. Dark-black hair cut short enough to curl luxuriantly on his scalp was perfect to run my fingers through. I never got tired of massaging his scalp and he always showed his appreciation by moving his hand, or hands at times, somewhere on my body to show his affection.

I moved my arm over the top of his body, the bedcover keeping us from actually touching. I didn't want to disturb my husband's sleep but I also wanted to yield to my desire to connect deeper with him.

Without opening his eyes, Jamal reached up underneath the quilt and pushed the cover back until he found my arm. Then he drew my arm down  until it circled his waist. He pulled the cover back up and fell asleep once more.

"I've never had sex," Jamil had told me after we seriously began dating. "So, you will be my first."

I remembered with what regret I had started to tell him how sorry I was that I had impetuously given myself to Alex and how my sexuality had been awakened by the man I had thought I was going to marry. "Life is never perfect the way we thought it would be," Jamal had shushed me. "You are a good man, Aaron. Having made a choice you now wish you hadn't, does not make you bad. We will make a life together because we love each other and the good in each of us will continue to overcome all obstacles."

287

Okay, okay, call me sentimental but I began to cry tears of joy. The deepest feelings of joy swept all over me as I felt his hand cover mine. Our sexual journey began after the wedding and continued to grow every day. We both knew our connection was much deeper than just having sex, which made sex even better. We had both been overwhelmed by our sexual journey and delighted in letting our sensual lives totally out of the cages we had voluntarily kept ourselves in. To have such a man love me so deeply, so intimately was even better than my wildest earlier imaginations.

"Those two can't keep their eyes off each other," Trevor had said at our reception. "Took them with me to a club one night and you would think they were the only two guys in there." The guests had laughed as Trevor described our outing.

"Guys kept coming up to them and sayin, 'Oh my gosh! You guys are so cute!' and 'You guys make me jealous! Your love is palpable And, it really was, and is," Trevor had continued. "You give me hope that I can find my special guy!"

We really are "handsy" as someone once described us. At home, we hold hands, we touch, we hug, and we seem never to be satisfied unless we touch as much as possible. "One of the things I see has happened to my nephew," Aunt Katie had said during the reception, for she really had shown up and I had been overwhelmed by my Aunt's love for me, "is how much more Aaron talks now. He could always talk but now, he talks and talks! He might even outdo his aunt, and she has had a reputation for years as a talker. 'I didn't know Jamil was so close to my age. I don't know why that makes a difference because I think I was always attracted to him, but I began looking at him with new interest!' On and on he talked, telling me how he had reservations about dating a younger man, for some odd reason."

I remember Jamil looking at me at that point and pretending to be astonished. As though I hadn't already told him more than once how my interest in him had made a turning point right then.

"Jamil took away one of my clients," Brian had added to the conversation. "Our last session was so filled with Jamil I had to remind Aaron I was also interested in his life."

I smiled at the man who had helped me so much in my journey. He had asked me privately if I minded if the guests knew I had been seeing him professionally. "They all know already," I had told him. "No, I am no longer ashamed of having sought help from a therapist."

Jamil sat up in bed and ran his hands through his hair. He yawned hugely and then rubbed his eyes and smiled at me. I think I shall never get used to seeing the contrast of his brown skin with the white of his teeth.

"Hi Handsome," I said, sitting up and facing him. "Are you awake now?"

"I am," he replied. "Did you sleep late?"

"I've been awake for a while," I replied. "Just lying here, looking at you and thinking back to our wedding evening. Hey, Babe, we are married."

"Sentimental man," Jamil laughed. "Silly, lovable, handsome husband."

"I love you," I said and kissed his mouth. Then I drew back. "Oh, do I have morning breath? I forgot."

Jamal smiled, "No. It's all good."

We had only been married for several days when Jamal had said simply, "Can you take better care of your dental hygiene? I love to kiss you but if you have bad breath, it kills a lot of the romance."

It was then I realized how fortunate I was to have someone in my life who was not afraid to say something that bothered him. I was used to having people in my life who would have easily taken offense at someone being blunt. "Thank you for telling me that," I had told Jamal and I took steps to take care of my oral health.

"I'm going to the bathroom and then I'll make coffee,"

Jamil swung his legs into a sitting position. "Stay in bed and I'll bring it up." He grabbed a robe and before he tied the sash, he turned to face me and wiggled his hips, a teasing look on his face. I made a leap towards him and he let out a laugh and raced swiftly down the steps to the kitchen.

I listened to the domestic sounds of Jamil making coffee. Yes, I had installed electricity in my house before our wedding. I didn't want to shock Jamil too much by forcing him to do without what all non-Amish consider a necessity.

I was lying on my stomach sketching when Jamil came upstairs with the tray. He placed it on the foot of the bed and then carefully lowered himself beside me. "New sketch?"

"I started it several days ago. I think it was while I was waiting for you to come home on Tuesday evening," I said as I shoved my sketch book towards him. I sat up and reached for my mug of coffee. "You dear man," I said as my eyes took in the slice of toast spread with marmalade, sliced in half and browned perfectly.

"I like this," Jamil said as he studied the sketch. I handed him his mug of coffee and asked," You sure you don't want some toast?"

Jamal laughed and said, "For the 58th time, no. But thanks for asking."

We laughed together. Jamil had made it clear earlier he did not want toast with his morning coffee. "Too many carbs. I have to take care of my body for you." He had teased me more than once.

We sat side by side, both of my hands busy with the coffee mug and my toast, and Jamil had put his free hand on my leg as he turned his attention back to the sketch. "It's us," he said simply. "It's you and me." I nodded with my mouth full of toast.

Jamil turned his head and looked at me. "Your brown eyes are more beautiful than ever," I told him after I had taken another sip of coffee. "I don't know how but the longer I live with you, the more I see your soul in those eyes."

My husband didn't say anything, but he reached out and stroked my bearded chin with his hands. "Mmmm," I murmured and pushed my face against his. I put my mug on the tray, reached out and took his mug and set it down, then I got up and put the tray on the nightstand. I knelt on the bed and put my hands on his shoulders and pushed him backwards onto the bed.

Jamil laughed as I lowered my body onto his and buried my face in his neck. Then I rolled off to my side and Jamil reached over and hugged me close to himself. Our kisses were the words and our hugs the paragraphs,  for we needed no other method of communication for another thirty minutes while our passion mounted, and we rode the waves of love together.

We lay, gasping and spent, side by side amid the tangled bedcovers. The autumn sun was shining in the window and our entire room was bathed in gold. "I shall need lots of color to catch all the shades of brown on your skin," I said, running my hand lightly over Jamal's chest. "I may even have to make up some new colors I don't have in my paint box."

"But you don't paint, you sketch," Jamil reminded me.

"I will paint. I've been wanting to and now I have so much more reason to do it." I reached for my sketch book.

"Maybe this will be the working sketch for my painting. 'You and me,' " I said echoing his earlier comment. "The first time I sketched this, it wasn't you. And it wasn't me. Just two men, lying beneath a shade tree, sharing a moment."

"You drew this before?" Jamil began paging through my sketch book."

"Remember?" I asked him. "The one I gave to my dad when I was found out?"

"Oh, that's the one your brother Levi saw," Jamil said slowly. "I remember you showing it to me and it took my breath away but I didn't know you gave it to your dad. Did the preachers make you do that?"

I nodded, "Funny thing about that sketch," I got up and went to my chest of drawers. I bent over and opened the bottom drawer. I pulled out a brown envelope and took it back to bed. "Here," I placed the envelope on the bed. "I'm going down to get more coffee. Hot! Somehow, your coffee has cooled off too much to drink. To think I love you more than my hot morning coffee. Yes, you are my morning Hottie!"

I went to the other side of the bed and picked up the tray and took it down the steps.

"If you gave this to your dad, how did it end up here?" Jamal's voice followed me down to the kitchen.

I poured fresh coffee into the mugs and took them upstairs. I climbed into bed again.

"I thought Dad must have destroyed this picture," I said. "But after he died, one evening Mom gave it to me. 'He couldn't tear it up,' she told me. 'You know, your dad was not one to use a lot of words, but he told me, "Aaron not only draws, he puts his feelings into his pictures." ' I was really deeply moved that my dad actually saved my picture."

Jamal put the sketches side by side. In the first, the two men could have been Amish, wearing collarless shirts, homemade pants and both were wearing suspenders. Their hats were tossed on the grass and although their faces were visible, they could have been any two middle-aged men.

In the second sketch, the prone positions of both men were similar to the first, but this time, neither of us were wearing shirts, just jeans. Jamil was lying on his back, his head turned sideways so he could look into my face, his one arm around my leg, clutching at the denim of my jeans, his other hand sprawled onto the grass. I had drawn my left-hand tousling his curly hair and my right arm reaching down and resting on his stomach.

"You are good," Jamil said. "That is us. You and I. Amish and Muslim. Two men in love."

I handed him my notebook. "I wrote this for you. For us." Jamil began to read.

*"Spirit and body merged into a coalescent world where time stood still.*

*We lay, arms entwined and embraced our space of two into one*

*Our hearts beat fast for we had gone beyond our expectations*

293

*The hunger of our need melded our bodies together with passion.*

*The sun came out and covered us all over and our kisses opened our souls with love."*

Made in the USA
Coppell, TX
26 February 2024

29449660R00164